D1348078

'... cool action sequences ... you need to read some Swierczynski stories.'
Wired.com

'A high octane, cinematic delight that uses film techniques of fast pace and quick cuts and highly visual scenes to rivet the reader to their chair. I loved it'
Joe R. Lansdale

'The compelling premise pulls all our paranoid strings, and Swierczynski, like a mad scientist twirling dials, ratchets the tension ever tighter . . . Stay tuned for part three of what may be the most unusual thriller series in a long, long time.'
Booklist

'Duane Swierczynski is a much-needed breath of fresh air in the book world . . . This guy is a great storyteller.' Michael Connelly

'More exciting than whatever you're reading right now.' Ed Brubaker

'The tale packs enough indestructible villains to satisfy a *Die Hard* fan, and each chapter ends on a cliffhanger . . . Written in deadpan sentences and funny as can be, this first installment of a projected trilogy left me greedy for more.' *Bloomberg*

'A furiously paced tale that cries out to be filmed . . . such breathless enthusiasm and good humour that it is easy to settle back and devour the book in a single go. Great fun.' *Canberra Times*

'Duane Swierczynski puts the rest of the crime-writing world on notice. So learn to spell the last name. He's going to be around for a while.' Laura Lippman

'Oh, what style!' *Kirkus Reviews*

'Duane Swierczynski has ideas so brilliant and brutal that one day the rest of us will have to tool up and kill him.' Warren Ellis

'I guarantee you won't want to put it down until its dénouement . . . Infectious and highly recommended.' *Milo's Rambles*

'Cracks along like many a reckless driver along Mulholland Drive itself' *Books and Writers*

'A mile-a-minute crime thriller – fearless, funny and utterly accessible – fit to leave you breathless by its last, explosive moments.' *The Speculative Scotsman*

Duane Swierczynski

Point & Shoot

A Charlie Hardie thriller

MULHOLLAND
BOOKS

HODDER

First published in Great Britain in 2013 by Mulholland Books
An imprint of Hodder & Stoughton
An Hachette UK company

1

A CIP catalogue record for this title is available from the British Library

Paperback ISBN 978 1 444 70760 1
eBook ISBN 978 1 444 70761 8

Printed and bound by Clays Ltd, St Ives plc

Hodder & Stoughton policy is to use papers that are natural, renewable and
recyclable products and made from wood grown in sustainable forests. The
logging and manufacturing processes are expected to conform to the
environmental regulations of the country of origin.

Hodder & Stoughton Ltd
338 Euston Road
London NW1 3BH

www.hodder.co.uk

For David J. Schow,
straight shooter

Tu proverai sì come sa di sale
lo pane altrui, e come è duro calle
lo scendere e 'l salir per l'altrui scale

Paradisio
Canto XVII, lines 58-60
Dante

And if you still can't see the light
God's gonna buy you a satellite

The Hooters

POINT AND SHOOT

Get up.
Grab your gun.
Where is —
Oh God, where's your gun?

1

This isn't going to have a happy ending.

—Morgan Freeman, *Se7en*

Near Brokenland Parkway, Columbia, Maryland—Seven Months Ago

A TWENTY-THREE-YEAR-OLD HUNGOVER intern with a broken heart saved the day.

The intern's name was Warren Arbona, and he was in a stuffy warehouse along with five other interns scanning endless pieces of paper and turning them into PDFs that nobody would ever, *ever* fucking read. The whole operation was strictly cover-your-ass. The interns' bosses wanted to be able to tell their government liaisons that, yes, every page of the flood of declassified documents they released had been carefully read and scanned by an experienced member of their legal team.

"Experienced" = interns who'd been on the job for at least two months.

The new president had made a big deal about declassifying everything, the shining light of freedom blasting through the deceptions of the previous administration. A democracy requires accountability, he said, and accountability requires transparency. Which sounded awesome.

But before the PDFs could be uploaded, the president's intelligence advisers insisted that no sensitive secrets harmful to the security of the United States would be leaked to the general public. This still was the real world.

So a white-shoe law firm specializing in government intelligence was retained to painstakingly review every line on every scrap of paper.

Nobody in the firm wanted to deal with that bullshit, so they put the interns on it.

And Warren Arbona, the intern in question, wouldn't have noticed a thing if it hadn't been for his cunt ex-girlfriend. He couldn't help it. The name just jumped out at him.

He stopped the scan and looked at the paper again. Were his eyes playing tricks on him?

Nope. There it was.

Charlie Hardie.

No, it wasn't Christy's dad. Her dad was named Bruce or some such shit. Balding. Big asshole. Deviated septum and beady eyes. But this Charlie guy was an uncle, maybe? Some other relative? Warren had no idea.

And really, who the fuck cared. Christy didn't matter anymore; he'd do best to put her out of his head and finish up with this scanning so he could go home and get good and drunk again.

They were all working inside the abandoned warehouse set of a canceled television show, *Baltimore Homicide*. The rent was absurdly cheap, and the set already had the delightful bonus of real desks and working electrical outlets, thanks to a subplot featuring a fake daily newspaper office.

So all the law firm had to do was arrange for the reams of paper—nearly three trucks' worth—to be backed into the building, plug in a bunch of laptops and scanners, and then set the interns loose. See you in September, motherfuckers.

The working conditions were less than ideal. While an industrial AC unit blasted 60,000 BTUs of arctic air into the fake office via ringed funnels, the warehouse itself had diddly-squat in the way of climate management. So every time you left to drag in another set of files, you baked and sweated in the stifling summer heat. And then when you returned, your sweat was flash-frozen on your body. No wonder everybody was sick.

Warren had been fighting a cold since May, when he first started scanning the documents. He believed that if he polluted his body with enough tequila, the cold virus would give up and abandon ship. So far, it hadn't worked.

But the tequila also helped him forget about Christy Hardie.

Almost.

Now the name popped up, and Warren couldn't help but be curious. He started to read the document, which was a deposition.

Seems Charlie Hardie was an ex–police consultant turned drunk house sitter who was later accused of snuffing a junkie actress named Lane Madden.

Warren kind of wished someone had snuffed Christy after she confessed that she'd been blowing his best friend for, oh, *the entire first year of law school*.

Anyway, Warren remembered the Lane Madden story from a bunch of years ago. Apparently she'd been raped and killed by this house sitter guy who used to be a cop and kind of lost his mind. But the rest of the deposition was kind of boring, so Warren stopped reading and fed the pages into the scanner. Yes, they were all supposed to eyeball each page—even the partners weren't foolish enough to tell the interns to actually read them. But Warren and his colleagues dispensed with the *eyeballing* crap somewhere in late May. If fingers touched a page, it was considered read. Osmosis, they decided.

Warren looked at the clock. Just two more hours until his brain went south of the border.

But at fifteen minutes until closing, something strange happened.

Warren saw the name again, in another deposition, from another year.

Charlie Hardie.

The same fucking dude!

But a totally different file!

To have the same name pop up…with the same surname as his skanky cunt ex-girlfriend…well, that was too big a goocher to ignore.

There wasn't time to read it all, so Warren broke a series of federal laws by stuffing the relevant pages into his North Face backpack and slipped out of the building a few minutes early. He made his Jose Cuervo run, put his feet up on a wobbly Ikea coffee table that was improperly assembled, and settled in for an evening of reading.

Now when Warren had started the scanning project, the partners had told him to look out for anything "unusual." Like what, Warren had asked.

You know, they'd said. *Unusual.*

This seemed to qualify.

Charlie Hardie, it seemed, had also been involved in a top-secret military project *years before* he'd been accused of killing that actress. And not just your usual creepy top-secret military project. This one messed around with you at a genetic level and resulted in…well, that was the frightening part. Few survived, and the project was shut down. Dumb fucking luck? Not likely. Warren didn't believe in synchronicity. Exhibit A seemed pretty clearly linked to Exhibit B.

This made Warren's night, because all summer he'd been dreading the idea of not reporting a single thing to the partners. This would prove he hadn't been dicking around all summer (even though he had). This was a genuine *catch*. This was justification for his summer. For his entire life.

The next morning he pushed the scanner aside and wrote a short memo, including his thoughts on the Charlie Hardie depositions, then copied it and Fed Exed it to the partners.

The partners, also happy to be able to report something to their friends in intelligence, passed it along.

This document would later be known as the Arbona Memorandum. Its shock waves would be felt around the globe.

But at first, it started with a brutal mass slaughter in Philadelphia.

One Mile Outside Philadelphia—Now

Of all the shocks Kendra Hardie had endured over the past few hours—the dropped call from her son, the chilling messages on the alarm keypad, the thudding footfalls on the roof, the wrenching sounds in the very guts of her house, the missing gun, and the awful realization of how quickly her situation had become hopeless—none of that compared to the shock of hearing that voice on the other end of the phone line:

"It's me."

Kendra's mind froze. There was a moment of temporal dislocation, distant memory colliding with the present.

Me.

Could that really be…you?

It *sounds* like you, but…

No.

Can't be you.

But then how do I know, deep in my soul, that it *is* you?

"Are you there? Listen to me, Kendra, I know this is going to sound crazy, but you have to listen to me. You and the boy are in serious danger. You need to get out of the house now and just start driving. Drive *anywhere*. Don't tell me where, because they're definitely listening, but just go, go as fast as you can. I'll find you guys when it's safe."

Kendra swallowed hard, looked at the face of the satellite TV receiver. Three thirteen a.m. A little more than four hours since she'd stepped into her own home and into a living nightmare. Eighteen hours since she'd last seen her son. And almost eight years since she'd last heard her ex-husband's voice. Yet there it was on the line, at the very nexus of the nightmare.

"Kendra? Are you there? Can you hear me?"

"I'm here, Charlie. But I can't leave."

"You have to leave, Kendra, please just trust me on this…"

"I can't leave because they've already called, and told me I *can't* leave."

Earlier in the evening Kendra had been out with a friend downtown, at a Cuban restaurant on Second Street in Old City, but found that she wasn't really into the food, didn't want to finish her mojito, and was tired of hearing about her friend's first-world problems, such as arguments with interior decorators and the headache of maintaining three vacation homes on the Delaware shore. Kendra excused herself

9

and just... *left.* Paid for half of the tab and split, handed the valet her stub, and drove back to the northern suburbs, leaving poor Derek to complain to somebody else about having too much money. Maybe one of the Cuban exile waiters would give a shit.

It had been that kind of listless, annoyance-filled week, and Kendra now felt foolish for thinking that a night of moderate drinking and inane conversation could turn that around.

During the drive home her son, CJ, called. He told her he was just calling to check in—which was just about as unusual as the president of the United States dropping you an email to see how everything was going. CJ didn't check in, *ever.* As CJ grew to manhood, he became increasingly like his father, complete with the delightful ability to cut off all emotional circuitry with the flick of an invisible switch. All the abuse her son had been dishing out over the years hardened her into exactly the kind of mother she'd vowed never to become. The kind of mother who said things like:

"Cut the shit, CJ. What happened?"

"Nothing, Mom. I just..."

Mom. Oooh, that was another red flag. CJ hadn't called her Mom in...months? CJ barely spoke to her, and when he did, it was little more than a grunt.

Now a tiny ball of worry began to form in Kendra's stomach. Was he hurt? Was he calling from a hospital or police station? Her body tensed, and she prepared to change direction and gun the accelerator.

"Where are you?"

"I'm at home, everything's fine. Look, Mom, I know this is going to sound weird, but...what did you do with Dad's old stuff?"

"What? Why are you asking me about that?'

First Mom, now...*Dad!?* For the past seven years, CJ hadn't referred to his father as anything but "asshole" or "cocksucker" or "psycho." Before Kendra had a chance to hear CJ's answer, the phone beeped and went dead. NO SERVICE.

Kendra continued in the same direction but gunned the accelerator just the same, all the way up the Schuylkill Expressway, then the endless traffic lights up Broad Street and finally the hills and curves of Old York Road out to the fringes of Abington Township. Home. She didn't bother pulling the car into the garage, leaving it parked out on the street. Something in CJ's voice... no, *everything* about CJ's voice was completely wrong. Dad's old stuff? What was that about? Why did he suddenly want to see the few possessions his father had left behind? The thought that CJ might be drinking crossed Kendra's mind, but his voice wasn't slurred. If anything, it was completely clear and focused, in stark contrast to the moody grunts she usually received.

And whenever CJ did go on a binge, his heart filled with raw hate for this father, not fuzzy nostalgia.

"CJ?"

The alarm unit on the wall to the left of the door beeped insistently until Kendra keyed in the code. She closed the door behind her, locked it, then reengaged the system. It beeped again. All set.

"CJ, answer me!"

And then began the nightmare.

No CJ, not anywhere. No trace of him in his room, no tell-tale glasses or dishes in the sink. The house was *exactly* as Kendra had left it when she left for Old City earlier in the evening. Had CJ even called from home? The call had come from his cell, so he could be anywhere right now.

Not knowing what else to do, Kendra tried him again on her phone, but still—NO SERVICE. What was that about? She could understand a dropped call when speeding down the Schuylkill, as if a guardian angel had interfered with the signal to prevent you from sparking a twelve-car pile-up on the most dangerous road in Philadelphia. But in her own home?

Maybe she could get a better signal outside. Kendra went back to the front door and keyed in the code. Two digits in, however, her finger stopped, and hung in midair before the 6 key.

The digital readout, which usually delivered straightforward messages such as SYSTEM ENGAGED or PLEASE ENTER ACCESS CODE, now told her something else:

STAY RIGHT WHERE YOU ARE

"The fuck?" Kendra muttered, then lowered her finger for a second before blinking hard and stabbing the 6 button anyway, followed by the 2. Which should have disengaged the system. This time, however, there was no reassuring beep. There was nothing at all, except:

KENDRA, THAT WON'T HELP.

Then:

DON'T MAKE A SOUND.
DON'T MOVE.
NOT UNTIL WE CALL YOU.

And Kendra, much to her own disgust, did exactly as she was told, staying perfectly still and silent...

...for about two seconds, before realizing *fuck this* and grabbing the handle of her front door. She twisted the knob, pulled. The door didn't move, as if it had been cemented in place. What? She hadn't put the deadbolts on when she'd come in just a minute ago...

The phone in her hand buzzed to life. There was SERVICE, suddenly. The name on the display: INCOMING CALL / CJ.

Oh thank God. She thumbed the Accept button, expecting to hear her son's voice, maybe even hoping he'd call her *Mom* again.

But instead, it was someone else.

Now, four agonizing hours later, during which Kendra heard the sounds of her own house being turned against her...she was listening to the voice of her ex-husband—an accused murderer long thought to be dead. And he had the audacity to be grilling her!

"They called me and said if I left the house I was dead."

"Who told you that? Who told you you were dead?"

"A woman. She didn't give her name."

"Did you call the police? Anyone at all?"

"They told me not to call anyone, or do anything else except wait."

"Wait for what?"

There was a burst of static on the line, and then another voice came on the line. The one who'd called four hours earlier, from CJ's phone.

The evil icy-voiced bitch queen who had her son and who claimed to have the house surrounded.

"Hey, Charlie! It's your old pal Mann here. So good to hear your voice after all this time. Well, that magical day has finally arrived. In about thirty seconds we're going to kill the phones, and the power, and everything else in your wife's house. We've got her surrounded; I know every square inch of every house in a five-block radius. You, of all people, know how thorough we are."

Charlie ignored the other voice.

"Kendra, where's the boy? Where's Seej?"

Seej: Charlie's old nickname for CJ—See. Jay. Over time, shortened to Seej.

"Shhhh, now, Charlie, it's rude to interrupt. You're wasting precious seconds. Now I know what you're going to say. You're going to tell me that if I touch one hair on your family's head, you'll rip me apart one limb at a time...or maybe some other colorful metaphor? Well, you know, that's just not gonna happen. Because you lost this one, Chuck. There's not going to be any cavalry rushing in, no last-minute saves, no magic escapes. And you know what's going to happen next?"

What *should* have been going through Kendra's mind at this moment was something along the lines of:

Charlie, where the hell have you been, and why have you surfaced now? The last time we spoke it was stupid and petty conversation about a late credit card bill and I think the last word I spoke to you before disconnecting was *whatever.*

Or maybe:

Charlie, why didn't you call me before tonight? Do you know how many late nights I stared at the ceiling, trying to physically will you to call me? Not to change anything or explain anything, but just to tell me what happened? Do you know how hard the *not knowing* was? How much it consumed me over the years, digging in deep, way past the regret and guilt and into the very core of me?

But instead Kendra thought:

Goddamn you, Charlie.

Goddamn you for doing this to us.

*   *   *

"What's going to happen next is," the ice bitch queen continued, "your family's going to die. And there's not a fucking thing you can do to stop me."

If Kendra had any doubts that the voice on the other end of the line belonged to her husband, they vanished when he spoke again. Because his words were infused with a rock-hard defiance that had once been familiar to her, over a decade ago.

Charlie Hardie told the ice bitch queen, "I can stop you."

2

Space is big. You just won't believe how vastly, hugely, mind-bogglingly big it is.

—Douglas Adams

Low Earth Orbit—Three Days Ago

THE TRANSMISSION WAS supposed to start at 12:30 p.m. universal time, but by 12:55 it became clear that wasn't going to happen.

Hardie told himself it was just a little trouble with the signal. Someone down there was diligently working on the problem, and pretty soon he'd be seeing his family on the monitor. Just a few more minutes. They wouldn't leave him hanging much longer, right? This was the only thing that kept him going, and they knew it. They wouldn't mess with him like this. That would just be cruel.

After four hours of being frozen stiff, Hardie unstrapped his legs to stretch them. Starting at 1:00 p.m. UT he had a checklist of duties to perform. They had better start the transmission soon. Otherwise...

And then the transmission began.

One hundred and sixty-six miles below, life went on.

Below, on the surface of the earth, at almost 10:00 a.m. eastern standard time, which was three hours behind universal time, Kendra was making chicken soup. Both she and Seej were fighting colds. Kendra had already taken apart the chicken and was now chopping thick carrot slices. Her furious motions made Hardie nervous—her fingers moved so quickly, chop chop chop chop chop chop chop, even though her fingers were curled under, just like you were supposed to do. Still, fingers could slip. And if something should happen...

Seej was in the living room, holding up an imaginary gun-sword thing and blasting and slashing away digital opponents on a flat screen. Hardie had no idea what the boy was playing. The last video game he could remember the kid playing, more than a decade ago, was something involving Italian plumbers and giant magic mushrooms. What the hell kind of game involved a gun and a sword? If a gun didn't do the job, did you really need the sword to finish off the bad guy? And why slash at him with a sword if you've got a gun at your disposal?

Still the boy was enraptured. Nothing real, except the sick delight on his face. You could tell when he got off a particularly gory shot, because his eyes lit up in a certain way. Partly appalled, partly amused. Much as Hardie didn't want to admit it, he looked like the kind of kid who might shoot up a school someday.

This was Charlie Hardie's family. Right there in front of him. Flesh and blood, living their lives, struggling with their problems.

Utterly unreachable.

For the past nine months, Charlie Hardie's life boiled down to mind-numbing routine. Open eyes. Crawl out of the harness that held him in place while he tried—and failed—to sleep. Evacuate bladder in a separate harness setup—which up here entailed a seventeen-step process. Climb over to the control panels. Check the levels, comparing the numbers against the ones in the manual, even though he knew them by heart. Stand to eat a bland meal, because sitting made his stomach hurt too much. Wash self with moistened towelettes. Do sit-ups and pedal an ergometer to get strength back. Push the same sequence of buttons again. And again. And again. A monkey could do this. But they didn't want any old monkey.

They wanted a monkey named Charlie Hardie.

It had been a year since Charlie Hardie *almost* shot that nice woman in the face.

And every day in this cramped-ass satellite, Hardie thought about what life would have been like if he *had* shot that woman in the face. Probably would have been short. As in "a few seconds long" short—because if he'd killed that woman, her armed minions would have blasted the meat from Hardie's bones with a dazzling array of heavy artillery. A few seconds may even be generous.

Instead Hardie had agreed to not shoot the woman in the face, and to surrender to the Cabal and pretty much do their bidding.

The Cabal...oh, they had so many names. When Hardie first encountered them, he knew them as the Accident People who worked for the Industry. Back then they'd nearly killed him...but he'd hurt them bad, too, scuttling a deal worth billions and *really* pissing them off. So much so that the incident (a) stole five years of Hardie's life, and (b) stuck him in a secret prison and forced him to be the warden. Needless to say, this really pissed *Hardie* off. So when Hardie finally busted out he set out to destroy the three known members of Secret America—which is what the inmates in that prison called the Industry.

But when Hardie asked the nice lady he almost shot in the face what they called themselves, she chuckled and said, "Call us the Cabal."

Hardie wanted to crack a joke like, "Kebob? As in chunks of meat on a stick?"

But it was hard to make a joke with so many guns in your face, ready to end your life in a fusillade of lead.

Oh, Hardie had tried. Just before finding himself in an un-winnable standoff, he had embarked on a mission of blood-splattered revenge. It was, to be honest, kind of a mixed bag. The first leader of the Cabal? Killed without a hitch. You might even go so far as to call that a smashing success. The second leader? Hardie thought he'd killed that son of a bitch, but it turned out that he had survived after all. Maybe. It was all kind of unclear. And the third leader?

Well, that was the nice lady he *almost* shot in the face but didn't.

Which brought them to their current arrangement. In exchange for a year of indentured servitude, the Cabal promised Hardie that the slate would be wiped clean. The Cabal would not actively seek to kill Hardie, and they would not seek to send the Accident People after his estranged wife and son. That's all Hardie wanted, of course. To have the threat of death finally removed from the heads of Kendra and Charlie Jr. So Hardie had lowered the gun and agreed to work for the Cabal.

We just want you to guard something, they said. That's what you do, right? You guard stuff?

Yeah, Hardie said, I guard stuff.

Only they didn't tell Hardie he'd be guarding something in *freakin' outer space.*

Okay: "low earth orbit."

Same damned thing, Hardie thought.

The very idea of it sounded insane. But the Cabal insisted that it was not only possible but practical, too. Certain things were way too valuable to keep on the surface of the earth, where they could be hacked or dug up and breached in countless ways. For as long as people had scuttled across the planet, they had been devising countless ways to steal the possessions of others. For total security, you had to remove the planet from the equation.

That required some expensive technology—but in the long run, it was not as expensive as maintaining an ultra-secure facility planetside. Once you shot the thing up into low earth orbit, you could be assured that only organizations with the resources of the Cabal could get up there, too. And no one had the resources of the Cabal.

But you also needed a human presence, because machines, no matter how well built, could malfunction. Hence the need for a guard.

Hence the need for Charlie Hardie.

Hardie shifted his body in the cramped space near the monitor, trying to stretch his sore body, get the blood flowing. He forgot his pains, though, when he saw his family.

On screen, Kendra cracked eggs into a glass bowl to prepare the batter for French toast. Hardie was instantly hurled back in time, a decade ago, watching her do the same thing on a Sunday morning, back when she *was* his wife. Same glass bowl. Same stainless steel whisk. Same plug-in electric fryer on the countertop, passed down from her mother. The sight of the familiar kitchen gear made it feel like they were still married, still together.

He knew they weren't legally married anymore. Too much time had passed. If she were smart—and Kendra was the smartest woman he knew—she would have declared him legally dead and collected an insurance payout.

Even if Hardie were somehow able to magically teleport himself down to the surface of the earth, inside that kitchen, what would she say? Their last days together, those years before all that madness in L.A., had been awkward and painful and tense. Back then, Hardie swore that if you could somehow liquefy and bottle Kendra's angry glares, you'd have the most potent weed killer on the market. He'd ask what was wrong. Kendra's mouth would say, *Nothing, I'm fine.* But her eyes would say, *I hate you with every fiber of my being.*

Kendra left the kitchen. The camera should have cut away to the dining room, but it didn't. Which was strange.

Whoever was in charge of giving Hardie his daily dose of family time was usually pretty good about making sure those few minutes were worth it. Hardie couldn't help but wonder how often the same person—male or female—watched over Kendra and the boy the rest of the day. Was it constant surveillance, or just the occasional check-in to make sure they were still alive and thus useful to the Cabal? Was this person a perv? Did he or she watch Hardie's family in his/her spare time?

Usually Hardie couldn't think thoughts like these—not with him trapped in low earth orbit and unable to do a thing about it.

But sometimes he spoke aloud to this mysterious Watcher, on the off-chance he or she could hear.

Which he knew was ridiculous, because this was a one-way transmission—they had stressed that during his training. *We'll be able to monitor you through various sensors, but don't bother talking to us. And fuck you very much!*

Still Hardie couldn't resist.

"Come *on.*"

He spoke out loud just to reassure himself that he had a voice. He almost wished he could time travel back about a year and visit himself in that lousy secret prison and tell himself, *Look, buddy, at least you've got people to talk to. Even if they are crazy. So enjoy it while supplies last.*

Hardie would say all kinds of things to himself.

You know how screwed you are, Chuck?

Chuck. Always Chuck. Nobody in real life called him anything but Hardie, and that would have included Kendra most times. But after he was almost shot to death nearly nine years ago, the media decided that he was Unkillable Chuck. And he was up in this tin can, still alive. So he must be Chuck.

Right, Chuck?

How we doing there, Chuck?

Morning, Chuck, you big asshole.

How'd ya end up in a satellite anyway, Chuck?

There was only one way up to the satellite. You basically had to own a rocket, possess the technology to dock with the satellite, then force your way into the orbiting craft—which was not much bigger than a Honda Odyssey. But *if*... and this was a HUGE *if*... you could manage to clear all of these hurdles, then there was one last fail-safe:

Charlie Hardie would be waiting for you, ready to point and shoot.

The only entranceway—a long tube that didn't feel much wider than a hula hoop—was lined with machine guns. If you stepped inside and Hardie pulled the dual triggers, you would be cut to ribbons, then jettisoned back the way you came, along with your intruding craft. In lots and lots of chunky, frozen pieces.

Hardie almost *wished* someone would try to break in, just so he'd have something interesting to do. Instead he languished inside a satellite parked 166 miles above the surface of the earth—passing over the United States, according to one monitor.

What was so important about this satellite? Hardie has no idea. But his life had boiled down to three duties: (a) press a few buttons to perform simple maintenance, (b) keep himself alive, and (c) shoot anyone who showed up.

Hardie still didn't fully understand why he'd been chosen for this particular mission.

I'm no astronaut, he told them.

That's fine, they told him. We don't want an astronaut. We want *you*.

Why?

You're a survivor. We realized this when you survived what happened in L.A. five years ago. This was confirmed when you managed to work your way out of an escape-proof prison facility. It's you we want. But first, we have to make a few modifications.

Yeah. *Modifications.*

You see, astronauts typically remain in orbit up to six months. Any longer than that exposes the astronaut to weakened bones due to loss of gravity and exposure to solar and cosmic radiation. (Not to mention the psychological stress of being so far from any other human being for so long.) But they claimed to have procedures that would limit the risks. Hardie wanted to know what they were going to do to him; they more or less flatly refused to tell him any detail. *Proprietary secrets,* they said. *Fuck you, it's my body,* you said. *Is it really?* they said. And they had a point.

All he knew is that after surgery, his head had ached for a really long time. And more or less hadn't stopped hurting since then, as if they'd sawed open the top of his skull, moved some stuff around, and then put his head back together a millimeter or two *off*.

Anyway, that had been nine months ago; there were three to go on his contract. Besides the hellish confined spaces and the constant low-grade headache, it wasn't complete misery. There were perks. In addition to Hardie's family being permitted to live, he was allowed to watch them for a few minutes a day, via secret cameras inside Kendra's rented home just outside Philadelphia.

Each transmission from Earth was torture and relief at the same time. Hardie supposed that's what ghosts must feel like. Watching your loved ones live out their lives while you were completely powerless to affect them. Hardie began to suspect that watching these little snippets of his family every day had driven him insane. But what was he supposed to do? Stop watching?

After his contract was up, he would (supposedly) be allowed to return to them.

Hardie didn't believe this for a minute. The lizard cop voice inside his head told him that this would never happen. *They will kill you after this job is over. They will kill your family, too...* So Hardie knew he had only three months left to figure out a plan to escape, rejoin his family, then disappear with them. That, of course, was presuming his wife and son would want anything to do with him.

Still the faithful husband, his nemesis had once told him. *Which is really impressive, considering how long since you've seen them.*

For now Charlie Hardie's life was simply mind-numbing routine in a super-confined space. And the occasional pleasure of watching his ex-wife make breakfast.

But now Hardie was staring at the surveillance image of an empty kitchen. He tried to project his thoughts across the atmosphere and straight down into his ex-wife's head in Philadelphia. Come on, Kendra. Just walk back into the kitchen for something. You forgot something, didn't you? Maybe you didn't turn off the fryer? Give me something. Anything.

But there was nothing.

Seej, where are you? Don't you want to raid the fridge for a post-breakfast snack? The boy, who was pretty much now a man (as much as Hardie didn't want to admit it), was lean and strong and ate like a trucker. Whereas Kendra seemed to consume small, birdlike portions, Seej could put away the provisions for the working staff of an entire farm. And then be hungry again for lunch by midmorning. He looked nothing like his father, but he ate like him.

So, c'mon. You must be hungry again, Seej. Let me see you. Or have you gone out somewhere? Maybe to meet a friend? Or a girlfriend?

But there was nothing.

After another few minutes of nothing, the transmission came to an end. Hardie was beginning the process of unstrapping himself when—

Whoah.

He felt the satellite jolt.

3

The last man on earth sat alone in a room. There was a knock at the door.

—Fredric Brown

HARDIE TICKED DOWN the extremely small list of things that could possibly jolt a $3.7-billion-dollar satellite.

The best-case scenario: an off-schedule food delivery drone. But that couldn't be. The last had arrived two weeks ago, and there wasn't another scheduled for at least six more weeks. There's no way his employers would send extra, because (a) they were super budget-conscious, and (b) everything up here was planned down to the ounce. Which left . . . asteroid? A collision with a piece of space junk?

Sure *sounded* like the food delivery drone docking, though. The noise and clatter was like someone slamming an SUV into the side of your house, followed by magnetic deadbolts, locking it in place.

CLUNK-CLUNK-CLUNK-CLUNK

Hardie pulled himself over to the gateway hatch, using the hand-holds to make his way. He checked the sensors that usually told him when a delivery drone was ready to deliver a payload. He waited. Nothing appeared on the screen. This wasn't a delivery drone. This was something else. The very thing they assured him could never, *ever* happen... because they'd taken every possible precaution so that it would not happen... well, it seemed to be happening.

Fuck.

Hardie decided he wanted a beer. Like, yeah, right now. It was the morning in Philadelphia, but it was afternoon here in space. He should have insisted that they install a cooler in this damned thing, maybe arrange for monthly shipments of quarter-kegs or even a couple of six-packs. Beer is packed with nutrients, right? If you're going to stick a guy in a tin can, at least give him a couple of cans to open every now and again.

But no. The satellite was too small for such an extravagance as a beer.

His entire world was in the shape of a bullet, and it flung itself around the earth many, many times a day.

There were two main sections: the bulbous part where Hardie lived and performed his pointless daily tasks, and then the skinny-ass metal gateway tube that led to a small rear hatch, where the delivery drone would bring fresh supplies of food and water and also accept waste. And, boy, was that whole process fun.

Then again, ordinary life up here in space was a Black & Decker funhouse of pain. Hardie was forever banging random body parts (elbows, knees, toes, skull) into the metal gizmos on the interior of his living quarters. As a result, he moved throughout the craft perpetually stooped, limbs tucked in close to himself at all times. Sometimes all Hardie wanted in the world was the opportunity to stretch. A *real* stretch, where you reach your hands to heaven and you can feel the vertebrae pop. Such a stretch was impossible inside this claustrophobic tin can. And taking a leak? Back on Earth, guys were blessed with the ability to find a semi-hidden spot, unzip, and let it fly. Up here Hardie had to contort as if he were doing yoga in a closet. If the vacuum seal wasn't tight, then he'd enjoy the sensation of his own gravity-free piss droplets smacking into this face.

Most days Hardie thought he'd have been better off languishing in that secret fucking prison.

The living area was about the size of a minivan. The interior, however, was so jammed with subsystems (thermal control, environmental control, avionics, communications, guidance computers, and a bunch of other crap he couldn't remember) that to Hardie it felt like a minivan jammed with crap for a cross-country family vacation. To do pretty much anything—sleep, eat, shit, shave—he had to strap himself in to one kind of harness or another.

Strapping myself in here, boss.

Go on, Charlie, strap yourself in.

For fun, Hardie could open the hatch and crawl into the gateway tube. But seeing as how that was lined with machine guns and didn't offer much in the way of entertainment value, such excursions were brief and unsatisfying. Sometimes he could look through one of the four tiny windows and check out the groovy solar arrays sticking off the sides of the satellite like robotic dragonfly wings. But that got old fast, too.

There was nothing else to do.

No place to go.

His only diversions were the heavily pixilated transmissions from Earth, showing his wife and son live their lives without him.

And if Hardie wanted his family to go on living, he knew that he had to take care of whatever might show up in that gateway tube.

*   *   *

The docking mechanism made a last, loud clunking sound. Hardie knew this was basically his front door being unlocked. Usually, he was the one doing the unlocking. To hear it being done with unseen hands was genuinely disturbing. This was no asteroid. This was some sentient being on the other side of the hatch, *unlocking it on purpose.*

Hardie's hands were wrapped around the dual triggers; here we go. All he had to do was point.

And shoot.

But a dizzying wave of thoughts raced through his head. He wondered how loud the gunfire would be. And would his employers bring him back down immediately, or would they force him to remain in orbit with the dead chunks of whomever still clinging to the sides of the gateway? Hardie heard himself sigh. Was he really going to do this?

The speakers crackled and popped.

"Charlie Hardie," a voice said.

Oh boy.

Not only was there a sentient being on the other side of the hatch. But this sentient being knew his goddamned name.

"Hardie, can you hear me?"

Yeah.

I can hear you loud and clear, partner.

The craziest thing—and this was pretty much the maraschino cherry on a sundae full of crazy—the voice sounded *familiar.* As in, it sounded like Hardie's own voice. Which was insane, right? Maybe after nine months of talking to himself, his ears were tuned only to his own voice. And now every voice sounded like his own.

The only other explanation was that Hardie had finally lost his damn fool mind, that the voices in his head had escaped and had somehow taken possession of this spacecraft.

"Hardie, if you can hear me, use the audio communicator and let me know, okay, buddy? It's the third button down to the left of the monitor."

Sure. Yeah. The audio communicator. So I can talk to the voices inside my own head. A handy external manifestation of interior cuh-RAAAY-zee.

"Hardie, talk to me," his own voice insisted. "I'm here to save you, man. Eve Bell sent me!"

Eve Bell?

That was a name Hardie thought about almost every day.

Hardie and Eve had been bound together in the strangest way possible: They were old prison buddies. In her previous life, Eve Bell was a private investigator, a professional "people finder" who'd been hired to find Hardie. And find Hardie she did. But they'd ended up in the clutches of their common enemy, and both had to claw their way through hell (and its Prisonmaster) to escape...at which point Eve announced that she was quitting the people-finding business. No, instead she would be in the "destroying the Secret America" business, and wouldn't rest until it was dismantled, destroyed, in flaming embers, etc. She recruited other like-minded loners who'd been screwed by the people she called Secret America and waged bloody war.

Eve had said: "We can fight back. All of us. We can take these bastards down."

But the Prisonmaster shook his head and smiled. "You have family, Mr. Hardie. A wife and a son, isn't that right? They will be dead the moment you leave this facility. They'll see to it."

"Not if I get to *them* first. Who are they? Who are your bosses? I want names."

"That won't do you any good. You can't comprehend the complexity of the Industry..."

Eve said, "I hate to say this: Hardie, he might be right. Once they know we've escaped, they'll be relentless. They won't hesitate to take out your family. I know how they work."

Which made the decision clear: Only Hardie could slip out of the prison for now. Leaving Eve behind to deal with the other prisoners. Hardie promised he'd send help.

"Don't," Eve had said. "Take care of your family first."

"I can help."

"*Go,*" Eve insisted. "Leave this to me. This is no hardship. I've been at war with Secret America for two decades now. Thanks to this place, I now have an army. And we're going to kick their asses."

That was what Eve had promised, anyway. Hardie had no idea how that whole war thing was going, because he was stuck in outer space.

Hardie often wondered if Eve had been winning any battles down there. Or if she'd already been caught, silenced, and/or killed. If it was the latter, Hardie wondered if they had made it look like an accident.

Now this mystery man here (who sounded just like Hardie) was invoking the name Eve Bell. Which would be a pretty clever move on the part of the Industry, or Secret America, or whatever you wanted to call them. Maybe this was simply a test to see if he had the guts to pull the triggers after all.

But what if this guy truly had been sent by Eve Bell? What if she was winning the war, and she'd sent someone to rescue Hardie? In that case, it would be a major bummer if Hardie were to pulp his own rescuer into machine gun–style chopped ham and flush him out into the void of space. Either way, he had to be sure.

"Eve who?" Hardie asked, trying to sound oblivious.

"Eve Bell. I know you know who she is, Hardie."

"No, it really doesn't ring a—" Hardie stopped himself. Christ, he *had* lost his mind.

"Hardie," the strange yet familiar voice said, "time is critical here. You either have to trust me and open this hatch, or you don't. In which case we're *both* dead men."

"Well, I don't trust you," Hardie said. "I don't know you, or this Eve Bell, so why don't you just leave." The moment he spoke the words Hardie realized how absurd that sounded. This wasn't like telling someone to *get off my porch*. There was no gray area here. This was low-orbit *space*. He had to either let this guy in or kill him.

"At least let me show you my face," the voice said.

"Why?"

"Trust me. It's a face you'll recognize."

"If I know you, why won't you just tell me your name, then?"

"It's a bit more complicated than that. Please, Hardie, just let me open the hatch and show you who I am."

This boggled Hardie's mind. Which wasn't good, because Hardie was already convinced he'd gone crazy inside this tin can all of these months. Secret America or the Industry or who-the-fuck-ever wouldn't run some kind of freaky psychological experiment on him all this time, would they? No. They wouldn't do that to poor old Hardie. Not after all that they'd been through together.

"I'm opening the hatch."

"You can't," Hardie said quietly.

"Overriding the system now," the voice said. "Hang on."

"Don't, I'm warning you," Hardie said, but he had to admit — his curiosity was overwhelming.

Who could it possibly be? Why would Hardie know his face? Maybe it was his former pal Deke Clark, who somehow had convinced his FBI bosses to rent a rocket ship for the weekend. Or, for that matter, the president of the United States of America. Even better: Sylvester Stallone and Jason Statham and Arnold Schwarzenegger and Bruce Willis, teaming up to rescue him. Oh, the adventures they would share!

Hardie knew it didn't matter, though. He'd been given simple instructions: If anyone enters the tube, you shoot him.

Otherwise, your family dies.

Down below, the hatch unlocked and opened a few inches, as if a cat had playfully nudged it open. Hardie was ready. The target onscreen, fingers on the dual triggers. Again, he hesitated. Was he really going to do this? Pump buckets of bullets into a total stranger?

Hell, yeah, he was. If it means saving his family, he'd do anything. There was no choice.

Hardie was about to squeeze the triggers when the hatch popped open all the way and someone screamed, *Don't shoot! I'm here to save you!* The figure clawed at the latch connecting his helmet to his suit, shouting, *Wait! Wait! Wait! Don't shoot! Please!* Then the helmet came all the way off to reveal . . .

Hardie's own face.

4

Am I mad, in a coma, or back in time?
— John Simm, *Life on Mars*

THE SIGHT OF his mirror image left Hardie dazed, his vision fuzzy. As if his mind was struggling to apply some logic to the situation. *There's a guy down at the other end of that tube who looks just like you. Therefore, we don't exist. Therefore, I am shutting us down so as to avoid a time-space paradox.* Hardie dropped his hands from the triggers without even thinking about it. The tips of his fingers tingled.

"Relax," the Other Him said. "I can explain everything."

Hardie thought: no. Fuck no, I'm not going to relax. I need to pour hundreds of bullets into this guy *right this very second,* no matter who he looks like. But...

...but...

What if he *was* the salvation he'd been looking for?

All this time, spinning hundreds of miles above the surface of the earth, praying that God would grace him with even the tiniest glimmer of an escape plan. Was this it?

Hardie stopped himself.

What, *yourself?* You are your own salvation? For reals, yo? Are you hallucinating?

That was it. A hallucination.

Nothing more than a bit of undigested reconstituted beef or powdered NASA potato—*Scrooge in Space*–style.

So a hallucination wouldn't mind getting blasted into little red messy chunks by twin machine guns, would it?

"Who," Hardie said, "the fuck are you?"

"I told you, I can explain."

"Explain quick."

Hardie stared down the long, silver metal tube at his double. And the longer he stared, the more his whole body seemed to rebel. Tingling and trembling and going numb in random places. The resemblance was more than uncanny. It was freakish. Hardie had always hated looking at himself in a mirror, but this was even worse than a mirror image. Mirrors flipped you around, showed you a skewed version of yourself. Now Hardie was faced with how he looked in real life, to other people. Never mind that this was a physical impossibility. He couldn't be in two places at once. The very thought of it was frying his circuits.

"I'm not going to hurt you," the Other Him said, his voice trying to approximate a soothing tone. "I'm here to help you."

"Don't—" Hardie floundered for the right sequence of words. He settled for: "Don't you move!"

"I work for the U.S. government. Intelligence. I'm here to save you from the Cabal."

"The who?"

There, for a second, the spell was shattered. Hardie never used words like "cabal." No, he'd use something like "creepy pricks who meddle in people's lives and force them to have accidents and shove

35

them down into secret prisons and shoot them into outer freakin' space." Never *cabal*. Sissies used words like *cabal*. Abrams, the bitch who'd sent him up into space, had used the word "cabal."

Still, the Other Him pressed his case. "You know exactly who I mean. The people who sent you up here."

"They seem to have many names."

"Well, they've evolved."

Hardie mulled this for a second. Then he said, "I thought I told you to explain quickly."

The Other Charlie Hardie explained quickly.

Six years ago, the lawyers who ran the Accident People were a group of problem solvers, working in secret for the most exclusive and powerful clients in the world. (Usually, huge corporations.) Over the past few years, however, they'd evolved to *become* the powerful, with their claws sunk deep into the U.S. government at the highest levels.

"But you started to change all of that when you escaped from Site Number 7734," the Other Charlie Hardie said. "All of those people popped out of that secret prison just jonesin' for some payback, and they've been attacking their interests all over the world. Your buddy Eve Bell especially."

"You say you know her, huh?"

"She sent me to find you."

"You're telling me she's behind all of this?"

"She's working with some others, but yes. We want what's in this satellite so we can deliver the killing blow. Dismantle their operations permanently."

"What's in this satellite?"

"They never told you this...hell, why would they? But you're up

here guarding information hidden in this satellite. The most dangerous information in the world, as a matter of fact. It's too dangerous
to keep on earth, where it could potentially be stolen or hacked. But
it's also too important to destroy."

"That doesn't make any sense."

The Other Him sighed. Swear to Christ—he *sighed.* Like he was
troubled by all of this pesky explaining. Hardie decided right then
and there: The Other Him was an asshole.

"Let me give you a quick example," the Other Him said. "You
ever hear of the Borgias?"

Hardie paused for a moment, then replied: "You talking about the
casino?"

"No, the cutthroat Italian family. They...wait, you're totally
messing with me, aren't you?"

"Go on."

"The Borgias apparently came up with the most lethal poison on
earth. A poison they only dared to use once, and vowed to never use
again—the potential to wipe out the entire population of the earth
was too great. Even back then, there was the fear that someone who
possessed the poison would lose his or her mind long enough to try
to kill thousands. The poison was *that* powerful."

"Uh-huh. So you're saying there's a deadly poison on this satellite."

"No," the Other Him said. "I'm saying whatever you've got
locked up in there has the potential to make the Borgia super-
poison seem like salmonella. You're guarding the one thing powerful
enough to destroy them. Let's find it...then destroy them."

Hardie turned his gaze away from the Other Him. Shit, he needed
to stop referring to the Other Him as...well, *the Other Him.* He

needed to give him a nickname, because it was truly freaky to see yourself on a small monitor. A slightly younger, slightly more handsome version of you. One who hasn't had his ass kicked to hell and gone.

But what should he call the Other Him?

Chuck?

Phil?

Jimbo?

Asshole?

For now, "you" would just have to do.

"Anything else I can explain?" the Other Him asked. "Like I said, time is fairly critical here."

"Oh, just one small thing. Why the fuck do you look like me?"

See, that was the weirdest thing to Hardie.

It wasn't that somebody had somehow, against all odds, managed to dock with this allegedly top-secret satellite. And it wasn't that he was stuck inside a top-secret satellite to begin with. It was the fact that Eve Bell (allegedly) had sent someone who looked exactly like him. Why? Hardie had watched dozens of movies where long-lost twin brothers or sisters or even clones were the catalyst for implausible, harebrained plots. And, except for *The Parent Trap,* stories with twins or doubles or clones often didn't turn out too well for at least one of the twins. So what was this? Was this guy up here to save him, or kill him and replace him?

"I can explain."

"Dazzle me."

"It's the satellite itself. They made me look like this to fool the biometric sensors. Everything in this craft is tuned to *your* biometrics. If somebody else tried to open the wrong compartment, it would result in complete shutdown. They left absolutely *nothing* to chance. Only *you* can be in this capsule. So I went through a series of procedures to look exactly like *you*."

Hardie stared at him—himself?—for a good long while before finally saying, "Bio-what?"

But Hardie remembered the weeks of prep leading up to his "mission." They did take thousands of measurements, snap what seemed like a million digital photographs of his entire body, from the top of his head to the skin between his toes. Which freaked him out to no end, and more than once Hardie was prepared to say, "You know what? I changed my mind. Why don't you skip the eighty-seventh photograph of my right nipple and just shoot me in the head." But he thought of Kendra and the boy, and he endured it. At least they didn't catalog his junk. Whoever this Other Him was, he probably got to keep his own twig and berries. Hooray for individuality.

"How long did that take?" Hardie asked, gesturing with his chin. "Being made to look like me."

"I had the final surgical procedure a few days ago. My ears are still a little tender."

"They saved the ears for last, huh?"

"They heal the easiest, apparently. And I needed to get up here as soon as possible."

"So before you were me...who the hell were you? Why did they think you'd make a good me?"

The Other Him paused. "Nobody special. I was chosen because of our similar body types, ages. Though I'm a little younger."

"Naturally. So what now?"

"Now comes the part you're *not* going to like."

5

If they told you wolverines would make good house pets, would you believe them?

—Del Griffith, *Planes, Trains and Automobiles*

YOU DIDN'T LIKE it, either, but what choice did you have? This was part of the mission.

You're a spy, doubling as a man named Charlie Hardie.

A few hours ago you had been stuffed into a small metal box—not unlike what that crazy Yogi Coudoux used to do on that early 1980s show *That's Incredible!*—and launched into space, hoping that the rocket carrying the box would be able to guide itself to the Cabal's mystery satellite and dock with it. When you first heard the mission directive a few months ago, you asked a tech guy if this cockamamie scheme could possibly work, and the tech guy said—yes, he actually said this—"You know, I like your chances." Which wasn't exactly the most reassuring thing you could hear from an astrophysicist, but, hey, death and danger was all part of the job. The life of a spy.

However, the trickiest, most precarious part of the operation was next.

If you're perfectly honest with yourself, you don't like your chances very much at all.

There is little chance Charlie Hardie is going to go for it.

But you have to try anyway.

"Go ahead," Hardie said. "Lay it on me."

"Okay," the Other Him said. "For this whole rescue operation to work, I need to search the entire craft."

"To find that Borgia super-poison or whatever. Yeah. So you said."

"Thing is, there can't be *two* people in the main module at the same time. Otherwise, the automatic controls kick in, resulting in total shutdown. So . . . uh, you're going to have to wait down here in this tube while I do my search."

Hardie looked at his double, smirked for a moment, letting nonsense words like *automatic* and *controls* and *total* and *shutdown* dance around his head. And then all at once the words really sank in, Hardie realized what this guy was asking, and . . .

Well, the guy had been right. Hardie didn't like it at all.

"No," Hardie said. "No fucking way."

"I know how it sounds. You have very little reason to trust me. But I'm telling you, the sooner I search the module, the sooner we can both get out of this thing. The sooner you're back with your family."

"They'll kill us all anyway," Hardie said. "You think they won't find out?"

"Not if I find what I'm looking for. The moment I deliver it to my handler, it'll cripple them. Instantly."

"What is it? What could possibly shut them down instantly? Now you're just bullshitting me. Do you know how long I've been tangling with these assholes? Your precious Cabal?"

41

"Yeah, I know exactly how long."

Hardie looked around the module, as if he'd see something he hadn't already spotted in his nine months trapped on this spinning tin can. Maybe a little hatch with stenciled letters that read TOP SE-CRET STUFF INSIDE!!! WHAT TO DO IF SOMEONE SHOWS UP ASKING TO SEARCH THE CRAFT.

"And I," the Other Him said, "am not bullshitting you."

The tone of the guy's voice kind of said, *Yeah, I'm not bullshitting you.* Hardie could tell. It was the tone he used when he was trying to convince someone that he was not bullshitting them. Whether or not he in fact *was* trying to bullshit them or not. The truth would be impossible to untangle.

"Tell me where to look," Hardie said. "I'm sure I'll be able to find it for you. This place isn't that big."

"This whole thing will go much faster if I do the search. And like I said, we're up against a ticking clock here."

"And like *I* said: no fucking way."

But Hardie's mind was already considering the possibilities. Let's just say this weirdo lookalike was telling the truth, and his best weapon against these "Cabal" assholes *has* been at his finger-tips the entire time he's been stuck in low earth orbit. In a sick way, it all made sense. They didn't stick him in this tin can just to keep it running; there were thousands of other resilient mon-keys who could do the same time. No, they wanted him to guard something. Because that's what Hardie was good at: guarding shit. Mansions in the Hollywood Hills. (Well, aside from the Lowen-bruck place, but you could hardly blame him for that one.) Secret prisons buried beneath old military forts. And now, precious secrets inside this satellite.

And holy Christ on a crushed pepper cracker—*that's* why communication was one-way. Just on the off-off chance that Hardie *did* find these little secrets.

Okay, Hardie, he told himself.

Keep your head together.

You don't know this dude. He might be here to save you. He might be here to mess with you. There might be an Option C you're not even considering. Doesn't matter. He's down in that tube and you're not. You've got the upper hand. This is rare, so enjoy it.

Hardie repeated himself, just to drive the point all the way home:

"No fucking way."

"Okay, Charlie. I understand where you're coming from. None of this makes sense to you, I get it. But let me at least tell you what you're looking for. Can I come up a little further? I need to show you something."

Hardie was struck by the surreal sensation of hearing his own voice blasted back at him. His whole swagger, his attitude, the way he used to talk a perp down from a ledge. Of course, Hardie was usually just lulling the perp into a false sense of ease so he could either grab him or cold-cock him.

"Why don't you just show me from there."

"It's on a handheld device. You won't be able to see it from there."

"Throw it up to me, then."

"And then it slips out of your sausage-link fingers and shatters on the side of the tube here and we're both completely screwed."

"Hey," Hardie said. "My fingers are not sausage links. Come to think of it, blow me. You've got the same fingers!"

"Will you stop being a baby and let me help you out of this mess?"

Just what Hardie would have said.

Finally Hardie decided that this guy was going to keep hounding him until he showed him whatever was on his little device thingy. What was the worst that could happen? What, was his double going to throw a punch at him?

"C'mon up."

"Thank you."

Hand over hand, spaceboot over spaceboot, and the Other Hardie was just inches away now. Close enough to touch.

Which he did, of course. First he snapped a punch right into the center of Hardie's face so quick and powerfully that Hardie's eyes instantly teared up. Then his double grabbed a fistful of Hardie's uniform and pulled him down into the gateway tube.

6

Big kiss? I'll give him a big kick in the ass, that's what I'll give him.

—Jean-Claude Van Damme, *Double Impact*

A CYLINDRICAL METAL *tube, lined with high-powered machine guns, hanging 166 miles above the surface of the earth.*

Charlie Hardie could now add this exciting new entry to the long list of crazy places he'd ever had a fistfight.

The Other Hardie had grabbed the real Hardie by his uniform, seizing the material just above each of Hardie's nipples, and pulled. *Hard.* Now he was kicking his way back down to the hatch area, banging Hardie's head and shoulder blades against the sides of the narrow tube on the way down. Each blow made Hardie's teeth rattle. Hardie used his bare fingers to wrench the man's hands free, but they wouldn't budge. Not even a pinky. The man's space gloves felt like they were covering titanium hands.

Despite his military and police background, Hardie knew he wasn't an especially skilled fighter. Nor had his technique changed all that much since grade school. The thing to do in any fight, he thought, was to get in close and do as much damage as quickly as possible. None of this dancing around, butterfly-floating, bee-sting-ing bullshit for him. No, it was much better to pull your enemy close and just maul him. Which was a good thing, because there wasn't much room in this space tube for anything else.

Thing was…his opponent seemed to have pretty much the same thing in mind. And he'd struck first. Hard, relentless, fast, and brutal.

Once they reached the bottom of the tube and bounced up off its surface, the Other Him snap-punched him in the face again. The universe exploded. It was possible there was a follow-up punch, but if there was, Hardie didn't feel it. He started to sink into a numb, murmuring blackness until some words roused him back to attention.

"I don't want to do this," he heard the Other Him say.

Hardie grunted. That was all he could do. His mouth tasted like it had been stuffed with pennies.

"I mean that. We're wasting time."

Hardie spit blood in his (own) face.

The Other Him slammed Hardie's head against the tube again. And *again*. And then slammed a fist into Hardie's nose for good measure. It was amazing how much power he'd managed to pack into the blow, considering there was no room to wind up. Hardie knew he hadn't been getting into the best shape of his life up here in the vacuum of low earth orbit. But he also didn't realize how weak he'd become until this moment, grappling with a man who was essentially a younger, stronger, and way more fit version of himself. This was like wrestling with himself back when he was in the military, straight out of boot camp, as cut and lean and tough as he'd ever be in his life. Their weight was the same; Hardie supposed they had to be because of all that biometric nonsense. But while Hardie's muscles had atrophied to the point where he wanted to kick sand in his own face, his double's body mass was seemingly made up of nothing but bone and muscle.

Unconsciousness was becoming a serious and real option in the near future. Hardie tried to use his forearms to return some blows to his opponent, but such efforts were easily deflected. And he kept banging his own damn elbows against the sides of the tube. So Hardie flipped. Heaved his shoulders until he was facing the cold metal of the tube.

This seemed to confuse the Other Him, who started a flurry of punches up and down his back, as if trying to snap his spine in at least six different places. Hardie appeared to be immobile. What, was he playing dead?

Not exactly, fuckhead.

Instead, Hardie was prying open one of the machine-gun ports.

They gave Hardie a tour of his new shiny microhome before they shot it (and him) up into low earth orbit.

Okay, not really a tour, more like a fitting — a groomsman trying on his miserable tux. You have no choice in the matter; you have to wear the damned thing no matter what.

During one excruciating session he watched as burly technicians installed rows of guns into a tube, running wires from the guns to a control panel. (It wasn't until much later that Hardie realized that tube was part of the craft he'd be trapped in for the next year.) They were machine guns specially outfitted to be fired by remote control from outside of the tube. Hardie had seen these kinds of setups before, at places that specialized in forensic ballistics. Techs would call it a "gun machine" or the "hall of bullets."

Thing was: They also had manual triggers. Right there on the gun, mounted inside the tube.

You didn't need a wire. All you needed was a finger.

*   *   *

By the time the Other Him realized what he was doing, it was al-most too late. Hardie had pried open the gun port hatch and shoved his arm inside, fingertips brushing against the trigger. Just another couple of inches...

The Other Him screamed at Hardie and then got all MMA on him, wrapping a beefy arm around his neck and pulling his free arm in a way that resulted in agonizing pain and seemed to defy the rules of human anatomy.

"You can't do that!"

"Wuh.... Wuh...*watch me.*"

"We'll both die!"

"Yeah, maybe we will."

"Listen to me...this tube was designed to be jettisoned, so the walls aren't bulletproof. You pull that trigger...we're both dead, you stupid fuck! You want to do that to Kendra and Seej? Or do you want to save them?"

"They're dead if I don't kill you."

The Other Him loosened his grip, then untangled himself from Hardie. "I get it."

Hardie was suspicious. "You get w-what."

"You think the biometrics might be a little off, and the moment I step into the capsule, an alarm will go off and they'll send someone to kill Kendra and CJ."

Actually, no, that wasn't what Hardie was thinking. But it was a good enough reason.

"Yeah," Hardie said, huffing hard.

"*Fine.* You win, you stubborn old bastard. You search the craft, then. I'll do my best to tell you what to look for."

7

This ain't no goddamn way to start a partnership.
—Reggie Hammond, *48 Hrs.*

HARDIE COULDN'T EXACTLY chalk this one up in the *win* column, though. After scrambling back up to the main craft, he searched through every section of it, as instructed by his double. Through components labeled Propulsion. Avionics. Flight software. Communications. Power. Guidance. Environmental control. TCS. TPS. EDL. The Other Hardie called out each system like a drill sergeant, leaving Hardie to scramble to look for the label, then figure out how to pry the components open with his bare fingers, which left his fingertips raw, by the way, only to find...

...nothing.

"Nothing?"

"Nothing like you're describing. You sure you got it right?"

"I wouldn't travel a hundred sixty-six miles up into outer freakin' space unless I had it right."

What the Other Hardie had been describing: a small black square of shiny plastic, mounted on four corners with some kind of gummy material.

Hardie didn't see anything like that.

"We're running out of time," the Other Hardie said.

"You keep saying that. Why?"

"This mission's on a strict timetable. I don't get it right, then we splash down in the middle of fucking Oklahoma. Look, I understand your hesitation, but c'mon now. Let me trade places with you and take a look. I know what I'm looking for. If you just give me ten minutes this can be all over."

"Gimme that gizmo and I'll look. You told me it could find it instantly, right?"

The Other Him hesitated. "It's not as easy as that. It's not just going to light up and go ding ding ding when it finds something. I had to train for weeks to use this damned thing and learn what the numbers mean. It's taking very precise measurements of electrical impulses, and this craft is full of them, so..."

"You're saying I can't read numbers? That I'm some dope who can't tell a two from a three?"

"Argh. Will you just let me up there to look?"

Hardie considered this for a minute.

"You know, maybe it's down there," Hardie said. "In the gun tube, with you. Did you use your little magic device down there?"

The look on the Other Hardie's face was sort of priceless. He recovered and snapped, "Just keep looking." Then he ducked back down into the tube.

Why hadn't you thought of that first? Some spy you are.

It would be just like the Cabal to pull a fake-out move where the valuable object was safely hidden away in the disposable portion of the spacecraft.

The more you think about it, the more it makes sense. Put

Charlie Hardie, the armed guard, inside the craft, with access to guns inside the tube. On the off off *off* chance that somebody who looked exactly like Charlie Hardie would make his way up here, overpower him, then go looking for the dingus on the craft. The last place any sane person would look would be the gun tube, which would eject upon reentry and crash somewhere in the Pacific and presumably be forgotten. Unless...you were the Cabal, and had a secret way of tracking it, with a beacon or some other device.

So you start scanning the interior of the tube, as much as it galls you to admit that Hardie might be correct.

You weren't kidding about the program's being tricky. By its very nature, the dingus was designed to fool traditional forms of tracking. It emitted close to zero power, and any tiny bursts of power your tracking device did pick up could be attributed to random bursts in space. Detecting something that may actually be the dingus was a matter of interpretation; the device was meant to give you a possible nudge in the right direction, and then give you a place to start digging and dismantling.

The numbers tell you: nothing.

"Nothing."

"Nothing?"

"Not a trace."

"Is it possible you're mistaken, and I'm not guarding this super–mystery shit you keep going on about?"

"Then what else would you be guarding?"

"I don't know. This billion-dollar satellite would probably fetch a pretty penny in the scrap metal market."

"Har-har. No, it's got to be here. They've just been super-clever about where they've hidden it. Maybe somewhere between the outer skins, where even you couldn't get at it? No, that's too risky..."

"So what do we do now?"

"Well, I do have a Plan B," the Other Him said. "But you're *really* not going to like it."

8

Lucky for me this place is soundproof. That way nobody gets to hear me beating the truth out of you.

—Kurt Russell, *Tango & Cash*

HARDIE WAS ASHAMED to admit it, but his body did an involuntary jolt when he heard Plan B.

Sweet Jesus in heaven, this was the Other Charlie Hardie's plan:

"We're going to knock the satellite out of orbit, crash-land in the Atlantic Ocean, and then get scooped up by my handlers. We'll let the NSA tear this damned thing apart, one piece at a time."

That his body jolted when he first heard the plan was remarkable, because it took a few moments for Hardie to unpack and comprehend what this Other Him was suggesting. It was as if his physical body understood right away how painful—if not totally life-threatening—this plan was, leaving his brain to play catch-up. Hardie, with his slow lizard cop brain, picked it apart one awful segment at a time. Knocked out of orbit. Crash-land. Scooped up. Tear the damned thing apart. Not one part of that plan sounded good.

So of course Hardie told him, "That's a horrible plan."

"It's our only choice."

"No, it's not. There's got to be something else. Don't you get it? Once they notice it's missing, my family's dead. I'm not going to let that happen."

"We do have a decent window of time," the Other Hardie said. "I can have my handler dispatch a team of double-hard bastards out to protect your family as soon as we make contact."

"No. Think of something else."

"There is nothing else. This is the plan. This is what I've been training for."

"Goody for you. We're not doing that. You can just climb back into your fake-food drone there and go back the way you came."

The Other Him just stared at him. Even Hardie knew that was ridiculous. The food drones were one-way delivery vehicles. Once the food was loaded onto the craft, Hardie pushed a button and the food drone (containing his own personal waste products) was jettisoned back into orbit, joining the billions of other pieces of space junk floating around up here.

There was no way out for the Other Him. Not until three months from now, when a promised private space cruiser would dock with the satellite and bring him back home—presumably replacing him with another mook they'd blackmailed into freaky indentured servitude.

"There's no way out for either of us, Charlie," the Other Him said. "You realize this, right? What did they promise you—a year in space, and all would be forgiven?"

Hardie said nothing. That was exactly what they'd promised.

"Uh-uh," the Other Him said. "They're not going to let you go. You're up here for good...until you die. And they're kind of counting on you being the indestructible type. That's why you were chosen for this mission. You're Unkillable Chuck, the man who can't be killed."

"That's ridiculous. I can sure as hell *die*."

"Of course. And they know you're not immortal. But they've learned things about you over the years, leading them to realize that if they needed someone to spend an infinite amount of time in this orbiting tin can, that person should be you. Let's say there's a precious jewel at the bottom of a seriously deep lake. Who do you send to the bottom to retrieve it? The person who can hold his breath the longest. For all intents and purposes, out here in space? That's you."

"What are you talking about? There's nothing special about me. I have the worst fucking luck of anyone I know. That's about it."

The Other Him grinned. "You really don't know, do you."

"Know what?"

"We don't have time for this. C'mon up and I'll figure a way to strap us both in so we won't both get killed upon im—"

But the Other Him never finished the thought.

Hardie had been in these moments before—these supposedly do-or-die situations.

About a year ago he'd been in such a situation. He'd had a loaded gun in the mouth of one of his primary tormentors, some really smug bitch named Abrams who'd basically sentenced him to rot in a secret prison forever. He could have pulled the trigger. *Do or die.*

But he didn't.

Instead he found himself up here, in this satellite with a duplicate of himself, informing him what a fool he'd been to believe them, that he was basically sentenced to rot up here forever instead of on earth, where at least he could have had a proper burial.

Each time, every time, when faced with a do-or-die decision... Hardie always seemed to select the worst and most painful option possible.

His life, a series of bad decisions that led him to this, the worst predicament of all.

So no.

He wasn't going to do it anymore.

Hardie knew how this would play out. No matter what he said, this Other Him will try to take control of the satellite and crash it into the ocean or some such shit, promptly sentencing his family to death.

So for once in his life, Hardie decided to preempt the bullshit.

While the Other Him was busy talking about strapping the two of them in and not dying on impact, Hardie reached up, grabbed a fistful of fabric spacesuit, and yanked him with all of his might back down into the tube. The Other Him never saw it coming.

Hardie guessed that sometimes you really could outthink yourself, couldn't you?

The Other Him's body bounced once, twice...and then a third time at the bottom of the tube, near the food delivery hatch. The thumps sounded painful, and upon each impact the Other Him let out a strangled cry that sounded strange, because that was essentially Hardie's own strangled cry. But Hardie didn't give a shit. He scrambled back up into the control room proper and closed the hatch behind him. Engaged the locks. The Other Him was screaming something down there, but you know what? Too bad.

His body aching from all of the physical activity, Hardie slowly made his way to the main controls and sat down. He just needed a quiet moment to think through his next move.

On the monitor, he could see the Other Him, now standing again, and pounding his fist on the side of the tube, screaming something.

Hardie flicked off the image. Let him cool his heels down there for a while. He should be thankful he didn't machine-gun his ass out the airlock.

The audio receiver was still engaged, and Hardie could hear the anguished protests of the Other Him.

"It's too late! You don't understand! It's too late!"

Hardie stabbed a button with his finger. "Nope. *You're* too late."

For once, Hardie thought, he'd pushed back. Show those evil, sneaky, let's-control-the-world bastards he was a guy who couldn't be messed with.

Shit. It was almost a new lease on life.

But then Hardie glanced over at the rows of sensors and controls. Lights he had never seen before were blinking urgently. Stern little warning tones were going bonkers, like a GPS unit that believed you were about to drive into a superhighway column. He'd never seen the spacecraft do anything like this before.

Sabotage, Hardie thought. *Damn it, the lookalike prick had sabotaged him!* Hardie wondered if he should try to report this to someone, but of course communication only worked in one direction. They could talk to him; he couldn't say jack shit to them.

And his pre-launch question-and-answer session hadn't covered this contingency. *Okay, let's just say I'm really soft-brained after all of those months in orbit, and I, you know, kinda accidentally let someone board the craft who looks just like me, even though you told me not to do that, under any circumstances, no matter who it may be, including my dead grandmother, John Lennon, or Mahatma Gandhi . . . but I do, and then this guy makes the craft go all haywire . . . um, what do I do then?*

Meanwhile Hardie began to become aware of a muffled sound. Words. A specific pattern being repeated over and over again. It was faint, but that was only because it was coming from the sealed gun tube.

You, Hardie thought. What in the blue blazes do you want?

That the murmuring was the same string of repeated words led Hardie to believe that his double had something specific to share and wasn't just telling him how he was going to rip off his head if he ever got out of the gun tube alive.

What else could he do? Information was power, after all. Hardie went over to the control panel near the tube and stabbed the audio button with a finger.

The message came screaming through the speaker:

"—our reentry sequence!"

A pause, then the full message again:

"I've already started our reentry sequence!"

Oh.

Fuck.

Me.

Hard.

9

Do you know how they say "Fuck You" in this business?
"Trust me."

—Liam Neeson, *The Dead Pool*

THIS IS NOT going *at all* how you planned. Or how your handlers planned. Who can plan for a force of living mayhem like Charles D. Hardie? You might as well try to plan for earthquakes or spontaneous combustion.

Making things worse—at least in your own head—is the knowledge that you are the world's leading expert on all things Charlie Hardie, since you look just like him and have studied him so intensely. You should have called this sequence of events, right?

And now you are inside a steel tube that very soon will eject itself from the main spacecraft and you will tumble to your death. Fortunately, you'll most likely pass out from the intense heat as the tube starts to smash into the earth's atmosphere. Just like falling asleep in a tanning booth, you tell yourself.

This doesn't help.

So instead you do the only thing you can: try to appeal to Charlie Hardie's compassionate side.

The man has one. You've studied it. You've seen it in real life. On the run from the LAPD, Charlie Hardie risked everything to double back and go into a fire to save a family of four—TV star Jonathan Hunter, his wife, his son, his daughter. Risked everything—saved them, too—only to get his ass shot. He nearly drowned, and was abducted and drugged and put in a trunk and sent to a secret prison in the middle of nowhere and...

Well, suffice it to say that he knows all about risking everything to help total strangers.

You need him to feel the same compassion now. Granted, Jonathan Hunter didn't beat the living shit out of him inside a steel tube floating in space. Okay, so maybe compassion was a bit much to expect.

Brains, though...Charlie Hardie was smarter than he looked. And even a man with a low-wattage intellect had to appreciate that killing *you* wouldn't do a thing to save the Hardie family...

Killing his clone wouldn't do a thing to help his family.

If he sabotaged the craft, maybe he could be forced to unsabotage it.

Hardie yanked open the hatch, mashing the knuckles of his right hand in the process. Gah, crap, *hell*. The pain centers of his entire arm lit up. As if he didn't have enough to deal with. He grabbed one of the machine-gun triggers with his left hand, then looked down at his duplicate. The Other Him was bracing himself against the sides of the tube with his arms and legs.

"What did you do to the satellite?" Hardie asked.

"I've already done it. I've initiated the reentry sequence. We're going down."

"What...? Why? Why in the holy *fuck* would you do something like that?"

"I'm not going to lie to you," the Other Him said. "This has always been part of the plan, with or without your cooperation."

"Not going to lie to...I'll seriously kill your ass dead if you don't tell me how to stop it. And none of this let-me-back-up-into-the-main-craft shit. You tell me from there, and you tell me right now. If you don't, I'm going to squeeze these triggers and spray you into little tiny chunks. I'll make it hurt, too."

"Well, then, go ahead and shoot, because it's too late. I couldn't stop the reentry sequence if I was Stephen J. Hawking. We've already been bumped out of our orbit. And unless you let me out of this tube, I'm going to be jettisoned and die."

"I'm not worried so much about *you* dying. I'm worried about stopping this satellite from crashing into the earth."

"Listen to me," the Other Hardie said. "The satellite will not crash. It is designed for reuse. It will deploy parachutes to slow its descent. It will gently splash down off the coast of California. It has redundancies and backup systems, GPS and iridium locator beacons. This is what it was designed to do. Get recovered."

"You sure about that?"

"Absolutely. We did our homework. But that recovery just applies to the capsule portion. In a matter of minutes, maybe even seconds, this gateway tube is going to be blasted away, and I'm going to die, and you will, too, because you have the hatch door still open. And then your family's going to die, and this whole saga is going to have a very, very sad ending."

"Or I could just close the hatch, shoot your ass dead, and take my chances."

The Other Hardie narrowed his eyes. "It'd be the dumbest move of your life."

Hardie thought about it. "No. I don't think so."

Then he slammed the hatch shut. Just before it clanged shut he heard the enraged screams of his double. Hardie did not give a shit. Over the past decade he'd made a series of dumb moves. Leading the Albanian mob straight to his partner and his family. Not believing Lane Madden soon enough when she told him there were people trying to kill her. Not pulling the trigger when the gun was inside that evil lady's mouth. Hardie decided he was out of the dumb-move business.

He would pull the trigger now.

Do it, *do it*, don't hesitate. Hesitation gets you killed.

Hardie wrapped his hands around the dual triggers and squeezed. And there was nothing but a faint double *klik klik* sound.

Hardie knew there was no sound in space—that the booming explosions in *Star Wars* were bullshit. But he should have heard the guns echo through that tube, right? What the hell was going on? Hardie pushed the audio button with one hand and the triggers with the other. Again, a dull *klik*.

Over the tiny speaker: "I've disabled the machine guns, too, dumbass. Now, are you going to let me up so we can survive this thing? Or are you going to let both of us die?"

Hardie supposed he was still very much in the dumb-move business.

The Cabal's super-secret spy satellite continued its descent toward the surface of the earth.

10

Fuck you, spaceman.

—Dolph Lundgren, *I Come in Peace*

OF COURSE THERE was a debate over who should be strapped into the reentry gear. Hardie's double pled his case quickly: He was the one who knew how to signal his handlers for help once they splashed down. He was stronger and fitter and could tow Charlie Hardie to safety in the event of an emergency water evacuation. He could revive Hardie in case he was knocked unconscious due to the excessive g-forces. He could also defend them in case a Cabal recovery ship found them first.

"Wait, wait, wait," Hardie said. "Water evacuation? Knocked unconscious? What happened to all of that shit about a gentle splashdown?"

"We're plunging out of low earth orbit," the Other Hardie said, "not going down a log flume. It's going to hurt. You're never going to experience pain quite like this. Or so they told me during the briefing."

Hardie had to admit, he didn't think about coming down so

much. It had hurt enough going up; he kind of blocked the whole idea of *coming down* out of his head.

"Let's just say I let you strap yourself in with that harness. You'll be nice and cozy. What am I supposed to do? Hang on and pray?"

"No. There's somewhere else we could strap you."

"Where? This isn't a two-seater."

Hardie followed his clone's eye path across the craft and over . . . to the cramped toilet facilities. The only other place where a gentleman could strap himself in for the extended haul.

"Oh, *fuck you.* Seriously? How about you take the shitter? You're the unwanted guest here. I'll even throw in a magazine, in case you get bored."

"We don't have time for this. We keep arguing, we're both going to be knocked unconscious in a matter of minutes."

Hardie didn't like the bathrooms in airplanes, let alone this.

Yet that's where Charlie Hardie found himself, on a space toilet, during the most traumatic experience of his life. At some point in the descent he found himself incoherently thanking Christ that he was situated over a toilet because at one point the pressure was so intense it felt like his mashed internal organs were going to come launching out of his ass. On top of that, the heat was way more intense than he had dreamed possible—as if he were lying on a sunny beach the day God decided to crank the thermostat from 102 up to Fahrenheit 451. Toward the end, when Hardie had convinced himself that he was really going to die this time, his bottom lip and nose bust and began to gush blood, splattering all over his face. Hardie would not be looking his best upon his return to his home planet, that was for sure.

And then came splashdown.

It was the exact opposite of gentle.

In theory they were supposed to have parachutes to break the fall, but Hardie didn't think they slowed down at all. Their descent was as fast and fierce and relentless as the worst car wreck you could ever experience. As if Godzilla had loaded the vessel into a Godzilla-sized shotgun, aimed it point-blank at the planet, and pulled the trigger. Everything hurt all at once—the burning, the straps cutting into his body, the insane pressure on every square inch of his body, inside and out—as the craft slammed into the surface of the Pacific Ocean.

Hardie couldn't see if his clone was experiencing the same set of miseries. He could only hope and pray that he was.

You?

Well…

You pass out fairly early in the descent—just as things start to heat up nicely.

And you *stay out*.

In your defense, you've been through quite a lot in the past twelve hours—being whipped into orbit and back, with a wrestling match and a fistfight and a stressful (and unfruitful) search, for good measure. Even the toughest of pilots go grayout at four Gs, and few can withstand five Gs. That was it. The craft must not have been designed to cancel out enough of the shock. You're not to blame.

Unfortunately, you're not conscious, either. Right at the moment you very much need to be conscious.

Somehow Hardie stayed awake the entire time. At the high point of the hurt he thought for sure that he was going be slammed into that not so gentle good night. Alas, he did not. That would be a break from the pain, at least.

Instead he was left with that deeply rattled feeling you have after a multicar pileup. Nothing seems quite real, yet your senses are taking in every detail, as if recording it for future nightmare purposes.

The craft was bobbing up and down. Hardie reached up, mildly surprised he still had hands with actual fingers instead of fleshy blobs at the ends of his wrists. He unstrapped himself from the toilet and dropped to the other side of the craft. He had no idea he was actually hanging upside down.

Ow.

Once he climbed to his feet and threw his arms out to balance himself, Hardie's earthbound bearings seemed to kick back in. Yes, he was inside a billion-dollar tin can, bopping along the surface of an ocean. Hopefully his clone was right and it was the Pacific. Then again, his clone lied a lot.

And look at him now. Strapped into the good seat and completely unconscious. Hardie made his way over to him. He was hanging from the straps like a puppet hanging inside a net. He felt for a pulse: beating and strong. Still alive.

"So," Hardie said. "What was that shit about reviving me? Or signaling for help?"

The double said nothing.

"What are you gonna do if the Cabal pirates show up to reclaim their little satellite, huh? What's that?

The double said nothing.

"Riiiiight, you're gonna do nothing at all, because you're passed out like a freshman at his first kegger. Dickhead."

Hardie thought about slapping him awake. Not just because it would probably make him feel really good. But also because it made sense. If they were indeed drifting on the open ocean they were going to need rescuing. He'd read a story once in an in-flight magazine about three boys who were cast adrift in a fishing boat for something absurd like seventy days and ended up eating their own fingernails and chunks of their own scalp. That sounded like a special brand of hell.

Then again, Hardie could always snack on his double. Would that be autocannibalism?

What the hell is wrong with me, Hardie thought. The crash must have scrambled my brains for me to be thinking about this stuff. He needed to pry his way out of this tin can pronto. After a few minutes of seasick searching, Hardie saw it:

PULL TO RELEASE HATCH DOOR

Easy enough, right?

Hardie reached up and pulled the handle. Nothing happened. He tried again. Maybe all of that time up in orbit had caused his biceps to wither away to nothing. Which would be amusing. Hardie imagined trying to twist his first beer cap in years and failing miserably. If that was the case, then what was he thinking? Did he really think he was going to bust out of this tin can and swim to shore and have beer like nothing happened?

He tried again, both hands now, giving it all of his might. Which, Hardie had to admit, may not have been much. This time, though, the handle yielded with a satisfying *thunk*.

And a microsecond later, the world exploded in front of his face.

11

Don't do me no favors.

—Danny Glover, *Lethal Weapon*

SEE, WHAT THE sign *should* have said, instead of

PULL TO RELEASE HATCH

was something along the lines of

PULL TO SET OFF A BIG HATCH-BLOWING EXPLOSION

THAT WILL KNOCK YOU ON YOUR ASS

And if Hardie hadn't been blown back into the opposite side of the craft, he might have seen the truly majestic sight of the hatch door bursting from the frame and flipping a few times before landing in choppy blue ocean water.

But instead, all he felt was burning fury on his face and hands...and then something heavy slamming into his spine. Which would be the opposite end of the spacecraft.

Hardie came to his senses a few seconds—maybe minutes?—later. Sunlight and water poured in from above. The first blue sky he'd seen in...Hardie didn't even know. The brightness and splendor of it all burned his eyes. Which paired nicely with his burning hands and face.

Where was he? No idea. The Other Him had said they'd be splashing down off the coast of California, but the Other Him wasn't the most reliable of narrators. Didn't astronauts splash down in the Atlantic, too? Which would be great. Hardie was sick of California. He's spent the better part of the last decade trying to escape it. Please, God, please let me be just off Key West or something. A quick swim to shore, a nourishing shot of rum, and then off to save my family.

Charlie Hardie's spacecraft did not splash down anywhere near Florida.

When the water started to fill the spacecraft in earnest, Hardie knew they were in serious trouble. Within a minute he was up to his waist in seawater, and that seemed to happen in the space of a blink. Was this supposed to happen? Or had he screwed something up when he blasted the hatch?

Whatever. Hardie needed to get out of here.

As he crawled along the side of the vessel, salt water lapped at his hands and burned like crazy. Which was going to make swimming fun. And that's what he was facing—a long swim. Without a life preserver. Somewhat stupidly he wondered if there were flotation devices hidden somewhere in this craft, as if he were aboard a commercial airline. There were no life preservers. Hardie had been over every piece of this damned thing for nine months; he would have noticed if there had been big inflatable orange vests. There were no seat cushions that could be used as a flotation device, unless by some miracle the toilet could float.

Worry about that later, Hardie thought. Get out now.

Then he remembered his buddy, the clone.

The cruel part of him wanted to shout, *Every man for himself!* And just split. But the human being inside him couldn't. The father and husband inside of him couldn't, either. He needed this guy if his family had any shot at survival. Even if his story about the NSA and Eve Bell and rescuing him was complete and utter bullshit, *somebody* had to be backing him. Sure as shit wasn't the Cabal, breaking into its own satellite. And any enemy of the Cabal's was a friend of Hardie's.

"Come on, pal, let's get you unhooked. No, really, it's no trouble at all. You just rest and relax and I'll take care of the whole thing."

You can't respond.

You're out. O-U-T. *Out.*

You don't sense Charlie Hardie unbuckle you from your harness, nor do you see the water rising at an alarming rate. You're not awake to see the panic in Hardie's face as he realizes the water is rising much, much quicker than he thought possible. You certainly don't feel it when Hardie accidentally bangs your skull on the side of the hatchway. Which is probably fortunate, because had you been awake it would have really, *really* hurt.

All you can do is be carried along.

Sometimes a much younger and more carefree Charlie Hardie would go swimming in someone else's pool (never his pool; his family couldn't afford a luxury like a pool, even those cheaper metal-and-vinyl above-ground pools). He'd play a game with himself: *How long can I stay afloat?* The rules were simple. He would pump his arms and legs to keep himself up in the middle of the pool without touching the bottom or sides. If he did, he'd lose. He'd imagine that he'd been abandoned in the middle of a vast ocean, and his life would be over the minute his arms and legs failed to move. The young Hardie never won the game, of course. Winning was impossible. Sooner or later his burning, tired limbs would give out, and he'd gently float down those few inches until his feet touched the vinyl pool bottom. Or someone would jump in next to him or throw a pool toy at his head.

Hardie never thought he'd actually be stuck in the middle of a vast ocean, with no land in sight, body aching and limbs already dangerously weak—and with his arm wrapped around a goddamned clone of himself.

Knowing that the moment his free arm and two legs ran out of steam, he'd be a dead man.

He'd give anything to reach down with his toes and somehow feel a vinyl bottom.

Charlie Hardie had no idea how much time had passed. It could have been anywhere from just a few minutes to a couple of hours. There were no landmarks, and there was no way to mark his progress. Or lack thereof. There was just water, water everyfuckingwhere, as a poet once said. The vastness of it was beginning to creep Hardie out. He tried not to think about it. But how could he not? He was a bug—not even a bug, a fleck of a bug part, struggling in this immense and ancient primordial force. Long before there was a Charlie Hardie, there was this ocean, and out of it sprang all life as we know it. Long after Charlie Hardie was gone, as well as the rest of life on earth, there would be this ocean. Charlie Hardie didn't matter at all. If he were to slip under the surface the ocean would not give a damn.

Thoughts like these did not help Hardie's situation. He started to feel faint. He couldn't tell if his chest was pounding from sheer exhaustion or from the onset of a heart attack. Rational, sane worry gave way to trapped animal panic. This was not good. He shouldn't have left the vessel. At least he could have drowned in familiar surroundings, and somebody would maybe find his fish-cleaned skeleton someday thousands of feet below the surface...

And then his weak, fatigued, oxygen-starved muscles finally gave out, and he slipped under.

12

THE CABAL NOTICED the problem with their spacecraft immediately. You don't spend billions on a project only to forget about it.

But notification wasn't instantaneous.

The whole point of this manned satellite was to render it unreachable by traditional wireless means, keeping the prize within safe and secure. But of course you had to be able to track the thing. An ordinary citizen with a telescope, a pen, and a piece of paper could track it. Which is who they employed—an amateur yet highly talented satellite tracker who would do this for fun. They even paid him a modest salary. The tracker saw the anomaly and immediately phoned it in. That call was forwarded to Abrams's office. The tracker was told to continue tracing the satellite's errant path, which he did dutifully, right up until the moment it fell out of the sky.

Which pissed Abrams off.

This entire operation was supposed to be a no-brainer, a simple way to contain two highly volatile elements far, far out of the hands of enemy forces during these challenging days.

Now this whole thing was going to become a highly annoying task, on top of the other annoying tasks she found herself facing every day. She could just *feel* it.

All of this was Doyle's fault—that stubborn savant cocksucker. He was the gadget-and-gears freak, and Abrams had the nagging suspicion that it was going to end in disaster for them all.

If Abrams'd had her way, Charlie Hardie's lifeless body would have been fed through a wood chipper and used to fertilize at least a dozen different states. "Unkillable Chuck" my ass—the man had caused too many problems as it was, and cost their movement untold billions. And Doyle wanted to throw *another* billion after him?

"You sure this isn't about revenge?"

She'd asked Doyle this as he was still recovering in a private hospital back east after his last encounter with Hardie. Doyle had been beaten senseless and hooked up to life support in the trunk of a car as Hardie drove down the Pacific Coast Highway. The only respite from the relentless nausea were stops so that Hardie could open the trunk, interrogate him, then beat him some more. *Doyle, buddy, we're going to Hollywood.*

"No," Doyle had said, clearly lying. "He's a resource. We don't squander resources, remember?"

"Uh-huh."

Doyle had sighed. "Fine. Perhaps there is a small, insignificant element of revenge. The man *did* leave me to die in the trunk of a car."

In the blazing sun of a long-term car lot at a California airport, no less.

But instead of destroying their enemies, which was more or less Cabal m.o. going back decades, Doyle had talked Abrams into sparing Hardie's life temporarily, squeezing some use out of him. Doyle had been talking about his fantasy of an "unbreakable vault" for many years now, to the point where Abrams realized she probably signed off on the venture just so he'd shut up about it already. For Doyle, the idea of an "unkillable" man inside his "unbreakable vault" became an obsession, an idée fixe, and it had finally come to fruition.

Now, apparently, it had blown up in their faces. There wasn't much Abrams could do about it except follow it through to its logical conclusion.

Originally there had been three ruling partners of their organization: Gedney, Doyle, and Abrams herself. Charlie Hardie had done the unthinkable and killed Gedney, though even Abrams had to admit that the man had it coming. You don't put someone as volatile as Charlie Hardie inside a secret prison and expect him to languish there forever. Wood chipper, people. *Wood chipper.* Abrams assumed her partners thought she was joking about the wood chipper, but they didn't realize it had been a fetish of hers since that infamous Coen brothers movie. You don't know bliss until you've walked barefoot through the freshly pulped remains of another human being. Especially if you've had a conversation with them not five minutes before.

Gedney's way: hadn't worked.

Doyle's way: failing miserably. The Cabal was hurting and was forced to hide underground while their enemies picked away at their various fronts and operations around the globe.

Which left Abrams's way.

"I'll take care of it," she said to Doyle on the phone now. Poor Doyle, even a year later, was still going through rigorous rehabilitation sessions at a private facility on the East Coast.

"This isn't my fault," he said. "The craft was impenetrable. All systems in place. Hardie had no way of knowing how to knock the craft out of its orbit, and there was no way anyone could have transmitted that information to him. It's a locked room mystery. An inside job!"

"I told you, I'll take care of it. I want your people reporting directly to me from here on out. No exceptions."

"You sound angry."

"I'm not angry. I'm annoyed," Abrams said.

"Because of what was inside the craft."

"Because of what had *still* better be inside that craft."

It was time to initiate her contingency plans: recovery teams on opposite sides of the country. *And* complete sedation for her old friend Doyle. Better he sleep through this next part. This was no longer a holy trinity. Abrams was God, and the world was about to feel her wrath.

Life had been pretty quiet for Factboy.

Which really sucked, because a quiet life meant *no money.*

For a while there, in the glory days, the frenzied big money days, he couldn't open offshore accounts fast enough. He and the wife didn't get along, but that didn't matter because the checking account was always fat, the credit limits on all of the cards were sky-high, and there were vacations galore. (Even if Factboy spent a lot of time in the bathroom.)

Factboy was an information broker for the organization that used to call themselves the Accident People. He was known as sharp, quick, and reliable. Not the best, to be sure. The top-tier guys were at another level entirely, and formed a tight little clique that called itself—and how freakin' pompous was this—the Architects. Factboy would never be an Architect. Nor would he want to be. He had enough to keep his family happy, and that was fine.

Until three years ago, when the work started drying up.

And the Architects snapped up all of the high-paying gigs, leaving everybody else with scraps.

Factboy especially.

Try explaining to your wife why your computer consulting job—one that had previously afforded them European vacations and the latest minivans and the fattest, tallest Christmas trees on the lot—suddenly paid a whole lot less, and they had to settle for the occasional trip to the beach, and hey, yeah, maybe we should just keep the Odyssey this year, it's been good to us, right, and wow, look at this artificial Christmas tree—a genuine blue spruce!

Ms. Factboy started to get suspicious, and Factboy started to get real worried.

It wasn't as if he could level with her. Tell her what he'd *really* been up to all of these years. Not only would that be a five-alarm security breach, and the next thing Factboy knew, he and the entire family would be wearing matching black hoods and feeling needles jabbed into the crooks of their arms. Don't worry, kids, everything's going to be allllllllllllllll

thud

No, honesty wouldn't work. Honesty never worked with wives. Factboy had come to learn this. Like the American Public, wives *wanted* to be lied to. But you had to do them the favor of lying creatively and plausibly. Otherwise, it was just insulting.

Factboy ran out of creativity and plausibility about, oh, two years ago. Marriage-wise, he'd been running on fumes ever since.

So Factboy was ridiculous, crazy, giddy happy when his cell phone buzzed one day and he picked it up and he heard the most glorious voice in the world: Mann's.

Crazy, creepy Mann. A voice that normally would chill him down to the marrow of his skinny, osteoporosis-in-the-waiting bones.

But now Mann meant big money.

Mann meant a return to the glory days.

Mann meant a lifeline.

Mann still frightened the crap out of him, but whatever.

With Mann, life would be good again.

"Sooooo good to hear from you," Factboy said, wondering if Mann could feel the soft impressions of his firm lips on her tender buttocks.

Mann had been waiting for this day for six years now.

Kind of sick to admit it, but she even fantasized about it in the hospital, after they'd removed one of her tits. Somehow it helped ease the aching loss and the horrible itch of her freshly scarred skin.

Just the *idea* of it.

Killing Charlie Hardie's family...and then Charlie Hardie himself.

Squeeeeeeeeeee...oh the sheer delight.

Mann knew it was ridiculous to pin so much fulfillment on one job—but Hardie had long ceased to be a job. He had become a bona fide obsession. You can look back at your life and see the places where you suddenly veer off in the wrong direction, recasting your entire life in the process. Mann had veered off when she failed to kill Charlie Hardie the first time, in that backyard in Studio City.

Now it was time to get it done right.

This was her dream assignment! To erase Charlie Hardie's wife and son from the face of the earth! And, of course, to make it look like an accident. Payback, at long last. She was told to plan it, scope it out, and prepare a suitable narrative within twenty-four hours...but not to pull the trigger until Abrams herself gave word. The family *must* be kept alive as leverage until Abrams said, "Sic 'em." Why? It was not Mann's place to ask why. Mann truly didn't give a shit *why.* She was the finger on the trigger, nothing more. Just the way she liked it.

Besides, what was twenty-four hours? Charlie Hardie was the outstanding balance in the accounting sheet of her life, and she knew that one day she'd have to set the numbers right.

Mann gave herself credit for bouncing back through some of the worst years of her life. For one thing, she thought her employers would *most definitely* have her killed after the monumental clusterfuck that was the Lane Madden job from seven years ago. Instead she'd been spared and allowed to make good on the Cabal's investment in her. That was a nice affirmation, even if they made her jump through countless hoops before she was allowed to direct an accident again.

There also had been personal trials. Mann had already sacrificed one breast to the Great God Cancer, but as it turned out, the god was not so easily appeased. It returned for more. Mann, though, was not about to surrender her other girl, so she dug in her heels and fought, all the while navigating the hopelessly complex alliances and internecine wars of the Cabal as it expanded. Some days she'd roll straight from chemo, ripping the plastic hospital bracelet from her wrist, and right into an assignment. Later she puked in little bags to keep her personal forensic materials away from the scenes of the accidents. She bought lots and lots of little bags.

After a few of those dark years, however, she beat back the Big C and emerged on the other side a stronger, sharper operative. Mann developed an icy detachment that helped her considerably.

Except in one area...

And that was Charlie Hardie.

Charlie Hardie

Charlie Hardie

Charlie Hardie, burning blinking neon in her brain, which

slammed her into wakefulness at 3:00 a.m. with a dry mouth and a racing heart.

So when the call came and Mann heard the name of her nemesis once again, she was full of conflicted feelings and emotions, and all of that hard-won icy detachment went bye-bye.

This was an old-school assignment; the Cabal wasn't as generous with supplies as it had been in the past. Abrams would never admit this to a freelancer, but the Cabal was clearly an organization on its ass. The instructions were to keep it cost-effective, small, and precise. No grand narratives. Just the basics. For such a thing, Mann knew she needed to skip the overpriced fact architects and bring in one of her old boys.

Besides, she knew he'd be grateful for the work.

"So great to hear from you," he said, and she could practically feel his cold, narrow lips on her ass.

"I need two things from you," Mann said. "One will be easy. The other, not so easy."

"Done," Factboy said, a little too quickly. "Um, we talking about the same rates? From, you know, the last time we worked together?"

We don't work together, Mann wanted to say. *You* work for *me*. You're like the guy behind the counter. I place an order, you deliver.

But you need to properly motivate a freelance contractor, not break him down completely from the start. She could apply threats and pressure later.

"Competitive rates," Mann said. "Does that work for you?"

"Of course," he said—again, a little too quickly. In that moment, Mann knew he needed the money and that he'd do practically anything for the paycheck.

13

If I am not me, then who the hell am I?
——Arnold Schwarzenegger, *Total Recall*

RIGHT NOW YOU have regained semiconsciousness. You're bobbing up and down in the cold salt water, being held up by who knows what, wondering what the hell has happened to you.

And then you sink down...

down,

down,

down,

sinking and flailing and wondering where it all went so gloriously wrong, to be drowning in the ocean.

Where *had* it gone wrong?

Well, it all started the day you drove to the quiet suburban office complex where you've been spending the past year and your handlers told you, *Congrats! You're going to become someone else, permanently leaving your own facial features and identity behind.*

You said sure.

Because what else could you have said? They have such a fierce grip on your balls it cuts off your vocal cords. Been that way for an entire year now, ever since you came in from the cold. You allegedly have your "freedom," but still your life is micromanaged to the nth degree. They know what time you get up in the morning, what time you take your first piss, what time you brush your teeth, what time you shower, what time you order your first (and only) cup of coffee of the day. They know how many reps you do in the hotel gym, how many miles you run on the treadmill, how many ounces of water you drink during your workout. They know the clothes in your closet and routinely inspect them. They watch you as you drive away from the four-star residence hotel and drive the 1.7 miles to the office complex; they watch you make the return 1.7-mile trip at the end of the workday. They know what you order for dinner. They know what you zone out to on the flat screen. They know when you close your eyes. They even know when you fall asleep for real.

So what else can you say other than: When do we start?

The trick to becoming someone else isn't selling it to others. Most people don't look too closely.

The trick is selling it to *yourself*.

If you're going to give yourself away, you'll do it to yourself first. You'll think, *I'm just playing around. My name's not really Charlie Hardie, it's* [REDACTED]. And then, boom, you've just given yourself away in a hundred little ways.

Hence, the year of intense study and surgeries. You don't mind the studies, actually. It's something else to wrap your mind around. The year you've spent being debriefed could only be described as a bureaucratic purgatory. Daily recitation and repetition of biographical and operational details, followed by the finest middlebrow American entertainment available, and then, all too infrequently, blissful sleep. But even that is interrupted by all of the recitation and repetition, so that you find yourself reliving huge chunks of your life on a nightly basis. As if your brain was taking its revenge for making you open up all of its secret cupboards and drawers and dump out the contents. *Hey, you wanted all these open, pal. So I'm going to keep opening them whether you like it or not. Yeah, yeah, I'm not getting any sleep, either.*

Someone else's life, however...the chance to wallow around in the weird and mundane and complex details of someone else's existence...that came as a nice break.

Your handlers tell you: You're going to become someone named Charlie Hardie.

You met Charlie Hardie before—briefly but intensely. Certainly not enough time for you to do a Rich Little–style impression of him or anything. But at least you did *meet* him, which gave you a definite edge over other candidates.

As if other people were lining up to be this guy? You thought this to yourself at the time.

They bring out these cardboard boxes of this guy's life. School. Military—a lot of it classified. Police files—so many Philadelphia Police Department files, it's sort of sick. What had Hardie been up to all of these years? As you flip through dust-filmed manila folders, you quickly realize the answer to your own question: A lot. Hardie was never officially a cop, he played the strong-arm/muscle to a genius crime solver named Nate Parrish. The more you read, the more you're convinced that Parrish should be given his own series of books, maybe even a cable movie of the week. Too bad he was killed in his prime. It was Moriarty who'd ultimately brought Sherlock Holmes down, tumbling with him over the Reichenbach

Falls. With Nate Parrish, it had been Hardie—and as it turned out, Hardie had survived the fall, too.

You read the case files and it's truly heartbreaking. And you're not the kind of guy to get all choked up over heartbreaking details. But Parrish, his entire family...wiped out because of a stupid Charlie Hardie mistake.

This is key to understanding the man. The thick layer of guilt that serves as the bedrock for everything else.

My God, you're going *method*.

But seriously, it all snaps into place once you've absorbed and digested these files, which are essentially an *Annotated Charlie Hardie*.

Hardie exiled himself because he felt guilty for surviving what should have, by all rights, killed him. Hardie exiled himself because he no longer felt capable of doing the one thing that a man is supposed to do: keep his family safe and alive. Hardie exiled himself across the country and drowned his emotions with booze and other people's dreams on DVD and thought that would be best for everyone involved.

But here's the thing Hardie doesn't realize but *you* do, because you have the *Annotated Charlie Hardie* sitting open in front of you.

Hardie—make that *you*—shouldn't feel guilty about not dying.

Because of the contents of a classified military record sitting open in front of you.

Oh, Chuck, you want to say. You could have been so much more. And yet you've squandered a decade doing...what? Running? Fighting? Thinking you were already dead?

Such a goddamned shame. Someone should have opened this file for you years ago. It would have cleared up so much.

Then you think to yourself, You know, it's not too late.

*　　　*　　　*

So you go through all of this insanity, with the studying and the surgeries and the slingshot into space, and you meet the real Charlie Hardie again and it's more of a psychological shock than you could have ever imagined.

You've studied him.

You've been tricked out to look just like him.

You've *become him*.

Still, nothing prepared you for the fact that he is kind of a giant dick.

And then because he is such a *stubborn* dick, you end up unconscious inside the spacecraft as it splashes down into the Pacific Ocean. Ideally, this would be an awesome time for you to be awake, because, you know, the mission is not over. Somewhere on the spacecraft is *the point to the whole goddamn thing*, a crazy-tiny hard drive containing the silver bullet that will slay the global werewolf.

So that brings you to the present:

Semi-conscious, bobbing up and down in the cold salt water, being held up by who knows what, wondering where it all went so gloriously wrong.

You rage against the ocean itself, pumping your arms and legs furiously because, of all the ways to die, drowning in the ocean is *not* one you're okay with.

On the way up, your lungs on fire, and just before you crash through the surface, you bump into...

Yourself.

That is, the original version of you.

Who is *also* drowning, the stupid, stubborn dick.

Part of you wants to just let him go, and watch his body sink into the deep, dark ocean, following the wake of the spacecraft . . . wherever the hell *that* might be.

But no. You can't.

Charlie Hardie still might be useful. All of the Cabal's tricks had yet to be revealed, and maybe something Hardie saw could help. Either in his time in low earth orbit or back in their secret lab.

So what you end up doing is scooping Hardie up. And you start swimming, one-armed, toward the shore.

You've got a vague idea of where you've splashed down. Somewhere in the fuzzy zone between *barely possible to swim to shore* and *no fucking way are you gonna live.*

This is not the way this mission should have gone.

By this point in the mission you should have been done, kicking back in the satellite as it bobbed up and down in the ocean, waiting for the cavalry to arrive. Miller Time, as they used to say.

But now you're a long, long way from Miller Time.

Legs pumping, arm pumping . . . your doppelgänger tucked under your other arm.

This would be so much easier if you could just go whoopsie and let him drop. Unkillable bastard would probably survive it, wake up with Ariel and her daddy and that goofy talking crab, and look around and wonder what had happened. Yeah, that would be the easiest thing to do. You didn't get into this line of work because it would be easy, though.

As you swim you try to forget about how much your muscles ache already, how hard you're breathing. Instead you ponder the mystery of the missing hard drive. You scanned the bejesus out of that spacecraft and there was no trace of it. The thing *had* to be up there. Why else spend so much money to launch a broken-down middle-aged man into low earth orbit? So it had to be an equipment failure. His hand-held scanner wasn't sharp enough to pick up on the hard drive's unique signature. That, or their intel was wrong. So in all likelihood, the hard drive was tucked away somewhere on that spacecraft, which was making an express trip to the bottom of the sea. Your people would just have to recover it before the Cabal. That part wasn't up to you.

So why work so hard to hold on to this 230-pound thug, when you yourself were struggling to keep your own 230-pound frame afloat?

Because there was a slim chance that Hardie knew where the hard drive was all along.

Maybe not consciously. But he could have a telling detail somewhere in that big skull of his. And you wouldn't want to explain to your superiors why you surrendered that telling detail to the ocean.

You keep swimming.

It's long, hard, exhausting work.

You come close to giving up quite a few times, giving your aching, weak, nearly numb limbs the break they're desperately crying out for. So what if the rest of you died. At least your limbs could have some peace.

You keep swimming.

Charlie Hardie is no fucking help at all.

He could be conscious, pulling his own weight, but no. He has to rely on you.

Fuck him for being a fat bastard, too.

Two hundred and thirty pounds isn't obscene, and he's a tall, wide-framed guy. A lot of it has to do with genetics; some of it has to do with his military experience. But still. Fuck. If he weren't so thick and heavy, you wouldn't be so thick and heavy. Back in your previous incarnation, when you had a different name, you were just as tall and wide but a lot thinner. Lean muscle. Your old self, you could have swum to shore (wherever it was) and back again—*twice*—by now.

No fucking help at all.

At a certain point you realize what you're seeing isn't a mirage or a reflection of the sun on the water. It's honest-to-fuck land, a beach, seemingly abandoned, even—which is perfect. You know you're somewhere along the central California coast. Where, exactly, you have no idea. It doesn't matter, because there is fucking land out there, people. Land. A tiny fleck of hope in an ocean of despair.

Even though you see the land, you're suddenly overcome with the oppressive feeling that you're not going to make it, your head is going to slip under the surface of the water and that little glimpse of beach will be your last, and hah hah hee hee hawwwww won't that be funny.

You keep swimming.

When you finally reach the shore you don't do that lame Christopher Columbus thing where you fall, exhausted, to your knees and then genuflect to kiss the grains of sand. No, instead you scream and drag fat fucking Charlie Hardie far enough up the shoreline so that the waves won't wash over his fat fucking face and drown him after all of that effort. Only then do you collapse next to him, eyes toward the sky, your limbs cursing you, you telling your limbs to shut up, and your chest heaving and your brain trying to supply countless demands for pain relief.

There's a noise not too far away.

A crinkling of paper.

"Whoah. You okay, man?"

You twist your head around to see a bearded guy standing there with a notebook in one hand and a cell phone in the other. Even upside down you can tell he's a hipster douchebag, central California version. The chunky glasses, the greasy hair, the tight misbuttoned shirt. He's in dire need of a shower and a hug.

"I'm doing just great," you say.

"Where did you come from?"

"Space."

The hipster douchebag, probably a fucking poet or something, doesn't quite know how to respond to that, so he focuses on the big dude lying facedown in the sand next to you. He crouches down next to you both.

"What about him? Is he okay? Wait a minute…are you guys wearing spacesuits? I thought you were just fucking around with me there."

Can't get anything past this guy.

"Can I show you something?" you ask, reaching for an imaginary pocket, and the moment his eyes track down to your hand you nail him. It feels good to take out some aggression on someone who totally doesn't deserve it. By the follow-up rabbit punch he's already out cold on the sand. Leaving you with two unconscious bodies on the beach. Let's just hope hipster douchebag has car keys.

He does.

So you pick up your fat-ass doppelgänger and drag up him across the sand all the way up to the road where you find the hipster poet's car, a late-model SUV. Inside, though, looks like what you imagine the guy's apartment to look like. Books and papers everywhere, the cloying scent of hash or potpourri or some blend of the two, and a pattern of stains that creep you out. You almost feel bad for fat-ass—he's the one who's going to have to be passed out facedown in some unidentified stain. You, well, it'll just be the ass of your spacesuit touching the seat.

You sweep the backseat clear of grad lit major bullshit, stow your human cargo, then try to figure out where the fuck in California you are.

The next few hours are frenetic and tense. You half-expect gunmen to turn a corner at any given second and blow the meat from your bones. But you can't think about that, because those kinds of things are out of your control.

You're in a small California coastal town somewhere north of San Francisco, but it has the things you need. A drugstore so that you can shoplift some essential supplies, a chain motel where you can break into an unused room.

This you learned from the *Annotated Charlie Hardie,* too. For a while there, after accidentally getting the Parrish family killed, Hardie was living in cheap motels, getting shitfaced, and forever losing his keycards. So he became fairly adept at using wire hangers to reach under the door and up and opening the handle with a quick jerk. When Hardie had been on the run in L.A. with the late Lane Madden, he'd perfected his technique to check into an unused room. He'd check the maid's pencil charts to see which rooms had gone unused. You choose a motel pretty far from the beach—one of those non-chains that pretend they're a chain anyway. You don't need the room for long. Just enough time to pull yourselves together, call your handler, then wait for the cavalry to arrive. A few hours of sleep wouldn't be a bad thing, either, while you're waiting.

Fat-ass, though, needs burn cream on his skin. It would be a lousy thing to have plucked him from the hot-cold vacuum of space only to have him perish from a skin infection. Unkillable or not, it was the little things that always did you in. As you work bandaging your body double, you can't help it—you keep checking the prepaid cell phone you stole, hoping for that call back that will mean this nightmare is over.

And then you see it.

On the back of his—*your*—head.

The scar that changes the whole game.

14

Don't start tryin' to do the right thing, boy-o. You haven't the practice.

—James Cromwell, *L.A. Confidential*

HUH.

Look at that.

Still alive.

Every time Charlie Hardie opened his eyes he experienced a sensation of mild surprise that he was still breathing air, still on this earthly plane of existence. Thing is, he never knew whether or not to be relieved or disappointed. For a good long while in his life, back when he was still house-sitting, he could have sworn he was in purgatory. And since you never die in purgatory, his continued existence was never a mystery. Since then, however, he'd gone through hell and back and had come to realize that he was indeed alive. But death could come for him at any moment.

Like *now.*

Hardie fully expected to wake up dead. The moment his head had slipped under the surface of the water, he had thought he'd drown in the Pacific Ocean, swallowed up and missing forever. Which was probably the fate he deserved, an anonymous burial at sea. So he was surprised to be on a too-soft bed in a dreary motel room with beat-up furniture. And standing across the way was...

Himself.

Huh. So it wasn't all some weird prolonged nightmare, was it? Somebody had been crazy enough to carve up some poor bastard so that he looked just like him.

The Other Him saw that he was being watched. "I can't reach him." His double had a disposable cell phone tucked between his face and shoulder. "I don't understand it. This line was supposed to always be open and available."

"Who?"

"My handler. I've been trying ever since I got the phone, waiting for a call back, but nothing."

Rising from the bed, Hardie felt like he was stricken with the most intense, bone-wearying flu he had ever had. Every individual part of his body seemed to hurt. Joints. Muscles. Bones. Even his hair follicles seemed to ache.

But nothing was worse than the searing agony in both of his hands, which had been taped up.

The Other Hardie noticed Hardie looking down at his paws. "Yeah, those are going to kill you," he said. "But hang on until we get to Nevada. I'll get you something that'll take the pain away."

Hardie turned them slowly, examining the bandage job. What little he could see of his actual skin looked ugly and purple and very unskinlike. God, his hands. The one thing Kendra always said she liked about him.

"Are they broken?"

"Well, I don't have an X-ray machine handy, but it's safe to say you banged them up pretty damn bad. Just like your face."

"My what?"

Hardie reached a taped-up paw up to his cheek, which set off twin waves of tear-inducing pain. The slight pressure on his fingertips sent lightning bolts down his hand all the way to his armpit. Simultaneously, his face remembered it had been burned to a crisp, and the pain centers lit up like a winning slot machine.

"Oh hell, my face. What the hell happened to my face?"

"I really don't know, because I was knocked out by the crash. I only woke up as you were slipping under, taking me along with you. When I managed to pull your head above water, I saw that it was burned to hell. I'm sorry, man. But in the grand scheme of things, I'd say we're both pretty lucky to be alive."

Which is what secretly worries you.

You two shouldn't be alive. That craft clearly wasn't meant to be recoverable—it crashed too hard and apparently sank way too fast. There were no NSA rescue teams waiting to scoop you up as promised. You were left in the middle of the Pacific Ocean to drown. Not exactly how they'd sold it to you inside that antiseptic over-air-conditioned vault of an office back in suburban Virginia.

Now that you've seen the little jagged surprise on the back of Hardie's head, you realize you've been fed misinformation from the start of the mission.

My God, you realize with a start.

Were you even meeting with the NSA over this past year? Or were you in the custody of someone else? You did the *one thing* you should never do in this game—accept something at face value. Just because you were remanded to the custody of US intelligence didn't necessarily mean you remained in the custody of US intelligence . . .

So what is going on? What part of the game board can't you see?

*   *   *

At the bathroom mirror, Hardie took a good long look at what was left of his face. The Other Him had done a thorough job. You couldn't see much of his flesh, other than the raw red charred meat around his eyes and his mouth. There were two slits in the bandages around his nose that allowed him to breathe. His ears were exposed, and they didn't seem too bad. Nor was his hair singed.

Hardie remembered an old Bogart movie called *Dark Passage*— based on a novel written by a fellow Philadelphian named David Goodis. Bogie spends a good chunk of the movie wrapped up in bandages following some back-alley plastic surgery, San Francisco–style. Hardie always thought Bogie looked kind of ridiculous—almost clownlike. He had to emote through his eyes, and, boy, did that old tough guy emote. Now the joke was on Hardie, because he looked just as ridiculous.

Okay, whatever. Who cares what he looked like underneath? He wasn't going to be entering any amateur modeling competitions at the mall.

Hardie's bandaged fingers found a loose piece of gauze under his chin and he started to pull.

"I wouldn't do that," the Other Him said. He was standing in the bathroom doorway behind him, with his fully functional face and hands.

"Why?" Hardie asked. "You about to eat lunch or something?"

"No. Because of the risk of infection. I should have taken you to a hospital with those burns, but we both know you wouldn't last long in a place like that. Not before they heard about it and took you out."

So the burns were that bad. Great.

"Hey, I did the best I could."

"Yeah."

"Be grateful you're alive at all."

"Didn't you hear?" Hardie asked. "We're unkillable. We can't die."

"You might be," Chuck said, "but the same doesn't go for me. I'm absolutely mortal."

Hardie shook his head. "Trust me, I can be killed."

The Other Him looked at him and smirked. A trademark Charlie Hardie™ smirk. Which creeped Hardie out, just as your reflection would creep *you* out if it started doing something different in the mirror.

"That's only because you've never heard of Project Viking."

"Project what?"

Project Viking had been buried for twenty years.

Nobody knew about Project Viking.

That is, until your handlers put together the *Annotated Charlie Hardie*—including a little shocking document they called the Arbona Memorandum—and discovered the truth about what had happened to Hardie in the early 1990s.

Back in the early days of the Iraq invasion, which had been treated like a field test for a lot of crazy stuff they'd been saving up over the years, a private corporation received the nod to treat a few soldiers with a series of hormones and vitamins that would amp up their endurance. The soldiers weren't told; nor were their superiors. But the idea was that if soldiers could last even a few hours more on the battlefield, modified to bleed out more slowly, or could be given extra blasts of adrenaline at the right moment, then the savings would be astronomical. You wouldn't have to deploy a new soldier if a bunch of old ones could last even a short while longer. Add those hours up, and you're talking billions.

Hence Project Viking. Soldiers were given doses during basic training, totally unbeknownst to them (they were told they were simply deficient in some vitamins and had to report for extra supplements). The creators of Project Viking thought they'd have a good old field test when the US Army kicked down Saddam's door and got into a serious rumble. The excitement was palpable. Would Crazy Hussein (in the membrane, Hussein in the brain!) use his rumored stores of chemical weapons? And if so, would the Viking subjects last longer?

As it turned out, Project Viking did jack shit in this kind of war. Didn't matter how many vitamins and hormones and supplements you gave a soldier: An IED was still going to turn him into chunks of lunchmeat.

And then the people in charge of funding fell in love with drone weapons and robots and all at once Project Viking was seen as a relic, a Captain America-ish dream that belonged back in the 1940s.

"You were a Project Viking test subject," the Other Him said.

"What are you talking about? I don't remember signing up for any experiments or tests. I was just there to escape my shitty neighborhood and my shitty life."

"These kinds of experiments, they didn't ask for volunteers. They just ran them. No permissions slips, no questions asked."

"They," Hardie said, anger building in his face as he tried to find the right words, "they just can't *do that shit* to people!"

"And yet they did. Look, the files were buried deep, but they exist. There's nothing more suspicious than a blank page in someone's biography. Well, the Cabal kept digging until they found it. And once they realized who they had on their hands, you suddenly

97

became hot property. Since then, we've dug up copies of them for ourselves. I've read them. I know what happened to you. And it's been a part of your life ever since."

"What do you mean?"

The Other Him gave a creepy look that bordered on pity. *Oh, you poor baby.* Which was surreal. Was that what Hardie looked like when he was trying to look sympathetic? No wonder everybody seemed to want to punch him in the face.

"You can stop beating yourself up because you lived and Nate died."

The words were like ice water through Hardie's veins.

"You may think you know what happened," he said quietly, "but every part of my life is not contained in a bunch of files somewhere."

"You lived because of Project Viking. Your body is able to rally and heal itself a lot faster than an ordinary human being's body. Just think about that for a moment. Think about what you could have done with that gift, rather than wasting it on...whatever it is you think you've been doing."

"If this is a pep talk," Hardie said, "you suck at it."

The Other Him smiled. "Maybe this is my version. Because, buddy, you and me got a long road ahead of us."

"They're going to find us anyway, aren't they? I mean, this is your all-powerful Cabal we're talking about. How long can we hide from people like this?"

"We can do this," the Other Him said. "We have to make it to my debriefing station. That's the only way now. I have to assume the field teams working the mission have been taken out, as well as my communication channels. It's in person, or it's nothing."

"Where's this station?"

"Somewhere in Virginia. I know it by sight."

"And we're somewhere in California right now."

"If we leave now, we can be there in two days."

"Wait...you mean drive it?"

"No other way."

"How about in an airplane, maybe?"

"They'd spot us within seconds. Especially with you, looking like the Mummy's ugly cousin. And me, wearing your face."

"Driving sounds insane," Hardie said.

"You don't understand," his double said. "I'm not giving you a choice here. This is how it plays out. Otherwise we're all dead. Including Kendra and CJ. We've gotta take down the Cabal while they're vulnerable."

"Uh-uh," Hardie said. "We get my family first. Once they're safe, then I'll do everything I can to help you bury these bastards. I'll do a drunken jig on their graves. But not until I know my family is safe."

15

*I'm gonna get us something from all four food groups: hamburg-
ers, French fries, coffee and doughnuts.*

           —Jim Belushi, *Red Heat*

THE GREASY SPOON on the ground floor of the motel was decorated
for Christmas. Strips of aluminum foil were meant to be tinsel, cot-
ton balls were meant to be snow, pine cones were meant to be...pine
cones. Plastic molded Santa Clauses and reindeer were affixed to the
walls and coated with at least two decades' worth of airborne grease
and dust, the remnants of past holiday customers and what they ate.

Appetizing.

Charlie Hardie had no idea what to order. He didn't know what
his stomach could handle after nine months of freeze-dried and powdered space food. Order a burger, and he could be seeing it again
within minutes. And it wouldn't be nearly as appetizing the second
time around. But he also knew he should be eating *something*. His
double had insisted: Eat now or hold your peace for three thousand
miles. Hardie realized the guy was right. His body needed fuel. He'd
be of no use to Kendra and the boy if he was passing out every few
minutes.

But what? Nothing on the menu didn't make his stomach pre-emptively clench. Everything seemed to be fried, breaded, or grilled—or covered in onions that were fried, breaded, or grilled. Wasn't this supposed to be California, land of healthy living?

Whatever he ordered, he was definitely going to pair it with a beer. It would probably hit him way hard, just like it did the last time. But screw it. A man who survives a crash landing from outer space deserves a cold one.

Hardie was still at a loss. "What do you recommend?"

"The pie's good," the counter girl said.

Yes. Pie. Wholesome, nourishing all-American pie. The staple of American diets since the colonial days. No, seriously. Hardie had read about it in an in-flight magazine once. How pies weren't just dessert. They were entire meals. Throw a bunch of ingredients into a dough shell and there you go.

"Pie," Hardie said. "Yeah, a big slice of pie."

"What kind?"

"Doesn't matter. There's no such thing as bad pie. And also, a beer. Doesn't matter what brand, either."

"Beer and pie. At 7:30 a.m."

"That's right."

"We don't serve beer. No liquor license."

"Then I guess it'll just be the pie, then."

The waitress nodded but lingered on his eyes a bit. Hardie could tell she wanted to ask him about the bandages on his face and hands but ultimately decided that she could live without that knowledge. She turned to the Other Him. "How about you?"

"Pie sounds great, any kind. Something different from my friend's order, okay? That way if we don't like it we can switch."

"I'm not switching pies with you," Hardie said.

"What, you don't want a beer or anything?" the waitress asked, not even the barest trace of a smile on her face, even though she was joking.

"Me? No. Not this early in the morning. My friend here's the drunk."

She went off to the cooling case to pull out two different pies. They were uncut, virginal. Hardie watched her use the knife on the pies and turned to the Other Him and said, "We need a name for you."

"What do you mean?"

"I can't call you Charlie, I'm sorry. You've got a real name, don't you? Before all this you were Secret Agent somebody, right?"

"I've had a few names in my career."

"So pick one."

"I can't. They're all classified."

"And your birth name?"

"It's been so long I've forgotten it."

"Uh-uh."

"Okay, it's classified, too. Look, they take this stuff seriously. But more than that—if you start calling me another name, it'll mess with my mind. The key to being you for all of these months? Truly believing that I am you. It's hard enough being with you right here. The bandages help a little."

"What do you mean, believing you're me? You're not me. We've established this already, right?"

"The thing is, some part of me still thinks I am you. So you can't call me anything other than Charlie Hardie."

"You're fucked in the head, you know that?"

"Welcome to my world."

The waitress put the pies in front of them. Cherry for Hardie, Apple for He Who Had Yet to Be Named.

*   *   *

It could all end here, with a slice of apple pie.

You tell yourself: Be smart now.

Quickly you plunge your fork into the center and reach into your pocket at the same time. You ask Hardie to pass you a napkin, because (luckily) the dispenser is on his side of the counter. You jab the pie with your left hand, pinch the capsules in your right. Meanwhile, Hardie's distracted, looking for a napkin. His peripheral vision is crap, thanks to those bandages. Now. Make your move. Do it, and do it quick. Burst the capsules with your thumb and index finger. Sprinkle that shit liberally.

Hardie's picked up his fork now and is ready to plunge it when—

"Wait," you say. "I can't eat this. I'm allergic to apples."

Hardie's head snaps to the right and his beady eyes peer at you from behind the bandages. "I've never heard of an allergy to apples. Plus, you've already stuck your fork in yours. No thanks."

"The fork didn't touch my mouth."

"I don't care if it didn't touch your ass. I'm sticking with the cherry."

"Come on. Cut me a break."

"Order another slice then."

You're thinking fast, tap-tap-tap-dancing inside your own skull. Boy, this really could go in any direction right now...

Hardie plunged his fork into his own pie, chopped off a ridiculously large portion of it, and shoved it into his mouth. Cherry juice stained the bandages around his mouth.

"You're an ass," you tell him.

"Mmmmmm, mmmmm, you really should order a slice of this," Hardie says.

But you're not done yet.

Oh no.

"You've got cherry gore on your face," you tell him, then reach across him for a napkin.

"Don't touch me."

People are staring now, which is fine, because they're all focused on him and not on your right hand, which has the contents of three burst capsules in it—and now you're sprinkling that stuff right into the gaping wound in Hardie's cherry pie.

"Come on. Let me clean you up."

"What are you, my mother?"

"I'm not driving cross-country with someone who looks like he's been snacking on small woodland creatures."

"Whatever. Let's get out of here. I'm done with this."

"Will you just finish your pie? After all of that bullshit about ordering it?"

Now Hardie realizes that, yes, he's the toddler making the scene in the nearly empty diner, everyone is looking his way, and well...he'd better shut up and enjoy his damn pie. He takes another forkful, not quite as large this time, but that's okay. Because that one forkful has it all.

Go ahead, eat up.

Enjoy your pie.

And then get *realllll sleepy.*

Now that you know he's all right, and his head isn't about to go ka-boom, you realize you need Charlie Hardie unconscious for the next part of this trip. It'll make things so much easier. You're in charge; not him. You need him asleep and out of the way so that you can win back your freedom at long last. The tricky thing is giving him enough to knock him out but not kill him. His tolerance for poisons and gases is legendary, but you realize there has to be a tipping point. And Charlie Hardie may not be much of a bargaining chip if he's dead.

The second bite of cherry pie didn't taste as good to Hardie. Probably the damned fake freeze-dried space food ruined his taste buds for life. That or the sting of embarrassment ruined the whole thing. He wished they served beer here. What he wouldn't give for a beer.

The hipster poet pays for your pies, though he doesn't know it. You've already changed out the license plates on his SUV, but that ruse won't last forever. You need another vehicle as quickly as possible. But not any old vehicle. You've got a special vehicle in mind, one that makes you believe that all is not lost, that you can pull this off.

You look over at your twin. He should be feeling the effects of the pills by now. Just to be sure, though, you've still got a pocket full of them, and while Hardie goes off to shake the dew off his lily one last time, you're going to dose a bottle of water you've bought him.

This would be so much easier if you could have access to the usual array of tools, poison, and rigs. Alas, wish in one hand, crap in the other...

"Come on, let's get a move on."

Predictably, you both make a beeline for the driver's seat. He thinks he'd driving. That's funny, for many, many reasons.

"I always drive when breaking in a new partner," Hardie says.

"You were never a cop."

"Screw you! You got the driver's harness on the spacecraft."

"A lot of good it did me. Look, I'm happy to trade up somewhere down the road. But you've just been unconscious for twelve hours.

Who knows if you'll suddenly slip back under?" You clamp your teeth down on your tongue before you can say, *And you will. Oh, you will...*

"You were out before we even touched ground," Hardie replies. "If there's anybody who's at risk, it's you. Geez, what if we go more than fifty miles per hour? That might just knock you out again!"

"You're not driving. Want to know how I know that? Because I have the keys."

You want to scream: *Will you just fall asleep already! Yawn or something. Let me know the stuff is working on you.*

From behind the bandages, Hardie's beady eyes are fiercely trained on you. "I can take them from you."

This kind of banter goes on for a while until you finally just push your way past Hardie, open the stolen car, and strap yourself in behind the wheel. Hardie does the sullen teenager thing as he climbs into the passenger seat and leans back against the headrest. Finally. He's feeling it, isn't he? You key the ignition and peel out of the diner parking lot and start your high-speed cross-country journey. If he falls asleep, you think everything will work out okay.

Hardie does not fall asleep.

Even after a very difficult interlude where you manage to dump more of your home-grown knockout cocktail into a bottle of water you've packed and offer it to Hardie. He's grateful, because the sun streaming through the windshield is making him thirsty, and he gulps down half of it.

But he does not sleep.

And then he drinks the other half a few minutes later!

But he does not sleep.

You're feeling sleepy just thinking about all of the milligrams of good old-fashioned pharmaceutical night-night juice you've dumped into that water because it seems to have no effect whatsoever on this guy.

You think: *Project Viking, you can kiss my fat, surgically altered ass.*

Hardie was tired as hell. All he wanted to do was close his eyes for a few minutes and let his brain cycle down. But he knew that would just be asking for trouble. He could easily imagine waking up to discover his disembodied head floating in a jar of electrified water or some such shit. His clone may have yanked him out of the Pacific Ocean and bandaged up his face and hands . . . but he still didn't fully trust him yet.

Instead of drifting off, Hardie thought some conversation would help. Chances were his clone would say something to piss him off, and the adrenaline would go coursing through his bloodstream and keep him alert for the duration of this hell trip.

The first question being, "Tell me again why we didn't steal a fucking plane?"

America is a nation of roads and bridges and tunnels and buildings and wide-open spaces, his clone patiently explained.

"The Cabal," he continued, "is part of a shadow nation of roads and bridges and tunnels and buildings running parallel to those we all know."

"Right."

"You don't believe me."

"No," Hardie said. "I believe you. I was trapped in one of those shadow zones for longer than I care to remember. So your big idea is to speed across the entire country through these shadow zones, hope we don't killed, rescue my family, then zoom down to home base somewhere in Virginia?"

"Pretty much."

"They'll find us on the road and kill us. We both know this."

"Not if we use their own roads against them."

"Still think flying's quicker."

"They're going to come at us with everything they've got," the Other Hardie said. "But it'll be in the way you least expect it."

"Always is," Hardie said.

"No, you don't understand. You faced the Accident People all those years ago, right? They were good at orchestrating events at a single scene."

"Not that good."

"Good enough. But imagine that kind of care and planning on a national scale. That's what we're up against. So we have to hide within their system."

"How do we do that? We're in a stolen car on the open highway. I don't see these shadow roads you keep talking about."

"The roads are a metaphor. It's not the road but the vehicle."

"You're getting all Jack Kerouac on me, aren't you."

"No. I'm talking about an *actual* vehicle, bulletproof and untraceable, hidden in a secret storage unit in the middle of the Nevada desert."

16

You may not like what you're about to see.

—Peter Weller, *RoboCop*

ONE COLD MORNING, Ellie Clark started talking to her husband again.

It wasn't much, and no eye contact. It was merely: "You want some?" *Some* being the rest of the scrambled eggs she'd cooked up for the girls. Still, this was progress. Five weeks earlier, when Deacon "Deke" Clark had placed his wife and daughters in witness protection, Ellie vowed never to speak to him again. Usually Eleanor Jean Clark was a woman of her word. She was a loving wife and a wonderful mother. But she recalled grudges like people recalled their Social Security numbers.

Now, all these stone-silent and awkward weeks later, she asked him, "You want some?"

Some, meaning the sad little clump of slightly browned scrambled eggs tucked to one side of the cheapo frying pan they'd had to pick up at a Podunk grocery store.

To Deke, it was like she had proposed getting married all over again.

Which is why it was *really* going to kill him when he told her that he had to leave her and the girls for an indefinite period of time.

"Thanks, baby," Deke said. His wife wordlessly pushed the clump of eggs onto a plate and put the cheap frying pan and even cheaper plastic spatula into a small, stained sink.

They hadn't spoken about it (obviously), but Deke suspected that the kitchen gear was the thing that angered her the most. They had spent their nineteen-year marriage gathering good plates, utensils, silverware, and pots and pans. Nothing fancy, and by no means all at once. A guy on an FBI salary isn't splurging on an entire set of Le Creuset cookware. Ellie picked up a piece at a time, almost always taking advantage of a sale or coupon. Both Deke and Ellie used the pieces equally; they were a couple who truly enjoyed cooking.

When they had to enter the protection program, however, nearly all of their possessions were dumped unceremoniously into cardboard boxes and stacked in a ten-by-twenty-five-foot pen in some anonymous storage facility center near the turnpike. Would they see their belongings again? Deke assured his wife that, yeah, of course they would. But he wasn't so sure.

They weren't in the traditional FBI Witness Security Program—or WITSEC, as they called it. There is a little-known *alternate* witness protection program, meant for agents and cops and politicians and anyone else on the slightly more honorable side of the law. Entry into this program was rare and was always meant to be temporary—unlike participation in WITSEC proper.

The more Deke learned about the people who'd imprisoned Charlie Hardie, though . . . the more he wondered about his own family's safety.

Even tucked away here, in this town in the middle of South

Dakota. They could still be reached. Which was why he had to go and stop this thing. Absolutely and definitely.

Not like before.

Before—about seven years ago—Deke Clark was laboring under the delusion that his old not-exactly-pal Charlie Hardie had lost his mind and killed a young actress named Lane Madden.

When the call came, Deke was on his back deck in Philadelphia, grilling up some carne asada, thinking about throwing some peppers and mushrooms on there, sipping a Dogfish Head.

Call comes, from a guy Deke hasn't spoken to in years. Guy he hasn't *wanted* to speak to, tell you the truth.

Charlie Hardie.

Don't like him much now, never really did back in the day, either.

He says, *"I'm kind of fucked, Deke."*

Says: *"You don't think you can get out here sometime tonight, do you?"*

Here, meaning: Los Angeles, California. All the way across the country.

Hardie explains the trouble. So of course Deke packs a bag. That's the kind of guy he is, can't say no to a man full of trouble. Goes to the airport. The whole flight out to L.A. he's thinking about the crazy story Hardie told him. That Hardie was house-sitting in the Hollywood Hills and there was a squatter in the house—only the squatter turned out to be famous actress Lane Madden, and people were trying to kill her. Like, with exotic knockout drugs and speed-ball injections and shit. And now Hardie and this world-famous actress were on the run, somewhere in L.A.

Hardie had called them the Accident People.

"Deke, they're smart, they're connected, and it's only a matter of time before they find us again."

111

And that was the last trace of Charlie Hardie for...

Six years.

When Deke finally ran Charlie Hardie down again, it was the result of luck, dogged policework, and a last-minute flight to San Francisco. A lawyer named Gedney had been pushed out a window, and the trail led Deke to this private garage near the Embarcadero. And when he finally had the man pinned down, standing behind a car with the trunk open, all Hardie could say was: "Hi, Deke."

And all Deke could say in return was: "Where the fuck have you been, man."

"They sent me away."

"I know. Believe me, I know. They sent me pictures. I've been looking for you for five years. I hired people to go looking for you. But you vanished without a trace."

"Well, I'm back. So what are we going to do?"

Deke looked around the garage, saw the bodies lying in pools of their own blood. "You do that?"

"You would have, too."

"Who's the guy at your feet?"

"His name's Doyle. He's one of the ones who sent me away."

"From the law firm of Doyle, Gedney, and Abrams? The police found Gedney. On the roof of the St. Francis."

"Yeah. He's another one who sent me away. There's this one. Abrams will be next."

Deke tensed up. "You don't understand, man. Stop for a minute and consider your situation. The world thinks you're a killer. That's right. Far as everyone's concerned, you killed an innocent woman five years ago and went on the run. Now you show up and start killing more people? Don't you realize the road you're headed down?"

"You don't know what these sons of bitches did to me."

"I know, Charlie. Believe me . . . I. *Know*. They've been threatening to do the same thing to me, Ellie, everyone close to me. They deserve to die screaming for what they've done. But this isn't how we fight them. We drag their asses out into the light and we fight them."

Hardie said nothing. Deke Clark was one of the smartest and toughest guys he'd ever worked with—outside of Nate Parrish, of course—but now his eyes were full of fear. Maybe Hardie would have been the same way, had the roles been reversed.

"Come on, Charlie. Let's go. Let's get out of here."

"No. I'm not finished."

"Finished *what?* You have nothing to finish. You come back with me and you start explaining. Other people will finish this. You? You're done. You don't have to do this anymore. We can get help. You've got to stop now and come home."

Home.

That's when it occurred to Hardie.

"Do you still have people on Kendra and Charlie?" he asked.

Deke swallowed. "They're fine. Perfectly safe."

"You're not answering my question. Does the bureau still have a detail on my wife and son?"

Deke couldn't lie; he was practically incapable of it. Hardie knew that.

"Listen, Charlie . . ."

"Goddamn it, how long have you been retired?" Hardie asked. "The person who answered the phone said you were gone."

"It's been a while, man. Look, back when you went missing . . ."

"How long have Kendra and Charlie been without protection, god-damnit!?"

After a quiet beat, Deke said: "I look after them."

"What, do you sleep in your fucking car outside their house and keep constant vigil? Does Ellie join you? You living your life making sure nobody kills my family? Who's watching your family? You got a detail for that?"

"Hardie..."

Deke couldn't tell if the man was crying or ready to collapse or laughing from nervous exhaustion or what. All he knew was that it was finally time for Charlie Hardie to come home. He slipped the gun inside his jacket pocket and walked over to Hardie, put his hand on his shoulders, and told him everything was going to be okay, even though it probably wasn't. Right here, in this room, were three men Charlie had killed. Another on a roof just a dozen blocks away. No matter what had happened, you can't make murder go away. He could feel Hardie trembling a little under his touch.

Look at him. With a cane and everything. If the moment weren't so horrible Deke would have maybe found a little amusement in the notion of Charlie Hardie, baddest man in Philadelphia, having to get around with a cane.

Didn't explain where he'd been the past five years.

"Come on, Hardie," Deke said softly. "It's going to be all right."

Deke briefly looked past Hardie to see the interior of the car's trunk. At first it looked like somebody had shoved a bunch of medical gear inside of it—oxygen tanks, IV bags, tubing. But then he saw how neatly it was all arranged. "What the hell is that?"

Deke was so mesmerized by the contents of the trunk that he didn't feel the tip of the cane against his chest until it was too late.

He barely felt the shock.

And when he came to, Hardie was already gone.

*   *   *

Deke had exactly one lead left: this impossible-to-reach lawyer named Abrams. The *A* in DG&A, Deke Clark's least favorite law firm on earth. And that was saying a lot, because Deke hated most law firms.

Now, you'd think that an FBI agent could demand a conversation with pretty much anyone in America—but you would be wrong. Deke's first attempt, through official channels, was met with a stern OH NO YOU FUCKING DON'T from on high. A back-channel attempt was similarly smacked down, with a second reprimand from on high: SERIOUSLY, DON'T EVEN THINK ABOUT IT IF YOU VALUE YOUR CAREER. Abrams was clearly protected, as if the president himself had stamped a big old DO NOT TOUCH on her forehead in holographic ink.

That was Deke, going through the proper channels.

Instead, Deke wanted to take a page out of the tried-and-true Charlie Hardie Ultimate Playbook and go through another kind of channel.

The kind of channel where you stick a gun in somebody's mouth and let him taste the cold metal, maybe even chip his teeth a little, then ask a few questions.

All of this was laughably ironic because back in the day, Deke Clark was the most vocal opponent of the Charlie Hardie Ultimate Playbook. You just didn't do shit like that, Deke would complain to anyone who would listen. Hardie knew it, which is why the man would never become a real cop. He worked as a "police consultant," which was patently ridiculous. Either you're a cop or you're not. Either you follow the rules or you're a criminal.

So what was Deke doing now, after all that moral grandstanding?

Protecting his family, that's what he was doing now.

He'd gone off the reservation before. Just last year, in fact. The mistake he made then was tackling this thing alone. Like a god-damned fool. Not again.

Deke had a list he kept in his back pocket. A list of guys who left the bureau—or the DEA or ATF or Secret Service or any other government job involving a gun. Good guys who were either bounced for bad reasons or pulled the plug for good reasons and who might be willing to help a brother out down the road.

Now all he needed was to find this Abrams. Without the geeks at Quantico working the computers, Deke knew it was going to be tedious and grueling. But what other choice did he have?

Then, like a car crash or a lightning strike, Deke Clark was blind-sided by his first real Charlie Hardie lead in over a year. It popped up on the Internet.

Deke had long ago set up a Google automatic search for all things Charlie Hardie–related, including the search terms:

Hardie
Lane Madden
Accident People
Truth Hunters
Phil and Jane Kindred

Along with a dozen other terms related to the Hunter Family/ Lane Madden case from seven years ago. Those little seeds bore only random, useless fruit. Rehashes of the case, blog posts detailing amateur theories, conspiracy bullshit, et cetera, et cetera, ad infinitum.

Every day Deke Clark would skim through the dozens of Google search emails that would pop into his in-box on a regular basis.

But it was a random "news of the weird" report that caught his attention:

POET CLAIMS SPACEMEN STOLE HIS CAR

Deke almost didn't read it. He didn't dig poetry and he wasn't into science fiction or cars. Nothing about the headline spoke to him in any particular way. But the quote in the lede hooked him, and he ended up scrolling down far enough into the story to see a photo that punched him in the gut: Charlie Hardie standing on a beach, squinting in the sun, wearing what appeared to be a janitor's uniform.

At his feet: a guy whose face was wrapped in bandages.

What the *what*…

Deke dragged the image to his desktop and embiggened it. (Yeah, Deke knew there was a proper term for that, but he didn't care right now.) As he made the JPEG larger, the quality suffered…but goddamn if that wasn't Charlie Hardie.

Again: What the *whaaaaaaat?*

So many questions raced through Deke's mind it was difficult to prioritize them. Where had Charlie Hardie been for the past year? Why was he wearing that uniform? Who was the guy with his face wrapped up in bandages? Why did he—according to the poet in the story—seem to walk directly out of the ocean and up onto the beach? Why did he steal the poet's car? Where was he now? Why the freakin' hell hasn't he reached out in the past year—at the very least to check on his family?

Nothing Charlie Hardie did made sense.

But at least now Deke had a lead—the name of that beach town, and the name of a poet.

Now came the tough part.

The tough part: explaining to Ellie why he had to leave again, and not telling her where he was going.

17

How come the bad guys always have the good cars?
                    —Gregory Hines, *Running Scared*

THE SECRET CABAL storage depot turned out to be a mile down the road from a Nevada rest stop that featured the biggest cockroach Charlie Hardie had ever seen.

Getting there was its own special brand of hell. Don't get Hardie wrong. He was happy to finally cross the California state line after— what, seven, eight years of forcible detention? Sorry, the nine-month trip into space didn't count. He had been launched from California, and, God help him, he'd splashed down just off the coast of California, so you could forgive Hardie for thinking there was truly no escape from the Golden State. So Hardie almost didn't believe it when the Other Him told him they had just blown past the infamous Donner Pass (*"Hungry?"* he'd asked) and were approaching Nevada. Which is when Hardie started to feel seriously nauseated.

Hardie acknowledged that it could have been the mention of the Donner Pass and its attendant thoughts of cannibalism; but more likely it was that damned pie. After the disappointing skyline of

Reno came and went, the road was all four-lane blacktop with rocky desert, followed by plain old flat desert. Which went on for miles and miles and miles, broken up only by the occasional lane-shifting construction zones. Hardie tried closing his eyes and focusing on a pleasant memory, but that made him all the more sick. He tried the old trick of focusing on a point way off in the distance, but all he saw was desert, with no relief in sight. Finally, he asked his doppelgänger to pull over.

"What? Here? We're just about to the depot."

"I don't care. I see a sign for a rest station. We need to go there."

"The depot is just a mile past it. Trust me, the facilities will be much nicer."

"Pull over here or I'm going to vomit all over you."

That seemed to convince the Other Him to hook a right and spin around. The rest station was a concrete pad, on top of which sat six metal outhouses situated in a half-circle. The backdrop: utter desolation. And in the vast distance, the ghostly afterimages of atomic test blasts from decades ago. Gee, the state of Nevada really knew how to roll out the welcome wagon.

Hardie didn't care anything about that. He fumbled at the handle of their stolen SUV for a few seconds before hurling himself out of it and crawling across the concrete to the closest door. Which was locked. Inside, a young voice—female—screamed. Hardie mumbled an apology and tried the next one. The door yielded. Hardie barely made it to the toiletlike metal fixture before his stomach exploded up and outward.

You watch your double scramble out of the car and marvel at his tenacity. You read the Project Viking reports and understand (some of) the science behind it, but nevertheless it astounds you. Something about mitochondria reprogrammed to create redundancies, rather than the single-point failures in most human beings. Super-sized white blood cells for rapid damage repair. The kinds of things that made sense on paper but quickly devolved into bullshit once you took your eyes from the page.

But here's the thing you really don't understand: You put enough knockout medicine in his slice of pie to fell a stallion. But all it did to this guy was make his tummy upset.

How?

Did the white blood cells mop up all of the drugs like floating tampons? Or was Hardie just naturally immune to this stuff?

Whatever, you tell yourself. Doesn't matter now. You just need to sedate your bargaining chip, then go and do some bargaining.

And to do that, you're just going to have to try harder.

Fortunately, the answer to your problems might just be in that storage depot a mile down the road.

Hardie's aim was okay. Not that you could tell in a place like this. The bodily emissions and expulsions of countless unlucky tourists were all over the walls and floor.

He ran a bandaged thumb across his chin and looked down. Well, that was stupid. He went to the sink and twisted the handle. A spurt of water gushed from the faucet before turning brown and then stopping. The metal tower dispenser, the only relatively new fixture in here, was predictably empty.

Whatever. His Friendly Neighborhood Double out there said there were clean bathrooms a mile up the road. He could wash up then.

Hardie was about to leave when something on the sink captured his attention.

Namely: the biggest cockroach in the world.

Hardie had seen plenty of cockroaches over the years. The cockroach was the unofficial insect of Philadelphia, and Hardie had grown up among them. The only place a boy could hope for some privacy was in the basement of his row house, and basements were prime order Blattodea turf. He was forever swatting, crushing, repelling, hating the little fuckers. None of whom seemed to give a shit about his presence. They were resilient, they refused to stay dead. The E. G. Marshall sequence in Stephen King's *Creepshow* had been a favorite of Hardie's because finally someone nailed the terror of the cockroach.

This one, however, was not like the Philadelphia cockroaches.

This was an atomic test-blast cockroach: Roachzilla. Easily triple the size of an ordinary cockroach (or, as his grandfather would call them, "wadderbugs") back east. The insect's legs were thick, supporting an even thicker body that resembled a miniature brown armored tank. You had to respect a creature this formidable.

"Hey," Hardie said.

The cockroach said nothing. It merely held its ground.

"You look like a survivor," Hardie said. "Maybe you and I should team up. Go off and save my family, have adventures."

If the cockroach was entertaining this proposal, it didn't let on.

"Then again, you've probably got your own thing going on out here in the desert, right? Well, don't let me get in the way. Good talking to you."

The cockroach didn't return the sentiment.

As Hardie left the outhouse and harsh light blasted him, he felt a little stupid for having talked to an insect. Maybe it was further proof he had completely lost his mind. Then again, it was better than talking to yourself, right?

*   *   *

The top-secret Cabal facility was indeed a mile up the dusty road, exactly as promised. The squat two-story building was marked as property of the US Atomic Commission. If the legal jargon promising prosecution, prison, and quite possibly death by firing squad didn't dissuade you, then the faded yellow radioactive symbols might do the trick.

"Clever," Hardie said.

"Not really. This was just an abandoned government property the Cabal bought up. They left the signs alone."

"So how do you know about it?"

"I told you, we're at war with these bastards. When I wasn't in surgery, being cut to look like you, I was studying up on their methods and tactics. As well as how they've turned our own country's infrastructure against itself."

Hardie steeled himself for a lecture—he didn't give a shit about the Cabal, or the Industry, or whatever you chose to call them...outside of how they could be stopped. Or forced to leave his family alone. Thankfully, the Other Him dropped the subject. He pulled the SUV up to the front gate, pressed a button to open the driver's-side window, then tapped a few keys on a pad. There was a buzz. Then some clunks and a mechanical whine and the gates opened.

"No guards?"

"It's self-serve."

Sure enough, this secret facility was disturbingly close to a drive-in fast-food restaurant. Gates opened as the SUV piloted toward them, and closed behind them, seemingly unprompted. Maybe they were short-staffed, Hardie thought. What with all of their other employees being shot into space and all.

Inside was a tightly organized garage with three identical black vehicles resting in bays in the center. Hardie recognized those cars. Same make, same color, slightly later model. The goddamned Lincoln Town Cars. Or, as Hardie called them: "coma cars."

These were what the Industry or Secret America or the Cabal or whoever used to transport people around. The oversized trunk contained a full life support system for one average-sized adult human being. Breathing tubes, IV, catheter, the whole package. Stick a person in there and it's suspended animation-ville for at least a few days. You could even park the car, and a backup battery (and reserve supplies) would keep things humming along for a few days until you returned. Perfect for those weekend getaways!

Hardie had encountered these coma cars twice. Once, as a passenger in the trunk, the very thought of which made him break out in hives. The other time, he was a driver, which was much better, because he had someone he truly *hated* in the trunk. A man named Doyle.

You're going to leave me to die here, aren't you, you prick!

Oh, Doyle.

Hardie tried to kill him, but he was still out there somewhere. Probably still pissed off.

"Hey."

The Other Him was staring at him. This was still jarring to Hardie. So jarring, he wanted to punch his double in the face.

"There's a restroom across the way. Why don't you clean up while I gather some weapons and supplies? We've got a race ahead of us."

Even Hardie couldn't argue with that. He reeked of vomit, and he felt like he was going to throw up again. Funny how vomit did that to you. Vomit: All it wanted was more vomit. Anyway, better to do it in a clean bathroom.

*　　　*　　　*

You know there *has* to be one somewhere, in one of these lockboxes or containers.

You'd better start searching—there isn't much time.

You're looking for a device called a wasp's nest.

Back in the glory days of the Accident People it was a fundamental piece of gear, designed to be mounted on any surface—a door, a wall, a fixture. Set the trigger mechanism and you were good to go. Ultra-useful when you absolutely, positively had to kill someone in an instant.

That was possible because inside the wasp's nest was a bit of neurochemical magic: a weaponized poison that rendered you unconscious within a second, then killed you about a minute later by temporarily shutting down the part of the human brain that regulates the heart. After accomplishing that task, the poison breaks down into little untraceable pieces of nothing. A coroner could order all of the tox screens he wanted but wouldn't find jack shit. The targets almost never saw it coming, and didn't recover to tell the tale.

Except...

Charlie Hardie.

Seven years ago Hardie received a face full of the stuff, courtesy of the Accident People. He should have gone down like Sasha Grey. They were so sure that the poison inside the wasp's nest would kill Hardie, they even shoved his big dumb self into a body bag. Left him on the floor while they took care of other business.

That was before they realized they were dealing with Unkillable Chuck, graduate of the Project Viking School of Combat Efficiency.

But the wasp poison didn't work on him. Not the way it should have. It stopped his heart, knocked him out cold. However, it failed to kill him, and by the time he ripped his way out of that black plastic body bag, the man was more than a little pissed.

A wasp's nest is what you need right now, to knock Hardie out. You're pretty sure it *won't* kill him. Because that would be bad.

But it sure as shit would render him unconscious, wouldn't it?

If . . . you can find it.

You look for the organizational principle behind this supply center. There doesn't seem to be one. There are syringes. Black canvas bags. Surgical tubing. Pills in plastic vials identified only by bar codes. Handcuffs. Ammunition. Bottles marked with a skull and crossbones. Razor blades . . .

And finally, there it was. Ready to be assembled.

But then you hear water running through the pipes. Hardie's at the sink, washing up, coming back soon. You need to buy yourself some time.

When Hardie came out of the bathroom his double said, "I've got a surprise for you."

Hardie stared at him. "I wish you'd stop being so good to me, Boss."

The clone smiled. *"Cool Hand Luke.* One of our favorite movies. Tell you what, we make it out of this alive, and I'll boil up fifty eggs for you. Then we'll go down to some honky-tonk and get our photo taken with a couple of floozies. Anyway, I do have a surprise for you. According to the files I read, you lost this bag about seven years ago. Back in the Lowenbruck House up in the Hollywood Hills."

"What are you talking about?"

His double lifted his arm. Dangling from his fist was a black duffel bag.

No.

Couldn't be.

Hardie thought it had been lost forever. His black duffel bag, which he'd last seen seven years ago in the passenger seat of a Honda Whatever. Hardie believed there were two kinds of things in the world. Things that could be replaced, and things that could not. He'd spent his years in house-sitting exile giving away or tossing everything in his life that could be replaced. Which, of course, turned out to be most of the things in his life. Clothes, CDs, kitchen utensils, old books, plaques, magazines, shot glasses, movies.

But this duffel bag...

The one in his hand right now, the one he never used to allow to leave his side...

That was full of the things that could not be replaced.

"What... what is *this* doing here?"

"No idea. The Cabal hangs on to all kinds of strange stuff. Not wasting resources is a thing with them. But go ahead. Take a look inside."

Then he looked down at the paper tag behind a plastic window. There was a name scrawled on it:

K. CHAMBERLAIN

"Wait. This isn't mine."

"Someone must have stuck the wrong tag on it. Take a look inside. I think you'll find the contents very interesting."

"How would you know?"

"Because I *am* you, dummy. I'll leave you to it."

And with that, his double turned back to rooting through drawers for medical supplies.

Hardie stared at the name again. So, K. Chamberlain, who were you? Did they ruin your sorry life, too? You off somewhere having your own series of adventures? Or are you buried in an unmarked grave? With his bandaged fingers, Hardie unzipped the bag. He hadn't laid eyes on the contents of this bag since . . . forever. He could barely remember what was inside, other than irreplaceable fragments of his former life. Back when he was a husband and a father and mattered to people.

Halfway through the zip something clicked and hissed—

PSSSSSSSSH

—and Hardie felt cold drops spray his face. The Other Him was standing just a few feet away, holding a small gizmo. Before his brain could form the thought, his body said Here We Fucking Go Again. The canvas bag slipped out of his hand and landed with a thud on the concrete floor. Again, he felt crazy weak. Overcome with chills. Head spinning, and once again he wanted to scream, NO NO NO at his mind as if he could convince it to stay awake this time and

INTERLUDE WITH THE BEST SERIAL KILLERS EVER

Montreal, Canada — Now

THE PSYCHOPATHS CROSSED the northern border, looking for some toys.

Also, truth be told, the man wanted to try some poutine. His sister, based on the way she scrunched up her nose, seemed to find the idea repellent. Either way, the decision would have to wait until later, because they didn't have much time to waste and they were looking for a story. They found it in an underground mall.

The idea came when the girl saw the abandoned fashion outlet in a wing of the subterranean shopping plaza that was under perpetual construction. Her eyes danced over the dusty, pale, naked mannequins surrounded by rust-acned metal racks and cheap plastic hangers, and she silently giggled. The man glanced at her. "What are you thinking, Jane?" Jane gestured, making her ideas clear. Her brother Phil smiled. He got it instantly. They had that strange brother-sister telepathy where a few simple notions conveyed entire histories and philosophies.

So now they were arranging a fresh corpse, which had been cleaned and scrubbed and shaved, to take the place of one of the mannequins in the abandoned storefront. Their loose plan was to kill enough people tonight, plucking them from various corners of the labyrinthine mall, until the store was "populated."

But the clock was running against them; there was never enough time to play, it seemed. Phil and Jane were only three bodies into re-stocking the store when Phil's cell rang—their Minder.

"Where are you two?"

"Shopping."

"In a foreign country, I understand."

"*Barely.* It's Montreal, man."

Which was true. Montreal wasn't very far from the New York state border. Very drivable, with relatively unimpressive border security, even in these post-9/11 days. The two psychopaths had no trouble crossing with their bag of toys.

"Your deal pertains to the continental United States," their Minder said. "Not Alaska, not Hawaii. Lower Forty-eight states only. They could have me killed for this. Then they'd come after you."

"And that would be wicked exciting, wouldn't it?"

Their Minder sighed for a moment. The sigh turned into a cough, and then, after he couldn't contain it any longer, a few chuckles.

"You know, Phil, that would be," he admitted.

Phil and Jane had a deal with a secret branch of the US govern-ment. They were called upon, from time to time, to accept certain assignments. Usually, serial killers—the true, authentic DSM-IV-certified emotionless, remorseless, manipulative, and sadistic mon-sters—were not the kind of individuals you could use as field agents.

But Phil and Jane were not your typical serial killers. They were media-savvy and intelligent, and they had a fantastic agent. They also saw the benefit of accepting the occasional assignment. Because one meager assignment equaled one year of doing anything they pleased, with the complete support of not only the US government, but its various shadowy intelligence operatives who could cover up and even offer tactical support. Not that Phil and Jane ever asked for such a thing, but it was nice to know it was available.

Presently Phillip Kindred and his sister Jane were living in Charleston, posing as husband and wife in a town called Goose Creek. They were paid to keep a low profile. Sure, they could indulge in some of their freakier kinks, but only in private, and only in tandem with a set of professional Cabal cleaners on hand at all times.

The care and feeding of a pair of serial killers wasn't easy.

Most of the time they did a good job of staying below the radar. But at other times . . . well, they couldn't resist.

They sometimes cheated and listened to their old standbys: orchestral pop and psychedelic rock. They watched stacks and stacks of DVDs—the *Friday the 13th* series, *Maniac,* as well as *Breakfast Club* and *Pretty in Pink* and *Saw.* Even though they weren't supposed to have a copy within a hundred miles of themselves, they would also pop in *Truth Hunters Special: The Kindreds.* The show featured reenactments from previous installments, and, oh, how the Kindreds loved watching those. It fed into their kinks at a crazy deep level. Phillip and Jane Kindred loved to cruise the streets of any given city on "casting call" runs, abducting people who looked perfect for the roles they had in mind, then taking them to a closed "set" (usually an abandoned or foreclosed home, or a forgotten camp cabin or industrial warehouse) and forcing them to play out scenes from their favorite horror movies.

Or their own Truth Hunters special, which made it a real-life staging of a reenactment of their own real-life stagings.

It was all...so...grooooooovy.

The one reenactment that the Kindreds didn't like: About seven years ago their employers had tapped two loser actors to portray them and kill a family of four in Studio City in the San Fernando Valley. The Kindreds themselves would have loved that gig...geez, Studio City? Right down the road from Warner Brothers and Universal and the other dream factories where so many of their favorite horror movies had been created?

But at the time, the Kindreds were being "trained" in another facility. Back then, their employers weren't too sure that serial killers could be trusted on missions.

The Kindreds had proved them wrong.

With the right handler, there was nothing they couldn't accomplish.

And their right handler turned out to be a fellow psychopath with a law degree working in an office in Century City. He indulged his darkness on a regular basis in exchange for helping mind the Kindreds. See, he knew how to speak to them.

Their Minder, a slender lawyer named Abbott, told them, "We need you two in Flagstaff, then Philadelphia."

"In that order?" Phil said. "We're a lot closer to Philadelphia."

"I know that. But the order is important. Flagstaff's just a quick errand. Philadelphia is the real fun."

"What's in Flagstaff?"

"Just a family."

"Does it need to look like us?"

"No. It should not look like you. It should look random."

"That's no fun."

"But think of all the real fun you'll be earning."

"Ugh. I hate work for hire."

"Don't we all."

"Man, there's just no room left for independents. They end up controlling everything, don't they. Even us."

"They certainly do," Abbott said. "By the way, *they* also listen to our conversations."

"I know they do. Don't you think it's kind of cool to scare them every once in a while?"

The Minder chuckled. "You're putting me in a delicate position here."

"Ah, I'm just kidding, bro. Guess we're going to Flagstaff."

"I think you're going to have fun."

Of course Phil and Jane Kindred would have fun. This was their idea of fun, and it still struck Phil now and again how lucky they were to be able to indulge themselves like this. Most psychopaths weren't as lucky. At best, your average serial killer could look forward to a bullet in the head or a stack of life sentences in some supermax penitentiary in the middle of nowhere. Sure, a few got a TV movie of the week or a cheapo paperback. But not the Kindreds. They were blue-chip killers, with a publishing/film deal already in place with the biggest media conglomerate in the country. They were branded. They were untouchable.

They had four more people to kill before this tableau beneath Montreal was complete. "Let's get a move on, sis," Phil said. "We've got a busy couple of days ahead of us."

18

*I'm giving you a choice: either put on these glasses or start eatin'
that trash can.*

—Roddy Piper, *They Live*

THE LAST TIME something like this had happened to Charlie Hardie,
he'd woken up in a body bag. Thankfully, this time was different.

This time he jolted awake inside the trunk of one of those goddamned coma cars, with IV lines already shoved into his veins. And
hey, wow, bonus! The trunk lid was still open.

"Oh hell," his identical twin said, holding in his hand a clear plastic mask attached to a tube. Obviously he hadn't expected Hardie to
wake up so quickly.

"Fuck...," Hardie said. He went to lunge at him...only he
couldn't, because he was already strapped down into the gear. "Fuck
you, you fucking fuck!"

Hardie wasn't afraid to admit it: He had an irrational fear of the
trunks of these stupid coma cars.

"Listen to me carefully," his double said in a tone usually reserved
for the mentally challenged. "This is for your own good. For *your
family's* good. You're no use to me if you're weak and ready to pass

out every two minutes. I need you rested and rejuvenated if we're going to survive this thing. Only I know you're too stubborn to actually rest. So consider this a forced R and R."

"*Eat me!*"

"It's not as bad as you remember. They've made a few modifications to the design in the past year. See this?" His double held up the plastic mask. The face portion was soft and rubbery, shaped like a pear.

"This is called a laryngeal mask. No intubator, no hose down the throat. This just slips over your face and you settle into a nice, peaceful sleep. Think of it as going down on a woman. You have to admit, it kind of does look like a pussy."

Hardie could see that. Yes, the mouthpiece looked like a pussy, if the woman happened to be opaque and made of plastic. But he didn't care what the mask looked like, because there was no way he was spending any more of his life in a trunk of a car.

"FUCK YOU AND UNDO THESE STRAPS."

"Shut up. There's no time to argue. Your family's in danger, so I need to haul ass to get to them before the Cabal does. So, I'm sorry, please accept my apologies and all that, but it's night-night time."

"FUCK YOU."

Hardie lunged again. His right wrist snapped out of its binding with a pop. This surprised Hardie as well as his double. Hardie recovered more quickly, however, and gathered up a bunch of his double's shirt in his bandaged fist. Then he yanked back as hard as he could. His double's head slammed into the top of the open trunk with a satisfying *THUNK*. Blood spurted from the wound. The double's eyes rolled up, his mouth started trembling, and then he went down.

"Huh," Hardie said.

*   *   *

Ow.

Ow ow ow.

You wake up a short while later with a grand prize winner of a headache. It takes a second for your short-term memory to reload, but once it does, you understand why you can't move your arms or legs.

You also understand why Charlie Hardie is looking down at you, plastic mask in his hand.

"How about *you* eat the pussy now," he says, this crazy glint in his eye that frightens you, because it looks like a mirror image.

You shout in a last-minute attempt to explain, but Hardie doesn't give a crap. Not with that kind of glint in his eye. He slips the mask over your mouth and you can't help it—you have to suck in some air from the big plastic pussy eventually, and within a few seconds you're

19

Hi, Fred. We got a little accident. Could you send a tow truck, please, to 618 Elm Street? Hold it. It's the, uh, third floor, apartment 304.

—James Caan, *Freebie and the Bean*

AMERICA IS NOWHERE near as big as space. It is a mere sliver of an insignificant spec in the solar system, let alone the universe.

But from the ground, it can feel hopelessly vast.

Even when speeding down the blacktop at 110 miles per hour in a bulletproof coma car.

Hardie kept track of the mile markers, all the way through end-less (neverending) rocky, dusty, barren Nevada, past the gaudy pur-ple glam of Wendover—which seemed to be nothing but casinos and gas stations—directly into Utah and its infamous salt flats. All the while he checked the rear and side mirrors for a flash of red. Try explaining the body in the trunk to a state trooper. *Gee, officer, I had no idea he was hooked up to life support . . .*

Though if the Other Him was right, Hardie could jet down the highway in this Lincoln Town Car of Death as fast as he wanted and nobody would touch him. The coma car was a GET OUT OF JAIL FREE card on wheels . . .

He hoped.

Hardie's brain was fuzzy, his eyelids heavy. The thing he wanted most in the world was the thing he couldn't have right now: a nap. He'd never felt more tired in his life. Probably the residual effect of that goddamned spray he'd been dosed with. But there was no way anything resembling that could happen. He couldn't even afford to blink. Hardie had wasted enough time tangling in the Cabal storage depot, talking to a cockroach in a disgusting toilet, and eating cherry pie. Kendra and the boy were walking around with targets painted on their heads, and they most likely had no idea they were in mortal danger.

The salt flats were just as advertised, Hardie realized. Salty. And flat. As if God had decided to smite an entire city and this gray, expansive patch of harsh nothing was all that remained. Well, that wasn't true. Every couple of miles you could see a formation of rocks spelling out a name or two. Did people come out here for fun, just to leave their mark in the middle of all this desolation?

Hardie tightened his grip on the wheel, which sent new waves of pain down his burned fingers. He wondered how long he could keep this up. Not a good sign just a few hours into the journey.

His mental geography of this part of the country was sketchy. He was pretty sure Salt Lake City was on the other side of this stretch of flat, salty nothingness. And then beyond that...um, the place where they held the Sundance Film Festival, maybe? Hardie would have to stop for a map. Which would be interesting, considering his facial bandages. Nope, that wouldn't be memorable to, say, a gas station attendant. Who would immediately call his brother-in-law, who would just so happen to be the chief of police in SLC or some shit like that.

Did the coma car have some fancy-pants GPS or something? It must, right?

Hardie felt himself jolt.

What was that? Did he just nod off?

C'mon, buddy, let's keep it together.

Forget the bandages. Hardie knew what he needed. A drugstore. Raid the pharmacy shelves for some kind of uppers. Just like Kowalski in *Vanishing Point*. Jack yourself up and hammer the accelerator all the way to Philly. Probably could be covered in a day, day and a half, right? Of course you'd be spent when you arrived. And you'd still have to deal with your estranged wife (*"Hi, honey, I'm home!"*) and the son who probably grew up hating your ass—and somehow convince them that they needed to get in the coma car and travel with you to some secret location in Virginia...

Don't worry about the big-picture stuff, he told himself. The big picture was always overwhelming. Take it one little piece at a time. First piece: Stay awake behind the wheel until you could figure out your next move.

Still, Hardie couldn't help but think about what it would be like when he knocked on his ex-wife's front door. Starting with the door itself. Hardie had seen the surveillance shots of the inside of Kendra's new house for months now, but never the outside. Were they still near Philadelphia? Hardie thought so. She wasn't one to pick up and move to another part of the country. But right there—another problem. His enemies knew exactly where Kendra lived; Hardie didn't even know the neighborhood.

Stop thinking about it and drive.

The midday sun blazed bright off the flats. Hardie squinted a little, wishing he had sunglasses. Wouldn't that make him look badass. Bandaged mummy dude in shades.

Were there enemy agents inside the house right now, creeping up on Kendra and Seej?

And then, in a fraction of a blink:

BA-DUMP-BA-DUMP-BA-DUMP-BA-DUMP-BA-DUMP

Hardie opened his eyes and then the coma car started rocking up and down, shifting from side to side. Each jolt through his body was so painful it brought tears to his eyes. It seemed like it took an eternity to send the message from his brain to his foot: *Stomp on the brake*. He did. The car spun a few times before making a complete stop. Only when it rocked on its suspension did Hardie realize he was screaming.

Throwing open the door, he tumbled out into the flats. Touched the ground just to make sure it was there. How far away was the road? Very, very far. He'd somehow veered off the road and gone off into the great barren nothing...

Oh God, Hardie realized, with his palm pressed against the dead, hot earth. He'd fallen asleep at the wheel. And then he threw up, right through the bandages.

Deke Clark's FBI agent brain worked at lightning speed. He might be ex-FBI, and he wasn't getting any younger or handsomer...but he still had the moves. He quickly found the poet's abandoned SUV, then traced that to another stolen car—a Honda Fit. Traffic cameras along 80 from Vacaville to Reno picked up the Fit as it traveled just a hair above the speed limit all the way to the state border. Another set of cameras picked up the Fit, but then, strangely, the car disappeared between Winnemucca and Battle Mountain. Up in that desolate part of northern Nevada, there aren't many places you can go. Why would Charlie Hardie hole up there, of all places? Answer: He wouldn't.

Unless his accomplice wanted him here. The guy in the face bandages.

So either they're staying put here for a while, or they're moving on.

Deke knew they weren't staying put.

Whatever Hardie was up to—and Deke didn't even pretend to think that his investigator brain could puzzle out *that* one—it involved steady eastward movement. For some reason, after all of these months of silence and hiding, Hardie was headed home.

If it came to it, Deke could hop a plane and tuck Kendra and her son away somewhere safe, then sit in the empty living room, shotgun draped across his lap, and wait for his old pal Charlie to show up. *Hey, how's it going, buddy?* Actually, Deke wouldn't even bother with a question. He'd cold-cock the mysterious bastard with the stock of the shotgun and ask plenty of questions later. The last time he'd seen Hardie, the man had taken advantage of their friendship and Deke had woken up with piss-stained pants on the floor of a garage.

So that was one option. But Deke couldn't help but think that was a tactical mistake. It also didn't factor in the mysterious mummy man, who could be anybody from D. B. Cooper to D. B. Sweeney. While Deke was busy subduing his old pal Charlie, the other guy could get the drop on *him*. It was foolish to go there alone and just wait for trouble to come knocking on the door.

Which made Deke think that he had to do his best to capture Hardie while he was still on the road.

And to do that, Deke was going to call in some more favors.

You're vaguely awake, breathing through the plastic pussy.

It's not bad, really, except for the nagging idea that you're missing something important, that you're botching some important job...

And then the universe opens up its lid and unholy light shines down upon you. Rough fabric hands pull the mask from your face, the needles from your veins, the bindings from your arms and legs. Then you're pulled out of the trunk and deposited on hard earth and somebody is telling you:

"Okay, fine, you were right."

You blink until the sunlight is almost tolerable. You've been in a lazy half-coma for what's felt like days, a half-waking dream. All you wanted to do was tuck into the pillow and roll over...only you couldn't, because you were on life support in the trunk of a luxury car.

"C'mon, wake up already. If I'm going to apologize, I'd like you to be conscious to hear it."

All you can think is, *Asshole.*

In fact, you might have said it out loud.

"Don't be that way. You have to see it from my point of view. I think you would have done the same thing."

See it from my point of view. Oh, that was rich, you asshole. My entire life has become all about *seeing it from your fucking point of view.*

"Can you see to drive?"

There's a rough hand on your shoulder and you slap it away. Which is a good sign. You're going to need motor function to make a cross-country drive.

You tell him, "Yeah, I can see."

The urge for payback is great. So many scenarios involving Charlie Hardie's beaten and mangled corpse left out here in the middle of Utah. But that wouldn't do anyone any good. You probably needed him alive, and you *definitely* needed him on the East Coast. All you can do is suck it up (you eat the pussy now) and recover and move on as quickly as possible.

Vision's coming back. You take stock of your surroundings. Apparently Hardie drove off the road somewhere in the Great Salt Flats.

"I put a bag of supplies in the back seat," you say. "Is it still there?"

"Yeah."

"Bring it to me."

"Your legs broken?"

"I can't feel them yet. But if you bring me the bag," you say, trying real hard to be the grown-up here, "then I can fix that, and we can go save Kendra and Seej."

Hardie gives you a weird look.

"What?" you ask.

"Don't call him that. He's not your boy. You're not allowed to call him that."

"Call him what?"

"Seej. That's my nickname for him. You call him Charlie Jr. In fact, don't even say his name at all."

There is a chill in Hardie's eyes, behind that mask of bandages, that twists up your insides a little. Does he know? Does he suspect?

You dismiss the feeling and ask for the bag again. Inside the bag is the rest of the goodies you stole from the pharmacy on the coast. Your shopping list was full of ingredients that could rev a human being up or down. Right now you're only interested in the stuff that will rev you up. Because you know that your surreal half-nap in the trunk of this car was the last sleep you're going to enjoy until all of this is over. No rest until you win your freedom. No rest until your new life begins.

"What's that?" Hardie asks as he gestures at the mix of pills in your trembling hand. You ignore the question and chew them down dry, one palmful at a time.

"You're not going to go into a seizure or anything, are you?"

Chew, chew, chew, swallow.

You wait for the pills to kick in. You wait for the feeling to come back to your extremities. But then again, you've been in the waiting room of life for some time now. The finish line is within view yet so many miles away.

Hardie reaches out his bandaged hand to you. You clasp it, only realizing halfway up that it's wet with something. Blood or vomit, most likely.

"We tag-team the wheel. You understand me? None of this riding in the trunk shit. We're going to have to work as a team if we're going to save my wife and son and then get you back to your little home base."

"I didn't think you were a team player, Charlie Hardie."

"I'm not. But you're my clone, so it doesn't count. Now can we go already? I think I can see flashing lights out there in the haze."

Deke Clark knew how to call in favors. He still had the FBI patter down. He could steamroll over almost anybody—DMVs, local sheriff's departments, DOTs, whatever—until he dug out the information he needed.

Sure, they could call their local field office and find out for themselves that one Deacon Clark left the agency quite some time ago and in fact has retired to parts unknown. But that probably wouldn't happen for some time, and Deke has given this last-ditch effort no more than a day. It can't go on for more than a day. This thing stretches out past the next twenty-four hours and it's a death sentence for everything involved. And that can't happen.

So Deke has called in favors along the one road leading out of that desolate part of Nevada: Route 80. Favors in Northern Nevada, favors in Utah, favors in Wyoming. He's given access to traffic cams and incident reports. He prayed for something, anything unusual. And then a few hours into his search, Deke's prayers were answered:

An incident report, about a car losing control and veering off into the Great Salt Flats.

But that wasn't the weird thing.

The weird thing was: *The incident was erased just a few minutes after Deke saw it.*

Deke knew his aging eyes weren't playing tricks on him. He'd seen the incident, jotted down a few notes on an index card. But then the damned thing vanished. In all of his experience in law enforcement, he'd only encountered one group who could make things—incidents, accidents, people—vanish completely. They were the same people who'd threatened him years ago. The same people who'd sent him and his family into hiding.

Would you like us to continue, Agent Clark?

Hardie called them the Accident People.

And for some reason, they'd just made an incident on Route 80 in Utah . . . disappear.

Deke hit the traffic cams. There was nothing much near the mile marker originally mentioned in the report, so Deke checked the time, did a quick-and-dirty guesstimate, then hopped eastward on 80, hoping to see anything that screamed "Charlie Hardie."

Just outside Salt Lake City, Deke indeed saw something that screamed "Charlie Hardie." Same make, same model. Last time he'd seen a car like that he'd woken up in wet pants and with the worst headache of his life.

Deke wasn't a man to curse much, but even he let a "motherfucker" glide across his lips as he picked up his cell phone and prepared to call in three, possibly four, more favors. Deke would be cashing in all of his markers for this one, and would be indebted to the types of men he used to pursue when he was a federal agent.

But, as they say in all of the bad movie trailers: *It ends tonight.*

Hardie had never quite seen anything like it. His hopped-up clone had been hauling ass across the salt flats, kicking up great plumes of . . . salt, maybe? . . . when barreling toward them from the opposite direction was a Utah state police cruiser, cherries flashing. Hardie was in the passenger seat and gave some thought to buckling his seatbelt.

"You see that?" he asked.

"Yeah, I see it."

"We going to do anything about it?"

"Hang on."

The clone hammered the accelerator and Hardie felt himself pressed up against the seat. The needle jumped to 70, 80, 90 . . . then 100. Which closed the gap between them and the friendly neighborhood Utah state trooper within seconds. Hardie knew the car was bulletproof. But he was pretty sure it wouldn't survive a head-on creepy David Cronenberg–style collision.

"You sure you can see?" Hardie asked.

At pretty much the moment Hardie thought he'd be inhaling shattered glass, his double careened off to the right, and the state trooper to the left, and both vehicles slammed through mini-asteroid belts of flying salt. Behind them, the trooper's siren screamed. The clone behind the wheel apparently didn't give a fuck. The accelerator needle wilted back down to 90, 80, 70 . . .

"You're slowing down?" Hardie gasped.

"Just giving him a look at my ass."

And as the needle slid back up the impossible happened: The trooper gave up. Sirens off, cherries off. He resumed normal speed and faded into the rear distance as they found Route 80 again, slowed down enough to merge safely, then peeled down the asphalt.

"What just happened?"

"I told you," said his double, "we're cop-proof. Once he saw my license plate and started to call it in, he had to let me go. Whatever incident he may have reported is now being erased from the police data banks. We're invisible. We could drive over the bodies of nuns and toddlers from here all the way to the Hamptons and no cop would be allowed to touch us."

Hardie shook his head. "I used to be a cop. Work for them, anyway. How did this happen? How did you get every cop from coast to coast to go along with this?"

"Things have changed a lot since you worked for the cops."

"The FBI, too?"

His double made a grim, laughlike sound. "The Feds, the CIA, the Secret Service, the Boy Scouts, whoever. The Cabal claims to be this country's greatest protector, and in exchange, they enjoy limitless immunity. But the information we brought down could end it all."

Hardie thought about Deke Clark and wondered where he was at this moment. Hopefully somewhere hiding out with Ellie and the girls. Not caught up in all of this stuff. Yeah, he felt bad about shocking the poor guy in that garage, but there was no time to rationally discuss things. And now Hardie was especially glad he hadn't bothered. That route, the calm, rational, white-hat cowboy route, would have landed them in graves immediately.

Meanwhile his double continued to speechify.

"Here's the real insidious part," he said. "The public has the idea that there's something seriously wrong, but they can't quite put their finger on it. They blame the usual suspects: the banks, the politicians, even the media. But they're missing the real culprit. They can't see the control room; they're too focused on the stage."

"You sound like you just walked off the set of *The X-Files*."

"*The X-Files?* Is that the best pop culture reference you can dig up?"

"Blow me. I've been in prison, I've been in space. Before that, I just watched old movies. Buy me a copy of *Entertainment Weekly* and I'll catch up. Anyway, you said we're all focused on the stage. What are these assholes doing behind the stage? What do they want, besides more power?"

"Are you asking me about their endgame? Here's my take on it: The Cabal knows the end of the world is coming. I don't mean rapture, or a giant asteroid, or a new ice age, or any of that Roland Emmerich shit. I'm talking about the fall of civilization. The explosives were planted during World War II, and everything's about to go up. The Cabal exists for one purpose only: to be the winners. That means having every available resource at their disposal, no matter what. They don't care if the public doesn't like it, or revolts, or camps out on their front lawn singing kum-ba-fucking-yah. It doesn't matter. They are ants scrambling up to the boot of a soldier."

Hardie saw the fringes of Salt Lake City on the horizon.

"You must be great fun at parties."

You like Hardie. In spite of everything, all of the studying and surgeries and the bad blood between the two of you, there was still something admirable about the broken-down old fucker. A tough, flickering spirit that only burned hotter and brighter when the wind picked up.

You'll almost be sad to see it snuffed out.

20

Don't eat the car! Not the car! Oh, what am I yelling at you for? You're a dog!

—Tom Hanks, *Turner & Hooch*

THEY MADE IT as far as halfway through Nebraska before Charlie Hardie was shot and killed.

After his doppelgänger's big apocalyptic speech on the outskirts of SLC, they settled into a serious driving groove. Nobody said a word. The sun went down, the terrain went from flats to mountains. Hardie tried to nod off but couldn't. Every so often an ambitious trooper would show an interest in their vehicle traveling at insane speeds, initiate pursuit, then drop off once the license plate was called in. What once was kind of a sick thrill became routine, especially when the troopers apparently called ahead with the word to let this black sedan pass. By the time they entered Wyoming, the pursuits had stopped entirely.

At some point Hardie did fall semi-unconscious, but it wasn't true sleep. Instead his brain had downshifted a gear or two, leaving one hemisphere in the real world and the other in a phantom zone of his own mistakes. He was at once aware of the hum of the engine and the sound of the tires on asphalt, but he also heard gunshot and cries and screams. His fingers curled his hands into loose fists.

Feels good, doesn't it, Charlie? Choke that bitch out. Go on. Break her little scrawny neck.

If his clone was looking over at him he would have seen Hardie's fingers twitch.

We want an actress who was cut down in her prime. Choked to death by a man who lusted after her. Murdered by you.

Would have seen his torso jolt.

And before you do open your mouth, I'd keep Kendra and Charlie Jr. in mind.

All at once he was looking down at Kendra and Seej. Both were lying on the cold concrete floor of a basement, eyes open. The strange thing was that this wasn't one of the surveillance-style shots Hardie had watched over the past nine months. He didn't recognize the basement or anything in it. And even though what he saw was a high corner of this mysterious basement, it didn't feel like he was watching the image on a screen. It felt like he was in the room with them, floating above them. And Kendra's eyes were blazing with the same kind of familiar hate. Staring right at him, as if she could see him. Could she? Was she wishing him dead right this minute?

Hardie couldn't look away. He was frozen in place, too, looking down at his family in torment for what seemed like a couple of forevers when he heard his own voice pleading with him—

wakeup

wake up

"Hardie, I think you'd better wake up."

Hardie sat up with a jolt. "What? What is it?" The car had stopped moving. Hardie squinted through the bandages, looking first out the windshield and then the back window.

The sun was hours away from coming up, but even in the pre-dawn gloom Hardie would have seen them. An unmarked sedan in front; the other sedan in back. Cherries flashing in both, cutting through the dark night. A classic two-car trap.

"I thought this car was supposed to be unpulloverable?" Hardie asked. "Remember.... limitless immunity? Or was that something you just made up on the spot?"

"Yeah, I thought so, too. Guess somebody didn't get the memo."

"I saw guns in that bag of yours," Hardie said.

"Yeah. But are you comfortable killing cops, if that's who these guys turn out to be?"

"Who else would they be?"

"If they're stopping us, there's a good chance they're not cops."

"Cabal?" Hardie asked. "Could they have made us, even inside one of their cars?"

"Anything's possible."

The two Charlie Hardies quickly discussed their battle plan, which was simple: point and shoot. Spray bullets at anything that moved. Make sure that the chunks of meat on the asphalt stopped twitching. Then haul ass out of the area and hope the Cabal didn't send any other mobile death squads after them.

Among the handguns the fake Charlie Hardie had shoved into the black canvas bag back at the way station in northern Nevada: Glock .23 semiautos, .40 S&W cartridge, plenty of loaded magazines. Smith & Wesson .44 Magnum and .38 Special revolvers, double action only.

The real Charlie Hardie took a .38 Special, stuffed it in a pocket of his spacesuit, then grabbed a .44. Outside, car doors snicked open. The noise echoed across the quiet Nebraska pre-dawn.

"This is it," the fake Charlie Hardie said, snatching up two Glocks for himself.

"I'll take the front, you take the back," the real Charlie Hardie said.

"Works for me."

A proper team-up.

Which of course was shattered when a familiar voice cried out, *"Charlie Hardie! It's me, Deke!"*

Deke Clark had called in four favors. These favors would soon become blood debts, held by four of the toughest gunmen on the planet.

The kind of people Deke Clark—in his former life as a federal agent—used to investigate, arrest, and remove from the general population.

But these rules had long broken down for Deke. He was tired of living with a gun to his family's heads.

So instead of cultivating a list of snitches, Deke had spent the past year cultivating a short list of hired muscle who could be called upon in a pinch to deal with a crisis. Of course, the crisis Deke had in mind was protecting his family against an onslaught of Accident People, or whatever the hell they were called.

This favor was different. This was about cornering a man speeding down a highway and taking him into private custody without anyone getting killed.

Only Charlie Hardie could answer certain questions about the people who had threatened Deke's family. And so God help him, if Hardie decided to do the stoic thing or try to escape...

Well, then, that's where his four favors came in.

By the time Deke's team was assembled—which didn't take long at all, since these men were prepared to travel at a moment's notice—Hardie and his mysterious black sedan were crossing the

Colorado state line. Deke calculated the time and agreed to rendezvous in Grand Island, Nebraska, and set up a two-car trap along Route 80. Nothing fancy. Just stop him. Pull him out of that car. Have one of the other men take control of the car (who knew what secrets it might yield) and go to somewhere neutral for some answers.

Deke kept tabs on the sedan thanks to favors called in to the Colorado, and then Nebraska, Departments of Transportation. Hardie was still headed east on 80, predictable as hell. The one strange thing that Deke didn't understand was the speeding. Hardie should have been pulled over a couple dozen times in Colorado alone. And Nebraska? Hell, the entire state was one big 104,111-square-mile speed trap.

Again, the steely voice called out on the lonely highway: *"Charlie, man, it's me. Deke! Come on out of there!"*

Inside the coma car, Hardie's bandaged jaw dropped. "No. Way."

"Is that—" His double lapsed into a brief dumbstruck silence. "Is that Deacon Clark? How did he find us?"

"No idea. But you know, Deke was always the best at the whole cop game."

"There's no fucking way he could have found us. We're *invisible.*"

"Well, he's out there asking for me right now. I guess I should go talk to him."

"I don't like it."

"I don't like any of this. But listen to me—whatever you do, do not shoot him. He's taken care of Kendra and the boy all this time, and—"

"You don't have to tell me. I know all about Deke."

"So none of that shit about pointing and shooting and spraying, okay?"

The Other Hardie nodded quickly. "But wait...you can't step outside. Remember, your face?"

Wrapped in bandages. Right. Deke wasn't X, the man with X-ray vision. He could be forgiven for thinking that a mummy had kidnapped his old pal Charlie, and would shoot first, check under the wrapping later.

"Let me go," his double said.

"No. What if he spots you for a fake right away?"

"I fooled all of those machines in the satellite. They thought I was a dead ringer for you."

Outside the car:

"Final warning, Charlie! Don't make me do this!"

"Deke's not a machine," Hardie said. "I have to go. Cover me in case it gets weird, okay?"

Hardie expected another fight, but instead his double just nodded again.

"Deke," the man in the bandages cried out, lifting his hands above his head. Deke could tell he had guns in the pockets of his uniform. Now that he saw it up close, it *did* look like some kind of spacesuit. "It's me! Don't shoot!"

"Show me your hands! Is Charlie Hardie in that vehicle with you?"

Hardie complied, lifting his bandaged hands up in the cool night air. "Deke, it's me. It's *Charlie.*"

"Step away from the car. Come all the way around."

"Deke, seriously, man. Listen to my voice."

"No. I don't know who you are, but I know you're not Hardie. Tell Hardie to step out of the car *now* or there will be serious trouble."

"The last time we met, you told me other people would finish this. That I didn't have to do this anymore. All I needed was to stop and come home. Well, Deke, you were partly right. All this time, I needed to come home. But I can't depend on anybody else. I put my family in this mess, and I'm the only one who can get them out of it. I hope you'll understand that."

Deke squinted, as if he could see past the bandages. Goddamn. Was this him? That was a conversation they had a year ago, alone, in a garage. That lawyer Doyle was there, but he was unconscious. The only other occupants of the garage were dead. Had to be him.

"Charlie?" he asked.

And then shots blasted out into the airspace behind Deke's head.

Abrams knew that Deacon "Deke" Clark would be useful one of these days. His weathered mug was the only face that Charlie Hardie trusted. Which was why Abrams didn't bother having an Accident team dispatched immediately to erase Clark and his family.

Instead, Abrams had his home—his supposedly "protected" home—bugged, right down to the wood under the carpet tacking. She steered Cabal-friendly gunmen and mercenaries in his direction, making Clark feel like he'd recruited them.

Abrams considered this a smart, relatively inexpensive insurance policy. Doyle would have gone all high-tech with it; sometimes, the old tricks work the best. And now it had paid off.

The gunmen had simple orders—grievously wound Charlie Hardie and bring him back to L.A. They needed him alive. He didn't have to be conscious. Just with a pulse. It was important if she was going to make her point heard and end these bitter little internecine squabbles with Doyle. Prove her way *worked*. Keep costs down, use forward thinking, not expensive gadgets and elaborate schemes.

If Doyle were in charge he would have probably sent heavily armed mobile death troops in dozens of bulletproof cars to hunt down and destroy Hardie. Which would have cost hundreds of millions and most likely exposed them in a number of small ways. Given the enemy something to exploit.

No, better to do this quiet and clean and cheap and easy.

Now it was nearly 6:00 a.m. East Coast time. Abrams leaned back in her first-class seat, picked up her orange juice, and eagerly awaited the status update.

The shoot-out was brief, as they tend to be. The gunmen behind Deke Clark opened fire. They were expert marksmen, ex-mercs who'd impressed the Cabal enough to be given retainers. They knew how to make shots designed to incapacitate. Kill shots were easy; the surgical ones required on-the-scene finesse.

There was no time for Charlie Hardie to speak or scream or protest or reach for the revolvers in his pockets. His body was thrown back against the vehicle, then slid down to the asphalt.

Deke Clark, still laboring under the delusion that these were *his* trusted men, spun around to face them, a stunned expression on his face. The gunmen knew the ruse was blown; they were under orders to execute Deke right after Hardie was taken out. His usefulness to the Cabal had come to an end.

Deke decoded the expression on their faces in a fraction of a second. He'd always been good at reading people, thinking fast on his feet. He opened fire; the gunmen adjusted their aim and returned fire at close to point-blank range.

Meanwhile another man emerged from the driver's seat and used a Glock .23 to open fire on the gunmen on the opposite end.

Those gunmen were momentarily gobsmacked; they had been

trained to kill Charlie Hardie; had studied various photographs until his image was burned into their minds. The moment that Deacon Clark confirmed the man in the bandages as Charlie Hardie—"Charlie?"—that man was taken out. So who was this man, *who looked exactly like him?*

This gave the double a small window of opportunity.

Headshot, torso shots. The double wasn't screwing around. He pulled a second Glock and started firing in the opposite direction, toward Deke and his gunmen—already engaged in a brief, bloodsplattered, close-range battle. Metal panged, glass sprayed, asphalt was ripped up by shots gone wild. The noise was as if the very air around them were full of firecrackers and all of them were popping off at the same time. Smoke obscured some shots. Agonized cries cut through the din and the fog and blood.

All told, the gunfight on that Nebraska road took maybe nine, ten seconds.

To all involved, it felt like forever.

Deke hadn't called an ending like this. Not for him, not for Charlie Hardie. He kind of saw the two of them as old men in a backyard, swilling beers they shouldn't be swilling, talking war stories while their grandkids milled about. While Deke and Charlie were never *friend* friends, he'd always hoped they'd mellow into some kind of grudging mutual respect as they grew old. And that would somehow transmogrify into real friendship.

None of this was right. It wasn't supposed to happen this way. Charlie Hardie, slumped against a black Lincoln Town Car, shot in every possible way a man could be shot.

Deke, breathing blood, feeling numb all over, knowing this was it.

As he died he mumbled words to his wife, Ellie, a confused tangle of apologies and sweetness. He sent his love to his daughters. He thanked his wife for the eggs.

The bullets didn't kill Charlie Hardie.

The sight of Deke Clark, shot up and dying on a cold Nebraska road...now that *killed* him, in the deepest way possible. This was a point-blank shot to his soul.

This was Nate Parrish all over again, but somehow worse, because when a man swears something will never happen again, when a man voluntarily exiles himself from his life and all that he loves so that it has *no chance* of happening again...

...*and it happens again*...

It was almost too much to bear.

Hardie got a good man killed. He always seemed to let good people die on his watch. Nate Parrish. Lane Madden. Now Deacon Clark. And somehow *he* went on living.

How? Project Viking? Was that bullshit even true? Was that his curse? To survive, even as good men were cut down all around him?

So be it.

He deserved the pain he had coming.

On the dizzy edge of consciousness—Hardie had to have lost a ton of blood in the past few minutes, because his clothes were soaked as if he'd gone swimming—he prayed that the Project Viking stuff was true. That somehow he was death-proof, maybe even immortal. That he could stand up now and the bullets would drop out of his wounds and go tinkling on the asphalt. And then he'd go save his family...

Hardie's eyes fluttered, then closed.

And in the end, you're the only one left standing.

You drop the Glocks, walk around the car to see what happened to the original Charlie Hardie. Your knees pop as you crouch down and reach out to feel his neck.

Please.

Please don't let him be dead.

Because that would ruin...everything.

21

You know, when I woke up this morning, I didn't expect to be trading nine millies with my friend.

—David Morse, *16 Blocks*

Undisclosed Location—Virginia Suburbs

ABRAMS HEARD ABOUT the Nebraska Incident and the death of the former FBI agent within seconds of landing at Dulles. The operation had been botched utterly and completely, which was something she was not used to. The wrong target had been killed—this mystery man with a face full of bandages. And Charlie Hardie had sped away, with the mystery man in his trunk.

Sure, they *could* waste more resources hunting Hardie and the corpse of his masked friend across the middle of the American heartland. But it was painfully obvious where Hardie was headed.

Home to Philadelphia.

While walking through the Terminal she texted the go order:

MANN YOUR TEAM IS UP

They would pin Charlie Hardie down and destroy his family and return his body posthaste. The only upside to this entire abortion was that Abrams would get to crow about it to Doyle. So much for an unbreakable vault, huh?

A Cabal employee took her to the private hospital in the Virginia suburbs where Doyle resided. There was nothing like a personal visit to emphasize the current power structure. If she had been a real dick, she would have forced Doyle to come to her in L.A. But the man was bedridden, and there was something to be said for looming over someone who's trapped in a prone position.

Doyle looked no better than when she'd visited him a few months ago. The assault had devastated him. Some men are able to recover after a violent trauma. Doyle was not one of those men.

"I hear that Nebraska did not go well," Doyle said as she entered the room.

"Have your teams recovered the spacecraft from the Pacific yet?" Abrams replied.

Attaque au fer, beat parry.

"Don't worry," Doyle said. "Your precious information is safe. There's no one who can pick up or decode the beacon, and almost no one with the diving capabilities required to recover it. Unless Jim Cameron decides to go looking for it on a whim. Come to think of it, deep sea is just as unreachable as deep space. Maybe I've been thinking in the wrong direction."

"That's not the point. I know the information is safe. But this was a very expensive mission, Doyle. And what did it get us?"

"For some pursuits, money should never be an object."

Doyle was a tinkerer. Always had been. While his profession was lawyer, his true passion was cobbling together strange devices in one of his many garages and labs scattered throughout the country.

He was the one who had given the so-called Accident People many of their untraceable weapons, from the wasp's nest to the coma car. Though Doyle probably regretted inventing the latter.

This was all fine when they ruled the Cabal as a triumvirate—Gedney being the brains, Doyle the hands, and Abrams the heart. With Gedney gone, however, the dual leadership of Doyle and Abrams resulted in an organization led only by hands and heart. Gedney had always been able to keep Doyle in check; over the past year, he'd run amok. And it was destroying them.

"I think it's time that you take a break, focus on your recovery," Abrams said. "Leave the day-to-day stuff to my care."

Doyle smiled and reached under his blanket.

The day-to-day has been left to your care, Doyle thought, *and you've done nothing but fuck it up.*

Oh, she must have been in her glory. Gedney gone, her other partner incapacitated.

But no more.

This organization used to be feared and respected; now it was simply too large and diffuse. Doyle believed they needed to focus on what they did best: arranging and tweaking and hacking the mechanics behind the reality everyone else saw. The reality everyone else accepted.

Abrams, meanwhile, had this ridiculous idea about taking over the world as it ended. Didn't she realize that with the proper planning and tweaking, you could choose the second, minute, hour, and day the world ended?

Something had to be done to properly refocus their organization.

So in the days after his attack at the hands of Charlie Hardie, Doyle stared at the tiled ceiling of his private hospital and came up with a way to resume command, to get things back on track. There was only one thing that Abrams had over him: the complete operational knowledge of their organization. She called it their heart. The heart was everything, and she'd tended it and cared for it and lorded it over them for years. The heart had purchased her seat at the table back when it was just Gedney and Doyle running the show. Doyle realized he needed to find a way to let Abrams voluntarily surrender the heart to his care.

And he had.

Boy, had he.

Convinced her that the only safe place for the heart was out of *everyone's* reach, including their own. The heart would be guarded in a hackproof bulletproof tamperproof and every other kind of -proof place you could think of, inside the head of an unkillable man who—get this—*didn't even know what he had in his head.*

It took a great deal of effort to convince Abrams to relinquish control of the heart, and even when she did, she insisted on being the one to help the team insert it into Charlie Hardie's skull. She oversaw every detail. Which made sense, because Doyle would have insisted on the same thing.

They launched the heart inside Hardie's head into space...and turned their attention to saving their organization from the threats attacking it from every direction.

Except Doyle had a side task. One he didn't tell Abrams about.

When you build something you believe is unbreakable, there's only one way to test it. And that is to find the smartest people in the world to attempt to break into it.

Banks routinely hire former heisters to test the security of their high-tech alarm and vault system; this was no different. Doyle set up a fictitious wing of the NSA (he picked the intelligence affiliation more or less at random), then tasked them with one goal: breaking into the heart in space.

It was disappointing that Doyle's satellite wasn't as impenetrable as he'd thought.

But it was so much better knowing that soon the heart would be in his hands, and there'd be no more need for Abrams.

For an awful minute Abrams thought Doyle was going to pull a gun from beneath his blanket, or worse...his cock. She flinched and reached down for her own piece, tucked away in her jacket. After Hardie had shoved a gun in her mouth, she never traveled without one. She never went to the bathroom without one, in fact.

But, no, it was just a small plastic trigger meant to release morphine into Doyle's IV drip. Go ahead, buddy. Ease back into that narcotic bliss.

"Forgive me," Doyle said.

"Do what you have to."

When Doyle thumbed the button on the trigger, something cold and wet hit Abrams in the face. She had only a second or two to realize that the spray had come from the IV bag itself and had been aimed perfectly at her eyes, nose, and mouth. The next moment she was on the floor, trembling for a few moments before settling down into paralysis.

Doyle didn't bother to peer over the edge of the bed. He'd invented this rig; he was sure it would work in exactly the manner he wanted.

"This is what I have to do, dear Abrams."

Abrams tried to reply, but all she could manage was a sloppy, stuttering "Suh.... suh.... *suh*...."

"We're going to keep you alive until we disable the kill switch. We'll keep you as comfortable as possible until then. This isn't personal, you know. Though I think I will try that thing you're always talking about. You know—with the wood chipper? I guess I'll have to rent *Fargo*. Do you know if it's available on demand?"

Another press of another button brought in his support staff, who'd been preparing for Abrams's arrival. One of his staff members brought him his secure phone and even helpfully placed the buds inside his ears and dialed the number of a lawyer in Century City.

"Send your people now."

Flagstaff, Arizona

Damn, it felt good to be an info gangster again.

Working with someone like Mann was always a trip. Don't get Factboy wrong. She was a total bitch. He loved to complain about her. Vowed never to work with her again. Complained to his wife about her—even though he had to disguise things, claim Mann was merely a "client" and not a crazy psycho death squad leader.

He had a large array of digital tools at his disposal, same as now, and his weapon of choice was still the national security letter, invented by the FBI over thirty years ago but really used to its fullest extent in the post-9/11 days. Hand someone an NSL and, boom, you had instant access to all of their files, no questions asked. Your tracks were covered by a built-in gag order, lasting until the subject's death. Factboy was a master of the NSL. It took him only a few minutes to put together a realistic digital version of one, and within an hour the answers would come gushing out like vomit.

No name, no voice, no trace... Factboy prided himself on being a digital ghost.

But in truth, Factboy was a forty-two-year-old man with a wife, two kids, an underwater mortgage, and a crushing amount of debt.

His family had no idea what he did for a living. He kept it that way by feigning irritable bowel syndrome whenever he had to respond to a request. The request for information could strike at any time, just like the sudden urge to use the facilities. Only with the bathroom door safely closed and locked could he relax enough to work his digital magic. There was nothing like the adrenaline rush of a Mann job. Or the money. Lately, the work had dried up so much that Factboy's wife was under the impression that the irritable bowel syndrome had cured itself.

But Factboy was back. And this new assignment was such a nostalgia trip, it should have been code-named DÉJÀ VU.

Seven years ago Factboy had assisted Mann in detailing the background of one Charles D. Hardie, a house sitter who interrupted a *huge* gig on Alta Brea Drive in the fabled Hollywood Hills. Now he was doing the same for his estranged wife, Kendra Hardie. They'd been apart for a decade. Ms. Hardie and their son, Charlie Jr. (*how original*, Factboy thought), had bounced around, address to address, trying to stay under the radar with the help of the FBI. Like that wasn't easy to see through. Their latest address was a rental under a few cut-outs and sham realty companies, but that was easy enough for Factboy to sort out.

And here was the déjà vu part, which cracked Factboy up:

Ms. Hardie?

She moved to Hollywood.

Not the one in California. No, the one right next to Philadelphia, about a mile from the city line.

There *was* such a thing; Factboy had the details within seconds. There was even a goofy science fiction novel from a few years ago partially set in this weird little enclave.

Back in 1917 a Philadelphian named Gustav Weber brought his

new bride to Los Angeles on their honeymoon, fell in love with the place and its Spanish mission–style architecture. When he returned to Philly, he bought a triangle of land just outside the city and decided to re-create a little L.A. back at home, with street names like Los Angeles Avenue and San Gabriel Road. Along these streets, he built a bunch of stucco bungalows with red-tiled roofs. Later, others built two-story homes, also in the Southern California style, and filled out the new town, dubbed Hollywood, nicely.

Of course it would have been completely insane if Ms. Hardie's rental house was on Alta Brea Drive...alas, there was no such road in this faux Hollywood. Instead, she was at the rather boring intersection of Fox Chase and Cedar roads.

Factboy's assignment was to dig up every last logistical detail that could help Mann lay siege to the home. Utilities, security, neighbors, neighbors' utilities and security...*everything*. Because at any given moment Mann might be given the green light to breach that home and slaughter everyone inside (whoops, sorry, Ms. Hardie! Sorry, unfortunately named Charlie Jr.!). No scrap of intel was too small, especially if Mann needed it in the clutch.

So Factboy locked himself away in the downstairs bathroom and began pulling everything he could.

As he tried to work, he heard a sudden loud thud. Probably his kids horsing around, with one tackling the other to the ground. They were full-fledged teenagers now but they still acted like idiot toddlers. Any second now Ms. Factboy would enter, yelling, which would be more of a distraction than the original thud.

Factboy went back to the task at hand. Maybe after this assignment, if there was enough money after paying down their cards and catching up on the mortgage, maybe he'd suggest a trip to the wife. Nowhere fancy, just somewhere to assure her that her husband still had earning potential. That the past few years were simply a road bump, not the new status q—

THUD.

What the hell were they doing up there?

Factboy coughed into his fist, then listened. Where the hell was the wife? She was supposed to have come out and tamed these kids by now.

"Hey!" Factboy shouted. "What's going on up there?"

Nothing but silence. Then, at the bathroom door, a small series of knocks.

"I'm in here! What the hell are you and your brother doing up there, anyway? It sounds like you're about to come through the goddamned ceiling!"

Then a voice, unfamiliar and creepy, whispered through the crack between the door and frame: "We're coming through all right, but not through the ceiling."

The door burst open, wood splintering, and Factboy tried to lift his laptop to serve as a kind of shield against the knife in the guy's hand that was already—oh God, it was *already stained with blood...*

"Families are fun," Phil said. Jane nodded appreciatively. She was raiding the dead family's freezer. Phil was thinking about the story-line to go with this Flagstaff slaughter.

To think they wasted all of those years copying other people's stories. They could have been making up their own fun, crazy stories *this whole time.*

Jane pulled out ice cream, but Phil had to be the one to break it to her: There probably wouldn't be enough time. They had a private jet to catch and a bigger, even *better* story to write on the way.

22

I would appreciate it if you would not act like a walking hard-on while we're on the job.

—Emilio Estevez, *Stakeout*

SO THIS IS where you are, at this exact moment in time:

You've got a dying body in the trunk, barely kept alive by life support—and thank Christ for the handy life support system in the trunk.

You're speeding across the rest of the country, trying like hell to make it to Philadelphia before another death squad tries to cut you down.

Everything is hanging in the balance, an anvil on the head of a pin, teetering between your old life and the new one . . .

And you can't help but be giddy.

Because your name is Charlie Hardie, and you're about to save your family. This is what you were born to do. This is what the military trained you for, spending untold millions molding you into an unkillable specimen of human being. This is the sum of all of your life's tough experiences, to do this one thing.

Save Kendra.

Save your boy, Seej.

You start to imagine what it'll feel like when you hold her in your arms. Your lips against hers, soft and full. Her breath, hot in your ear. The texture and scent of her hair. You've been imagining it for a year now, ever since they started feeding you information about her. At first it was an academic game. To become Charlie Hardie, you must hate what he hates, love what he loves. His motivations must be hardwired into your nervous system. You relied on your imagination. At a certain point, your imagined encounters started to feel real.

You know the difference between reality and fantasy; you're not that deluded. The difference is, you don't care anymore.

After many frenzied miles on the road, where the country around you faded into a blur of mile markers and billboards and road signs and trees and cars, you finally pull over near the finish line. You can't wait any longer; you want to hear her voice. And try your soon-to-be-new life on for size.

You pick up the pay phone, dial the number you've memorized so much that part of you truly believes it's your home number. A voice answers. You've heard this voice a million times in surveillance footage. Her voice. Kendra. A voice so familiar now it's almost as if you truly *were* married.

You tell her, "It's me."

She says nothing.

For a moment you wonder if the surgery, paired with endless hours of vocal coaching, wasn't successful. Maybe something about your voice is off, and maybe Kendra can tell.

"Are you there? Listen to me, Kendra, I know this is going to sound crazy, but you have to listen to me. You and the boy are in serious danger. You need to get out of the house now and just start driving. Drive *anywhere.* Don't tell me where, because they're definitely listening, but just go, go as fast as you can. I'll find you guys when it's safe."

Still nothing.

"Kendra? Are you there? Can you hear me?"

"I'm here, Charlie. But I can't leave."

"You have to leave, Kendra, please just trust me on this..."

"I can't leave because they've already called, and told me I *can't* leave."

You realize that things are already in motion. This is bad.

"They called me and said if I left the house I was dead."

"Who told you that? Who told you that you were dead?"

"A woman. She didn't give her name."

"Did you call the police? Anyone at all?"

"They told me not to call anyone, or do anything else except wait."

"Wait for what?"

A burst of static. Then:

Another voice.

"Hey, Charlie! It's your old pal Mann here."

This voice is familiar, too, but not in the same way that Kendra's is familiar. This is a voice from your own past, back when you were living under a different identity.

Mann.

Your ex-boss.

She continues: "So good to hear your voice after all this time. Well, that magical day has finally arrived. In about thirty seconds we're going to kill the phones, and the power, and everything else in your wife's house. We've got her surrounded; I know every square inch of every house in a five-block radius. You, of all people, know how thorough we are."

"Kendra, where's the boy? Where's Seej?"

Mann continued: "Shhhh, now, Charlie, it's rude to interrupt. You're wasting precious seconds. Now I know what you're going to say. You're going to tell me that if I touch one hair on your family's head, you'll rip me apart one limb at a time ... or maybe some other colorful metaphor? Well, you know, that's just not gonna happen. Because you lost this one, Chuck. There's not going to be any cavalry rushing in, no last-minute saves, no magic escapes. And you know what's going to happen next? What's going to happen next is, your family's going to die. And there's not a fucking thing you can do to stop me."

You tell Mann, "I can stop you."

What you don't tell her is: *Because I'm much closer than you think.*

23

You better be sure you wanna know what you wanna know.
—Meagan Good, *Brick*

Hollywood, Pennsylvania

UPON HIS RETURN home from another wasted night, seventeen-year-old Siege Hardie slid his key in the front door, twisted. The door wouldn't open. Granted, he was pretty drunk. Just like he should be on a Tuesday night. Too many pounder cans of Yuengling behind the Hollywood Cantina on Huntingdon Pike. A wasteoid named Eddie P. bought six-packs for him on a regular basis in exchange for a five-dollar surcharge or a pack of smokes, which was more or less the same thing. The Cantina owners didn't seem to care. They'd caught Siege drinking behind the place plenty of times and hadn't done anything about it. If the weather was nice, Siege would sometimes take his six to nearby Pennypack Park and sit in the stone foundation of a long-lost colonial-era mill house and get blitzed in the ruins.

Thing was, Siege wasn't being rebellious. When he drank, he was able to forget that creepy feeling of someone watching him.

The feeling was hard to shake, and it had only intensified over the past year. Worst of all was when he was in the rental house. (Siege didn't—couldn't—think of the goofy house they rented as "home," because to him, he hadn't had a real home since his father walked out.) Inside that weird fake-ass Hollywood house it felt like eyes were on him *all the time.* In the kitchen, raiding the lunch-meat drawer. In the living room, playing the Xbox. In his bed, in the middle of the night, when the beer would wear off and he would pop awake for no reason.

And just feel these *eyes* on him.

So he got shitfaced on beer, never the hard stuff, because his dad used to drink the hard stuff, so fuck him. He'd come home late, but not so late that his mom would call the police. Siege felt they had an unspoken agreement.

Tonight, though, the unease—Siege called it his Spidey Sense from Hell—was worse than ever. He couldn't shake the feeling that something was very, very wrong. The roiling in his guts was so bad even the beer didn't calm it down. He couldn't stay still and wandered from the bar to the park and back up around to the bar again. When he couldn't take it anymore, Siege did something extremely unusual: He called his mother. He could tell she was out at a restaurant. Probably with that asshole Chris. Still: He needed to check on her, reassure himself that his Spidey Sense from Hell was just as useless as ever.

"Everything okay at home?"

"Cut the shit, CJ," his mom said. "What happened?"

Siege should have expected this reaction. Why would he just call? He never called. Still, Siege hated how his mother could go from annoyed to flat-out *pissed* in two seconds flat, but he supposed he couldn't blame her.

"Nothing, Mom. I just..."

"Where are you?"

Siege decided to lie. Easier that way.

"I'm at home, everything's fine. Look, Mom, I know this is going to sound weird, but...what did you do with Dad's old stuff?"

"What? Why are you asking me about that?'

Siege grappled with the truth. Ever since his dad had left home there'd been this mythical steamer trunk full of his police stuff. Not that he was ever a real cop—no, Siege couldn't even take solace in that. But close enough. When Dad was still wasting his days as a drunk house sitter—and not a fugitive wanted for the murder of some junkie actress—Siege would sneak down to the basement, crack open the steamer trunk, and look through the stuff. Most of it was of no interest to a boy. Manila file folders. Mug shots. But then he saw the baggie full of bullet casings and an idea bloomed in his mind and he started digging more furiously until his fingertips brushed it: his father's gun. Siege had taken it and hidden it in his room and honestly sort of forgot about it until Mom found it and went NUCLEAR. There were talks, there were loud screaming arguments with Dad over the phone, which, come to think of it, may have been the last conversations before Dad snuffed that actress and went on the lam. Oh, happy times. All Siege knew was that the gun went back into the steamer trunk and the trunk suddenly had a padlock on it. Which told Siege that Mom hadn't disposed of the gun; that it was still locked away under all of those files...

But how could Siege tell his mom that he wanted to know where Dad's gun was because his general feeling of unease and being watched was at an all-time high?

"I just wanted to," he said. Then the line went dead.

Now that was weird. Did she actually hang up on him? Was she that pissed off that the very mention of his dad sent her off into a tailspin of rage?

Whatever. Fuck it.

Siege had more beers and wandered the park, but neither activity did anything to ease his lunatic, annoying Spidey Sense. If anything, the alcohol made it worse. He'd never felt it this intensely before. He felt faint. His heart raced. He was too young to be having a heart attack, right? Maybe he should just go home. It might be worse at home—the feeling always was—but he couldn't stay out forever.

That's the one thing he swore to himself, no matter what. Don't be your asshole father. Always. Go. Home.

The walk from the Cantina to his front door was two short blocks up Fox Chase Road. Siege paused to look out at the intersection.

Three of the corners were suburban housing, but the fourth corner was a field. Populated by horses.

Yeah, goddamned horses. Barely a mile from the border of Filthydelphia.

Siege liked to look at them from the upstairs window. Mostly they ate. Sometimes they ran. Once in a while, they mounted each other, which would have been amusing to him when he was a preteen, but now it was just a bitter reminder of how fucking lonely he was.

Right now, the horses were just standing there, giving Siege sidelong glances.

"Hey."

Which was *for horses.*

Enough of this.

Time to slip inside, hope that his mom wasn't awake or at least would ignore the question about his dad's stuff. Otherwise he had an hour-long monologue ahead of him. All he wanted to do was kick off his shoes and pass out in bed. The beers he'd knocked back—ten? eleven?—should kick in at some point.

As he slipped his key inside the lock, Siege could smell woodsmoke. Somebody was burning a fire on this freezing night. Lucky them.

The key refused to turn.

Siege tried the key in the door again, wondered what he was doing wrong. Wrong key? Wrong door? Wouldn't be the first time. Squinting, he saw that the deadbolt was engaged. Great. Mom was clearly pissed as hell. The deadbolt was never locked unless both of them were already inside the house. She wanted him locked out. She wanted him to knock like a pathetic loser. She wanted to confront him now—not tomorrow, not after school, *now*.

Might as well bite the bullet.

Siege pulled his cell phone out of his jeans pocket, pressed the auto-dial number for Mom. He waited. Nothing happened. Siege looked and noticed there were no bars on the screen. What the hell was up with that? There might be a horse pasture across the street, but this was still Philadelphia.

He thought about having another beer, even though it was late at night and he would be expected in class in a matter of hours. Just go crack your last beer, go head back down to the park, and let Mom sit up all night worrying. Maybe by the time he returned in the morning she'd be singing a different tune.

Yeah. Sure.

He had a system for breaking into the house, despite the deadbolted front door and the alarm system (which was sure to be engaged). From time to time he'd forgotten his house keys at school and made it home before Mom, so he'd improvised.

As he slid his keys back into his pocket, he pulled himself up by the cement edge of the door frame and put a sneaker on the ledge of the front window. Hopefully no one would see this from the road and call 911.

There were people watching, but they were not about to call 911. Not yet, anyway.

"Who's this?" Culp asked over the wireless com system.

"Just the boy," Mann replied.

"Looks like he could be trouble."

"No. I've practically watched him grow up. He won't be any trouble."

Culp didn't know what to say to that. Was that meant to suggest that Mann knew the target? That was weird. Usually teams were dispatched to neutralize strangers. Personal conflicts lead to mistakes, errors of judgment, botched assignments. After all, accidents were supposed to be random acts of fate.

This job would be Culp's tenth, but his first with an actual code name. Previously, he had played support roles (working his way up to assistant director) in four engineered automobile wrecks, two drownings, an untraceable poisoning, a suicide, and the one that made his career: a complicated amusement park accident that really wasn't an accident after all.

The client had wanted something spectacular and blood-splattery and headline-making, which all would be a distraction from the real reason this individual had to be removed from this plane of existence.

And the real tricky part: No one else had to be injured or killed.

The stunning success of that assignment bumped him up to the higher-paying name slot and this higher-profile assignment. Last thing he wanted to do was have it go wrong, because then he'd be right back to support roles and career oblivion.

Tonight's job was surprisingly straightforward but with many moving parts. The narrative, as Mann explained it during their initial script reading, was as follows:

An estranged—and deranged—husband returns home after many years away. He's already an accused murderer and a fugitive, and his last known sighting was a year ago on the opposite coast. But now he's back for revenge. He's heard that his wife has been seeing some guy named Chris, a real estate speculator, and he's consumed with anger, guilt, and jealousy. He returns home, kicks down the front door, finds his wife alone—despite his suspicions. But then he finds the receipt to a fancy Cuban restaurant downtown, puts it together, and chokes his wife to death right in her bed. See, this deranged husband had done this sort of thing before. Minutes later, the son wakes up and discovers his father next to the corpse of his mother. The son runs back toward his bedroom, where he left his cell phone. The father pursues. The son trips. The father is on top of him. The son fights back. The father snaps the boy's neck. See, he knows he's real far gone now, that there's no coming back from this. Which is when the father marches downstairs to the basement, finds a metal chair and a sturdy length of clothesline, and hangs himself from the rafters.

A common narrative, the familial murder-suicide. But that's what made it believable. The public was prepared to hear that exact story, and practically programmed to shake their heads in momentary sorrow (*Isn't that awful?*) before going about their lives. The best death narratives, Culp knew, were the ones people completely expected.

The trick tonight would be arranging all of those steps to fool even the best forensic examiners. Not that the best would be sent out to investigate this murder-suicide. When local police (not Philly

PD, Culp noted) heard the name Charlie Hardie, they'd already have the narrative preloaded in their minds.

Now it was just a matter of arranging the physical evidence to tell the tale.

As he climbed, Siege Hardie caught his reflection in a window. He had no illusions; he knew exactly how he appeared to the outside world: He looked like a kid who would shoot up a school. God knows he'd never do such a thing, but it was handy social armor. Most of his classmates tended to leave him alone. At first it started as an act to avoid hassles in the hallway. At some point, though, it became his real personality. Siege supposed he had his father to thank for that. He wished he could tell him now.

Thanks, Dad.

No, really.

Thanks.

You flipped out and took a long California vacation and snuffed some actress you were probably trying to bang (stay classy, Pops) and then tried to cover your tracks and then went on the lam. Leaving a wife and a ten-year-old kid home to...well, do whatever. Not as if you gave a shit, right?

The weird fake-ass California design of the home made the place easy to climb. Even drunk. Plenty of ledges, footholds, and a tiled roof that allowed Siege to crawl up and over the house. Halfway across, he glanced down at the backyard below. He could see their small gardening shed, their charcoal grill under a vinyl tarp.

And through a clearing in the trees, right in the middle of their own yard, a woman in a parka sitting in a plastic Adirondack chair.

Siege froze there on the roof, looking down at her. Mom? Why the hell would Mom be sitting outside on a bitter night like this? She wouldn't. She'd be waiting inside to yell at him. So who was this? Siege was reminded of a million horror movies where an ordinary woman turns out to be demonspawn from hell at the merest touch of her shoulder...

Whatever.

Ignoring the woman, he pressed his belly against the edge of the roof and stretched a leg down to the rusty railing outside his bedroom window. This railing was a design element and pretty much the most useless thing ever, as there was no porch, not even a mini-porch, to go along with it. Useless...until now.

Siege crouched down on top of the railing and started to pull up the screen. He kept his window unlocked for such situations, and he'd also disabled the alarm sensor on his window a long time ago. He only paused to look back at the woman, who was still resting in that plastic Adirondack, calm as could be, seemingly talking to herself. Creepy.

"What's he doing?"

"Breaking into his own house," Mann reported.

"Do we want him inside?"

"I'm thinking about that right now."

The easiest thing, Mann thought, would be to let the boy slip inside. Then they could seal off all of the exits and pump in some paralyzer and keep them on ice until Hardie showed up. But the boy...well, if he was anything like his father, he'd start trouble immediately. The last time Mann had let a Hardie run amok in a supposedly locked-down house...well, frankly, that's how she'd ended up here. Missing an eye, a tit, and sitting in a freezing plastic Adirondack chair on the fringes of Philadelphia. This was not where she'd seen her life taking her.

So Mann looked up at the younger Hardie and pointed.

The boy squinted. Perched up there, he looked like a Peter Parker who'd forgotten his red-and-blue tights at the dry cleaners.

Mann curled her index finger twice. *Come here.*

The boy paused for a moment, then, God bless his soon-to-be-still heart, began to scale down the side of the house, using ledges and cement door frames until he was safely on the ground.

"I'll babysit him for a while," Mann told her team. "Get yourself ready to breach the house at my command."

24

"HI, CHARLIE," THE woman said.

This freaked Siege out. Whoa, was he supposed to know this woman? Maybe a relative on his dad's side. There weren't many of them, but Siege hadn't seen any other Hardies for something like ten years, since he was a little kid. Mom always described the Hardies as a weird clan. Sitting in the backyard, with an eye patch? Yeah, this person could very well be a Hardie.

"Do I know you?"

"Take it easy, Charlie. Pull up a chair."

"That's not my name."

"I know. You call yourself *Siege,* right? How very punk rock of you. But I find it more than a little sad that your father gave you, his only son, his own name, and here you are casting it aside."

"Like I said, Who the fuck are you?"

"You didn't use profanity the first time, which I thought was much classier. C'mon. Pull up a chair and I'll explain everything, buddy boy."

A few yards away was a matching Adirondack. Mom had bought the two of them earlier this summer with the idea that they could sit out back together in nice weather, but that never seemed to happen. Sometimes Mom would sit out here and read or just decompress. Once in a while Siege would sit out here and try to sober up a little before entering the house.

"C'mon, I'm not going to bite you."

The only other option was climbing back up into his bedroom window, but Siege realized that wouldn't solve anything, either. A conversation with this creepy woman was unavoidable.

So Siege pulled over the matching chair, positioned it so that they'd be sort of facing each other, sort of not, then lowered himself into it.

"Do you have any beers left?" she asked.

Siege tried not to be creeped out by the question. How did she know he had a can of Yuengling in his jacket pocket? She couldn't know he'd been drinking at all unless she'd been following him, *watching him.* Goddamned Spidey Sense was right!

"You're such a worrier," she said. "I can see your eyebrows scrunching up there. Look, I can see the bulge of the can in your lower left-hand jacket. A boy...sorry, a guy your age doesn't hide soda pop in his jacket pockets, so obviously it's beer. I can tell you've been drinking because you smell like a brewery. Not a bad thing, by the way. I have a lot of pleasant memories of boys who smelled like beer."

"Again, who the fuck are you?"

"So that would be a no on the beer, then? Fine. I'll remember this, Siege."

He sighed, then pulled the can from his pocket, cracked the top, took a sip, and handed it over.

"Oooh, we're sharing," the woman said, taking the beer. "Swapping spit, practically."

"You keep talking like you know me, but I don't know you, or why you're sitting here in my backyard."

The woman took a long pull of the beer. "You know exactly why I'm here, Siege."

"This is about my father."

"Oh yes it is."

"You know him?"

"Do I *know him,*" she said with a crazed smile on her face. She took another quick pull of the beer and held the can in her lap. "Oh, Siege, we could sit here all night and talk about your father. Unfortunately, we don't have the time. That story's going to have to wait."

"Who are you?"

The woman locked eyes—well, a single eye—with him, then handed the can of Yuengling over. Siege took a pull, just to prove he wasn't afraid of her cooties or what have you, even though he did find it more than a little gross to be swapping can spit with a one-eyed creepy woman.

"I've never told anyone this before," she said. "Not on an assignment, at least. You see, we all have code names, and a person in my position usually takes the name of a director. For about ten years now I've been known as Mann, after the director Anthony Mann. Not Michael, though I do admire his work. I'll admit it. I chose the handle *Mann* as a thumb in the eye to those who thought that directing was not suitable work for a woman. Now it strikes me as obnoxious. Much like your own nickname, Siege, will seem obnoxious to you in perhaps a decade, if not sooner."

Siege tipped more beer back into his throat, holding the can so that the middle finger of his right hand was prominently displayed.

"Ah, nicely played," said the woman who claimed her name was Mann. "But after tonight's assignment, I think I'm going to retire the handle. I'll need a new one and there are a few options I have in mind."

Siege handed her the can of beer. She shook her head and gave a little wave of her hand. He knew he shouldn't drink any more of it. That last sip hit hard, and he was feeling dizzy.

"You ask who I am," Mann said, "and tonight I'm in the mood to tell the absolute truth. My real name's Melissa."

"Nice to meet you, Melissa," Siege said, "but that still doesn't answer who the fuck you are."

"And back to the profanity. Your father would be so proud. Anyway, let me tell you what's going to happen tonight in as much detail as possible. First . . . hey, would you mind passing the beer?"

Siege was about to say, *Change your mind?*

Siege also meant to lift the can of beer and hand it to her, tell her she could finish the thing, for all he cared, he was done drinking for the night.

But he couldn't.

He could barely wiggle his fingers, a motion which made the half-empty can crinkle.

"Good, good," Melissa/Mann said. "You're feeling it."

Fuck.

Fuck, no, this wasn't happening . . .

"Here's what going to happen tonight. I've given you a mild paralyzing agent. Don't worry. It won't kill you. That'll come later."

Melissa/Mann tipped the rest of the beer into the grass and then took a plastic baggie from her coat and placed the empty can inside.

"I'm going to have my team take you inside, and then we're

going to give your mom the same type of paralyzing agent. Completely untraceable. I've used this stuff for years, and it's quite reliable."

Melissa/Mann pulled herself out of the Adirondack, joints popping. She slid the bagged empty can into her jacket pocket and crouched down in front of Siege, her hands on his thighs. She squeezed them lightly.

"Can you feel it when I do that? You should. See, you can still experience physical sensation, you just aren't able to respond to it. I could jab a steel skewer through your leg and you'd feel every excruciating millimeter of it. But you couldn't do a thing to stop me."

Melissa/Mann reached up and touched Siege's face. Siege wanted to scream but it was as if someone had ripped his brain straight out of his skull, severing all connections *except* for the nervous system. Her fingertips were cold and clammy.

"Pretty soon your father is going to come home. He thinks he's coming to save you, but it's already too late for that. He's pissed off too many people for there to be a happy ending. Instead, we're going to arrange it so that the world thinks your father came home to kill you and your mother. He's going to strangle your mom, because that's kind of *his thing*. That's how he killed the actress. I was there. I saw it all happen. Okay, since we've got this honesty thing going...I made it all happen."

Holy.

Fucking.

Shit.

All at once Siege made the connection, he knew who this Melissa bitch was and what she was doing here and...fuck, how could he have been so stupid?

This whole time Siege had thought she was a fed or a cop or a bounty hunter or some shit, looking for a bead on his missing dad. They'd bugged his mom enough over the years; Siege just figured that they were starting in on him now that he was almost eighteen. Never did he once think that this could be...

That the Accident People could be real.

Oh, it was hilarious back in the day when his dad first made international headlines and the kids at school put it together. An initial wave of sympathy lasted, oh, all of thirty minutes before the shunning and awkward silences began.

But the worst of it came days later, when those Hunter fruitcakes started talking about the Accident People, and how *they* were to blame for Lane Madden's death. All of the assholes in fourth grade refused to let that pass.

Look out, Chuck! The Accident People are waiting in your locker!

A sneakered foot smashed into his shin, a painful tumble, and then—

Hey, it wasn't me. Blame the Accident People!

Siege grew up hating the assholes among his peers, but he reserved a special white-hot brand of hatred for people who didn't even exist—the mythical Accident People.

Only, turns out they did exist.

They were here now, and about to kill him and his mother.

Melissa/Mann moved in close, almost as if she were going for a hug. Siege could smell the soap on her skin, the trace of conditioner in her hair. Instead she reached into his jeans pocket and pulled out his cell phone.

"Hi, Kendra. We have your son. I'm calling from his phone, which is all the proof you need. If you want to see him alive again, you're going to let one of my associates enter the house. He'll tell you what to do next. Cooperate and this will all be over soon."

Siege heard his mother yell

Fuck you!

through the tiny speaker of his cell before Melissa/Mann thumbed END. She frowned, then looked at Siege, a pitying expression on her face.

"Don't be hard on yourself, kid. You're not to blame for any of this. You want to blame somebody, blame your father. He threw you and your mom headfirst into this whole mess. So let me give you some free advice. Save your rage for him. You'll be seeing him pretty soon."

25

The older you get, the more you live with ghosts.

—Nick Tosches

I CAN STOP YOU.

Oh, if Kendra Hardie could only bring herself to believe her husband's words. Somebody letting you down *that* consistently—ten years running now—makes it awfully hard to stick your hand inside that blender one more time and hope they don't press the PUREE button.

I can stop you.

Can you? Can you *really*? They have our son, Charlie. They have him and Christ knows what they've already told him...or done to him.

Who were these people? What did they want?

Only now did Kendra begin to realize the full gravity of her predicament. Phones: off. Cell phones: jammed, except for incoming calls from that fucking bitch. Water: cut off. Gas, power, everything. This was survival mode.

Kendra Hardie, however, was not the type of person to fall apart under tense situations. Over the past ten years she'd become accustomed to them. When those Albanian scumbags had nearly shot her husband to death, she found herself in a black despair that was hard to shake. She hated feeling like that. She vowed never to feel that way again. Part of that vow, sadly, contributed to the gulf between herself and her husband. Instead of staying to fight, Charlie chose to go away. Which brought on a similar black despair. For a long time she didn't know the way out. She kept her head down and focused on raising her son. The house-sitting money Charlie started to send kept them financially stable for a few years. But when Charlie disappeared after being accused of killing that actress, so did the money. The cumulative effect was devastating, personally and financial. Cue: black despair.

Until the moment she decided to stop despairing and try something insane. Her life had been populated by well-meaning law enforcement types over the years, checking in on her and CJ. Emboldened by the fact that she had nothing left to lose, Kendra started asking about work. One cop gave her a lead on a job as a process server.

In many ways she was ideal for the gig. Kendra looked like a suburban mom, attractive yet not threatening in any way. The kind of person who could approach you and have it feel perfectly natural, as if you were about to be asked to give directions...and then, bam, you were served papers. Most importantly, it nudged Kendra out of the black despair and made her feel like part of her life was under her control again.

Sometimes the people she served would curse at her, threaten her. Strangely, Kendra didn't mind these people at all—they were tangible threats you could understand. Somebody in your face, yelling that they're going to rape and kill you...well, bring it on. It was the threats of the unknown, creeping just out of peripheral vision, that caught you unaware—now those were the ones she feared most. The kind that could appear when you were out visiting your mother, completely unaware that a team of gunmen were killing your good friends and their children, trying to kill your husband.

When threats were tangible, you could deal with them. If any of the people she served were to show up at her house to make trouble, Kendra had an ace in the hole.

Her husband's old gun, buried in the basement.

Time to dig it out.

"You're clear," Mann said, still crouched down in front of the boy, relishing the intense laser point of pure hate blasting from his dilated pupils. Buddy Boy was Pissed, with a capital *P*.

"How do you want me in?" the voice in Mann's ear said.

"Go knock on the front door. She may try to fight you, but never mind that. Use the aerosol paralyzer on her—"

Ooh, look at the raw naked *hate!* The kid really didn't like the sound of that. Paralyzing poor mum. If the boy weren't immobilized, Mann knew he'd lunge for her throat.

"—then drag her into the house then come to the back door so you can help me with the kid."

The gun was inside the steamer trunk in the basement. Kendra hadn't touched it since that horrible day she'd discovered it in CJ's room. Thankfully there were no bullets inside the gun, or anywhere near it, so he really couldn't have done anything serious. But the very idea of a weapon like that in her boy's room chilled her insides.

The cop wife cliché was that cops' wives hated their husbands' service pieces being anywhere inside the home. Back then, as Kendra met many cops' wives, she found that the cliché was simply not true. Most of them were kind of gun nuts themselves, and even participated in family outings at the shooting ranges downtown on Spring Garden Street.

Kendra—while not technically a cop's wife, since Charlie was never a cop—embraced the cliché anyway.

She hated guns before the shooting that almost killed her husband.

She hated guns even more after.

So why didn't Kendra sell the damned thing after discovering it tucked away in the corner of her son's closet?

She didn't know.

But fuck...at this very moment, she was glad she'd thrown it back into that steamer trunk.

Kendra was about to head down to the basement when she heard three loud, even-spaced knocks at the front door.

Fuck.

Fuck.

Fuck.

That bitch on the phone claimed to have CJ. If she didn't answer the door right away, would they do something to her boy? Did she have the time to make it downstairs, thumb open that combination padlock (and what the FUCK was the combination?), find the gun in all of those files and crap, pray there were bullets somewhere in there, too, and...

Again, not to put too fine a point on it:

Fuck.

There wasn't time. Kendra would have to open the front door and play along. Hope there was an opportunity to retrieve that gun...

*　　*　　*

"AD, you in yet?"

"Waiting for her to open the door."

"If she doesn't—"

"I know."

The same time Culp heard Mann on the coms, asking for AD, there was a soft crunching noise outside the van, on the passenger side. Maybe AD's boot, crushing a stray acorn. But you didn't earn a spot on a team like this by playing around with maybes. Culp knew it could be anybody. A cop. A mugger. A kid. A nun. (Hey, there *was* a Catholic high school for girls just up the road.) Whatever the case, Culp was prepared with everything from a cover story (just checking on a fiber-optic network problem, officer) to a handheld spray aerosol paralyzer that would incapacitate the victim for up to an hour. That was the weapon of choice tonight. He slipped the device into his hand and deactivated the safety mechanism and waited for the person to enter the frame of the passenger-side window.

What Culp wasn't prepared for, however, was a brick that came smashing through the driver's-side window, spraying glass over his neck and back. Nor the gloved hand with the surgical scalpel that, one second later, reached in and sliced across his throat.

"AD, did she answer?"

Nothing on the line.

"AD, come on. Quit screwing around and report back."

Siege stared at her. Oh, those eyes. Full of pure rage.

"Hang on, babe," she told him. "I'll be right back with you."

*   *   *

Again, more knocks.

"I'm coming," Kendra said, trying hard to keep the anger out of her voice.

But the three knocks sounded strange this time. They were muted somehow, as if someone had laced up a boxing glove and used that fist to pound on the front door:

THUMP

THUMP

A pause, and then—

THUMP

She flipped back the deadbolt, steeling herself for anything but, most of all, reminding herself that she'd do anything to protect her boy. When she opened the door she was confused by how heavy it felt. A second later, as it swung into the living room, she saw exactly why.

Jump on it!

Jump on it!

Jump on it!

Ah-oonga-oonga-oonga

Phil and Jane Kindred agreed to the raiding soundtrack in advance: The Sugarhill Gang's "Apache," a jam they both remembered from, geez...toddlerhood? The horns, the tribal drums, the shouting, the early raps, it all made their muscles loose and imbued them with a childlike confidence.

And it worked, too. Every mass murder, Phil Kindred liked to say, needed its own soundtrack.

Plus, they had arrows.

Phil did, anyway. Four years in a row of summer camp. Four summers of archery lessons. Four summers he'd thought had gone to waste until this very day, when he was considering the narrative they'd be spinning as they destroyed a woman named Mann and her so-called Accident People.

Jane chose a medical scalpel for her primary weapon. She'd skipped the archery lessons during the same summer camp sessions. She was usually too busy playing doctor with other campers roughly her own age. Her idea of playing doctor was vastly different from that of her peers. Back then, just as now, she preferred the intimacy of a blade. Lawsuits were threatened, but Phil and Jane's parents had deep pockets and were able to squash any potential scandals.

So they divided and conquered. Abbott, their lawyer/minder from Culver City, supplied them with the hit list: seven names total, along with permission to slay anyone who stepped into their path. These Accident People were the first and easiest. Predators were not often willing to admit or accept they could be prey.

Arrows. There was a man affixed to her front door with *arrows*. Kendra couldn't quite comprehend it at first, thought it was some kind of Halloween special effect or a joke. A lightweight rubber body, fake arrows with suction cups on the other side. But no. The body was heavy and real, the dark red blood dripping down the wood.

Before a scream could escape her throat, there was a tiny voice coming from the corpse's ear:

"AD, where the fuck are you?"

The horror quickly gave way to relief when she realized this wasn't her son, this wasn't anyone she knew, in fact...this human pincushion was one of *them*.

So why...?

The implications of this hit her barely a second later. Kendra Hardie had always been a fast thinker—able to leap ahead in a conversation with terrific speed while everyone else struggled to catch up. This ability served her well now. Because the moment she put it together, the moment she yelled and kicked the door shut, there was another loud

THUMP

of an arrow on the other side.

There were two sets of individuals trying to kill them. Good Christ, Charlie... what kind of curse did you bring upon our house *now?*

"Hang on, tough guy," she said, before moving behind Siege and hooking her hands under his arms. He hated feeling this helpless, hated how stupid he had been. She yanked him out of the plastic Adirondack and dragged him across the cold, damp grass. Dragging him inside the house where he could be killed in peace and quiet, wasn't that it? Siege prayed to be able to control his arms and legs again. Just for a few minutes. Just long enough to stop this bitch from hurting his mother...

Then, without warning, the bitch cursed and dropped him.

Siege's head lolled to the side—he couldn't even control that. Which is when he saw that they weren't alone.

Across the yard was a deranged-looking teenager with a blood-soaked scalpel in her hand.

Mann kinda wanted to call a time-out.

Never mind that there was a creepy girl with a knife leering at her. This was a surprise factor in tonight's fun and games, but nothing insurmountable.

No, what troubled Mann immensely was that the creepy girl *looked familiar.*

"Have we met?" Mann asked, more to buy a few more seconds than anything else. She tried to run through a few possibilities—an angry girlfriend of Charlie Hardie's boy, maybe? Those random knife-wielding serial killers you run across from time to time?—but the creepy girl didn't give her much time. She bolted forward like a thoroughbred at the crack of a gunshot.

Who the hell are you? And why are you interrupting my job?

Why isn't AD responding to me?

"AD, Culp, we've got a problem," Mann said, and then the creepy girl was on her, slashing away with that scalpel of hers, above the prone body of the kid.

Mann blocked two swipes; a third opened up a gash on her left forearm that was instantly troubling. Your body knows when it's been cut bad. Even before the pain strikes there's an emergency alert that hits your brain at a primal level that tells you: *This will not end well.*

The creepy chick slashed again. Mann leaned back quick and felt the speeding tip of the blade nick her chin.

Who the hell are you!?

Mann took a step back. The girl advanced. Mann blocked the next wild slash with her cut forearm—which hurt badly—and hurled a punch at the girl's eye. This angered the girl, who started slashing away more furiously than ever, the scalpel barely missing Mann's flesh each time. Then the girl pulled the scalpel above her head, Norman Bates *Psycho*-style, and plunged it straight into Mann's chest.

The only thing Siege could do was watch the strange battle taking place just a few feet away from his immobilized face. He couldn't follow all of the action; he saw the blade dancing through the air and heard Mann's grunts and cries. Siege didn't know whom he should root for. Would it be too much to ask for them to kill each other and leave his family alone?

Then he saw the crazy girl stab the older one...

Oh God.

Right in the tit.

Mann saw the scalpel enter her breast and plunge halfway in. She reached out and grabbed the creepy girl's wrist anyway, locking it in place.

The creepy girl looked at Mann's chest, then up at Mann, waiting for a reaction. None came. Creepy girl's face fell. Something was wrong with this picture...

"Breast cancer survivor," Mann said by way of explanation, then headbutted the girl. The blow caused Mann's entire skull to pulse with instant throbbing agony, but it was worth it to see the creepy girl's eyes roll back up in their sockets, her entire body staggering backwards, leaving the scalpel hanging out of Mann's fake boob.

Over the years Mann's falsie had served as an excellent place to hide poisons, weapons, and other assorted items. Now it had most likely saved her life. Had she known this, she may have been tempted to have both cut off years ago and a pair of Kevlar girls installed.

Mann yanked the scalpel out of her breast, fully intending to use it to carve the flesh from this little bitch's face (which, again, was so, *so* fucking familiar!), but then she heard a frenzied shout.

"Jane!"

She wasn't alone.

What was going on, then? Did Abrams double-book this job to really, *really* make sure they nailed Hardie and his family? No. That would be an act of blazing stupidity. *Wait.* Was this knife girl a mercenary, hired by Hardie himself to protect his family? He'd seemed so cocksure of himself on the phone. *I can stop you.*

If that was the case, then there was only one way to play this out. Mann dropped the scalpel into her jacket pocket and used her remaining good arm to continue dragging the younger Hardie toward the back door of the house.

Fuck you, Charlie Hardie. You're still going to lose.

26

*I never knew who anybody was. I could meet you the night before
and not remember you the next day. If they dug my mother out
of her grave I wouldn't know who she was.*

— Charles Bukowski, *Hollywood*

YOUR NAME IS Charlie Hardie. You're back in Philadelphia to save
your family from the Accident People. To finish a job you started
seven years ago.

Only you weren't Charlie Hardie back then. Sure, you've taken
over the role now, but seven years ago you played a vastly different
role. Back then, you played on the opposite team — which of course
was why they courted you for this role. See, you had a couple of encounters with the real Charlie Hardie — bastard almost killed you, as
a matter of fact. *Twice.*

And that would be fifty thousand volts, motherfucker.

Seven years ago you took the name O'Neal. You served as second-
in-command for the Lane Madden job. The assignment was supposed
to be simple; it turned out to be anything but...thanks to Charlie
Hardie.

You had Lane Madden pinned down in the house, but then the

asshole house sitter—your future identity—showed up. Wrong guy, wrong place, wrong time, wrong everything. At first you thought, no big deal. You'd take out the house sitter, then Lane Madden. You even caught the house sitter by surprise and tazed his ass but good.

Fifty thousand volts.

Fifteen seconds' worth in the back, then ten more to really discourage him.

And then you prepared to deliver the coup de grâce: an EpiPen full of a heart attack serum, perfected by a mobbed-up scientist back in the go-go 1960s.

You'd lifted up the house sitter's arm for a direct vein jab—goodbye, you stupid fuck, thanks for playing...

And then the house sitter executed something that could only be described as a break-dancing move, his limbs flying out wildly as he spun, sending the EpiPen full of sure-fire heart attack—

—straight into your own thigh.

What went through your mind right then?

Shit!

Shit Shit Shit...

You had no choice but to yank the pen out and make a hasty retreat back outside to the supply van, where you might—might— have a chance of getting out of this alive, all the while ignoring the vise grip in the middle of your chest, the jolts of pain in your arm, the sudden feeling of impending FUCK THIS HURTS AND I AM GOING TO DIE.

Thankfully you'd managed to find, load, and shoot enough adrenaline to counteract the heart attack special. The experience had left you shaken like nothing else you'd ever experienced. *And you killed people for a fucking living.* Mann, meanwhile, had enjoyed her own encounter with the house sitter, and it left her with a mangled eye that would later have to be removed.

The second time Charlie Hardie almost killed you was nearly as life-altering. You'd followed the house sitter and Lane Madden up the Hollywood Hills, near the peak that overlooked a dog park as well as the Hollywood Reservoir. You were in a speeding van; they were not. You ran them over the side of a cliff. You thought they were both toast.

They were not.

All you did was seriously piss off the house sitter—who punched you with so much raw power that your bladder let go. And then he hurled you off the same cliff. On the way down your body was riddled with hundreds of cacti needles and all you could think was what a stupid way this was to die, straight out of your boyhood night-mares of falling, unable to stop your descent...

This also did a number on your mind.

And then later that night, the life you knew ended.

This was the final showdown: House Sitter vs. the Accident People.

Lane Madden was dead, but that pesky Charlie Hardie was still among the living and determined to skull-fuck the rest of the assignment as hard as he could.

When the end came, you were a block away, on Moorpark, and you counted off the shots in your head. *Bang bang.* Pause. Bang bang bang. Still another pause—a little longer this time, and then finally *bang bang.* Seven shots total. Plenty for everybody on Mann's hit list: Hardie, a dad, a mom, and two kids, with two bullets to spare. You hoped they'd used those extras on Charlie Hardie, the stubborn pain in the ass.

You waited on that suburban street.

Soon this would be over.

You made a promise to yourself to sprawl out on your king-size bed and just sleep for days and days after this job, pausing only to eat, shower, drink, and then crawl back into your big, soft bed.

Then you heard Mann screaming over the line: "Get in there, my AD and Grip are down! Kill them all!"

And that's when you realized that this night was far from over. You pulled your gun and jogged down a green path between two houses that led to a lush, overgrown backyard. Something in your pocket vibrated.

Your other boss.

A lawyer named Gedney.

He'd sent you a text message:

WALK AWAY

See, you were the fail-safe on this job. If things went tits up on one of the Accident People assignments, your job was to report it to one of your bosses and await further instructions. Thanks to Charlie Hardie, things had been going tits up pretty much all day on the Lane Madden job, so you'd pressed the panic button four times throughout the day. Each time came the calm reply:

STEADY ON

But this time, the message was different. And, boy, was that a chilling message to read. Not for your own sake. But for Mann's. You could practically hear the grade-school sing-songy voice in your head: *You're-gon-na-get-in-truuuuuu-ble.* But you followed orders. You slid the gun back into your pocket, plucked the earpiece out, snapped it in half, put the pieces in your pocket, crossed Moorpark, looking both ways, then headed north. You exited the scene, hit the nearest safe house, disposed of the gun and the broken earpiece, then disappeared.

You never worked with Mann again.

In fact, for the longest time, you assumed Mann was dead.

You had more assignments with other Accident People crews, under different names.

They never made you a director, and you were fine with that, always serving with the professionalism that was expected of you. Besides, being a director wasn't easy. Directors were the first to be blamed if something went wrong. The pay was fat but nowhere near compensated for the headaches. You told yourself: No, I'm happy in this role. Steady pay, lots of work. At a certain point you'd have enough to retire very comfortably, and then you'd look back at all of this and laugh. You had no real attachments, neither within nor outside the Accident People, but that was by design. This was the life you chose. You told yourself, *This life is enough.*

Even then, you knew you were full of shit.

Because you did crave more. The power of being a director, and the thrill of an intense connection with another human being that didn't involve death or a fistful of untraceable hundreds in the champagne room.

You realized that you dedicated your whole life to practice a highly illegal craft and . . . for whom? For what?

This realization was accompanied by a professional malaise and fits of depression and then finally . . . a mistake.

One that put you on the blacklist among the Accident People.

Which made you ripe for the picking when the spooks in the NSA came a-calling.

*   *   *

This whole time, you've been telling yourself:

The NSA doesn't know you're a fiercely independent operator. You are using them, not the other way around.

What *you* didn't know:

You weren't dealing with the NSA at all. Rather, you were still working for the Cabal. A secret division set up by Doyle himself, meant to test his own security devices.

A mindfuck inside a mindfuck.

Doesn't matter, though, in the end.

You know there's something valuable in Charlie Hardie's soon-to-be-dying head, and you'll be able to exchange that for a new life. You, your wife, and your son. Maybe you'll go to the NSA. Maybe somewhere else. Someone would be happy to pay for the information inside the Other Hardie's brain.

But first you had to deal with the Mann.

You worked for Mann only a short while before you knew she was trouble. Arrogant and reckless, all the while purporting to be a stone-cold pro. That's what annoyed you the most, because you know what? *You* were the quintessential stone-cold pro. Mann, on the other hand, always had to inject a little bit of personal into the equation.

These assignments weren't supposed to be personal! If you were running the show, you'd never send a damaged director like Mann against the family of the man who sent her life into a tailspin. Never.

Just another reason you're glad to be getting out of this business.

* * *

You park the coma car down the road, near a Catholic girls' high school. Across the street is a field full of horses. If you knew how to ride one of those things you'd pull a western on Mann and her crew. They were prepared for a thousand contingencies—but a guy charging in, guns blazing, on horseback? That would be amazing.

Alas, you grew up a city kid, hardly ever seeing horses, let alone riding one. You're going to have to do this the old-fashioned way.

Taking out Mann and her team one by one, on foot.

You know how these fuckers operate—you were once one of them. Mann would have at least two support team members: a right-hand man (or woman) and an AD. She could have brought in more personnel, but you don't think so. They've probably already got your future wife and son paralyzed inside the house, waiting for Charlie (you) to arrive to arrange some kind of psycho-comes-home scenario. The worst thing you could do would be charge right in and play into their hands.

For a minute you wished Hardie was not dying in that trunk but able to help. Two Charlie Hardies were better than one.

Oh, to have two Charlie Hardies on horseback even...

Stop this, you tell yourself. Fantasize later. When you're inside a secluded mountain resort with Kendra, working on repairing your badly fractured marriage. It would take work; your previous self botched this as badly as could be. But the situation wasn't hopeless. You could hear it in her voice. This could work...

And then, out of the darkness, came a man with a bow and arrow and a girl with a scalpel.

27

Come on in and experience some of my bullshit.
—Eddie Murphy, *48 Hrs.*

THE VOICE—MUFFLED, from the other side of the back door:

"Let me in or your son dies."

Kendra had been on her way down to the basement when she heard more knocking, and for a moment there—just a moment—she thought the back of the house was being riddled with arrows, too. She could barely, barely appreciate the absurdity of the moment. Because it seemed like the savage Indians were attacking, and it was up to Ma Hardie to defend the ranch with hot lead and a steely determination to save her brood...

"Time is of the essence, Kendra. Open this fucking door now."

She nudged the curtain aside enough to see...oh no, CJ *was* out there, in the arms of a woman with a patch over her fucking eye. Pirates and Indians. Her world had turned deadly and surreal at the same time.

Deadbolt, handle lock, handle...

The woman in the eye patch didn't enter so much as explode inside, pulling CJ along with her. Kendra pulled her son away from her. Eye Patch kicked the door shut behind her and flipped the deadbolt. There was blood dripping from the woman's forehead and right arm.

Kendra brushed the hair from CJ's forehead. His eyes were open but dilated. His mouth was open slightly. He wasn't moving.

Oh God oh God no no no...

"What did you do to him."

"He's fine. Temporarily paralyzed. It'll wear off within the hour."

"Fix him. *Now.*"

"We've got bigger problems than that right now. I'll be honest, Kendra. This is not how I saw this night playing out."

"Who are you? Why are you doing this to us?"

"Me? That's the funny thing. The whole game just changed, and right now, I'm the only chance you've got. Are we going to work together to survive this, or do we all die? Including your son?"

Mann had no intention of Kendra and her boy *surviving this,* of course. They were fated to die. But better to have them on her side now and deal with the new narrative later, when the bodies were either subdued or cooling.

This depended on the identity of the creepy girl outside. Her face was *so fucking familiar.* Why couldn't she place it?

So many murders over the years, so many faces. It was beginning to become a pulpy mass of yearbook photos.

It came to Kendra, all at once, as she stared into the woman's one good eye. "I recognize your voice. You're that bitch from the phone."

Hey, Charlie. This is your old pal Mann here.

Kendra didn't know the full story, how her estranged husband

and this one-eyed cunt knew each other, or what Charlie had done to make her so angry. But you know what? Kendra didn't care at this moment. Here was a threat made tangible, a threat she could do something about.

Kendra threw a fist straight into Mann's eye—her good one. She knew how to put as much weight as possible behind a punch, how to keep the line of her hand even with the line of her forearm. The blow connected with a satisfying POP, and Mann stumbled backwards into the back door.

You were expecting to deal with one set of psychos.

Now it appeared you had to deal with *a completely different* set.

You jog up Fox Chase Road in stealth mode, watching in part-admiration and part-horror as Mr. Bow and Arrow does your work for you—pinning one of Mann's team members to the front door of the house. Then the assailant disappears. You watch as the guy stuck on the door squirms briefly and dies.

You reach Mann's surveillance van and find another team member with his head barely hanging on the rest of his body. Glass shards, blood everywhere. Two down, probably just Mann to go. Who are these people? Who'd sent them?

And, fuck, were they already inside the house with Kendra and CJ?

There is another player on the board, which worries you. Who sent these assassins to kill the primary assassins? And why? The NSA, knowing he was going to double-cross them? No, they'd have a squad of ex-linebackers in Kevlar descending on this neighborhood, locking down everything tight. They wouldn't send some goofy guy with a quiver of arrows.

Who, why...it doesn't matter now.

What matters is you stopping them before they kill your new family.

Bad move, Ms. Hardie, Mann thought.

I'm already having a bad night, the capper to a pretty fucking bad decade. I'm not about to lose another eye and be fucking blind because of your asshole family. No. Just not going to happen.

Mann could barely see at the moment, but she *could* reach into her jacket pocket and pull out the wasp pistol.

And spray it in the general vicinity of where she heard Kendra Hardie moving.

"Good night, Ms. Hardie."

Kendra had simple goals: Pull her son down into the basement. Barricade the door shut. Open her husband's steamer trunk. Find his gun. Pray there were bullets.

Point and shoot at anyone who tried to come through the door.

She was halfway through Goal #1 when a burst of something cold and wet hit her in the face.

"Good night, Ms. Hardie."

Possibly she was imagining it, her nerves amped up to an insane degree, but the droplets of mist seemed to *burn* her skin, and then her chest seized up and her vision blurred and...

Siege was conscious for all of it and raged against his useless body, screaming at it, pleading with it, trying to command it to wake the fuck up already and save his mom.

But he was helpless as he watched Mom deck that one-eyed bitch (good shot, Mom) and the one-eyed bitch retaliate with a spray of some kind of poison gas. Mom was struggling to pull him down the basement stairs when she fell unconscious. Landing on top of him. Sending both of them tumbling down the stairs (carpeted, thankfully) into the half-finished basement.

As promised, Siege could feel every bump on the way down. He was sure his mom could, too. And both couldn't do a thing about it. Two of them, mother and son, at the whim of psychopaths. He couldn't even turn his head to look at that evil one-eyed bitch, even though he could hear her calling down to them.

"I'll be back for you guys in a little while. Don't go anywhere, okay?"

Mann slammed the basement door shut. Family taken care of. Now to see about the psychopaths outside.

And finally, at long last, Mann experienced a moment of déjà vu. Why hadn't she seen it earlier? We have a suburban home, prone family members, Charlie Hardie ready to emerge on the scene...

Jesus on a cross she hated sequels.

28

My daddy'll kick your daddy's ass all the way from here to China, Japan, wherever the hell you from and all up that Great Wall too.

—Chris Tucker, *Rush Hour*

YOU DUCK AROUND a front hedge, giving you a better view of the poor bastard stuck to the front door with arrows. Bet he thought he'd hit the big time, working for a legend like Mann. Been there, been fooled by that. There but for the grace of the NSA could go...you.

You make your way around the Hardie rental house, feeling like you sort of know the place from all of the surveillance photos you've been fed over the past year. Kind of like how you obsess over a photo gallery of a resort hotel in anticipation of a trip.

Making your way around to the back of the house, you see the guy with the bow and arrow.

Pointed right at you.

"Wow, the famous Charlie Hardie," the guy says with genuine amusement on his face. He's like a kid meeting a celebrity. It's that boyish smirk that enables you to recognize him: Phillip Kindred, professional psycho.

Not the *actor* who portrayed him seven years ago during the botched Hunter hit. No, this was the real thing. Whoever wanted Mann and her team dead cared enough to send the very best.

"I get to be the one who kills the Unkillable Chuck. Isn't that what they call you?"

Crazy Phil's got an arrow loaded with your name on it.

Fortunately, you've brought a gun to a bow-and-arrow fight. You smile and lift the gun and begin to squeeze the trigger.

Point and shoot, baby.

Unfortunately Phil's anticipated this. A fraction of a second ago he released the string, sending all of that stored-up elastic energy into the shaft of the arrow. The arrow cuts through the space between you then hits into your upper right arm with a meaty-sounding

TWOK

and pops out the other side. Your right arm is useless. Immobilized. The gun tumbles out of your trembling hand, and blood is already gushing down around your elbow. Now you've been shot before. Injected. Cut. Punched. Thrown. Never shot with an arrow in the arm.

Crazy Phil reloads his bow, almost laughing out loud at you. He won't stop until you're a St. Sebastian.

"Wonder how many arrows it takes to take down Unkillable Chuck?"

More than anything else—more than the pain, even—you're feeling the rage.

You're also feeling the grip of the second gun you've brought with you, tucked in the waistband of your pants. You pull it out now and in one fluid motion squeeze the trigger.

Crazy Phil releases the second arrow, but a fraction of a second too late. His face explodes.

He's not laughing now, is he.

In fact, his face is never going to register another emotion ever again.

Sadly for you, the second arrow slices right through your love handle and *stays* there, wobbling a little. *You've got two arrows in you now.* You stagger back, smoking Glock still in your left hand, wondering what the hell you can do about the two arrows in your body. Somewhat absurdly, your very first thought is: How the hell am I supposed to drive? You won't be able to close the driver's side door with that arrow sticking out of your side. And if you try to turn the steering wheel, you'll rip that sweet leather interior of the coma car.

But this is the least of your worries.

Topping the worry list, right this very moment:

The girl who's rushing forward, silent scream on her mouth, who is ready to utterly destroy you, because you just killed her brother/lover/partner.

Mann stepped out of the fake California house preparing to engage in the fight of her life. Instead she was greeted with a vision of pure delight:

Charlie Hardie, shot up with arrows, and being clawed apart by hooked fingers of the creepy girl.

Come to my arms, my beamish boy! O frabjous day! Callooh! Callay!

Mann *knew* there was another assassin out here. Pausing in the kitchen, ear to the back door, she heard a male voice: *Isn't that what they call you?* She braced herself for the reality that she was alone out here, her team dead, with two killers who had obviously been dispatched by enemies of the Cabal. Like all of the other Accident People, Mann had heard the rumors that the Cabal was at war with forces that had been unleashed by Charlie Hardie himself. For years, they'd stuck their enemies into a secret prison, but Hardie had managed to escape along with the worst of them. The Cabal had been paying for it ever since. There were even rumors of internecine struggles for control.

But that didn't matter now because

WAH-HOOOOOOO

Charlie Hardie was shot up with arrows and was now on his knees being savaged.

One glance to the right and Mann understood Creepy Girl's fury. Her partner was splayed out in the grass with a particularly messy gunshot wound to the face. There was, strangely, a bow in his hand. What, had they hired Robin Hood and his surgical resident girl-friend to kill them?

Mann watched her work and couldn't help but be amused. *Hey, honey, I'm with you. Dude has done me wrong more times than I care to think about. You take your time. You make it hurt.*

Mann couldn't let this go on forever, of course. Besides, she wasn't about to let this sorority girl claim her prize. Charlie Hardie was *hers*.

She reached for the scalpel inside her jacket pocket, pulled it out. Cleared the distance as quickly and quietly as possible. She had to use her left arm, which wasn't as strong or sure as her right—but her right was sliced open and dangling rather uselessly at her side.

Then Mann let the Creepy Girl have it all up and down her spine with jackrabbit stabs. She convulsed and threw her arms out immediately, like a cat who's been thrown from a fifth-story landing. Throughout the brutal stabbing the girl said nothing—but then again, she didn't seem to be much of a talker.

Mann finally pulled her off, let her drop backwards to the ground, then crouched down to give her a final slash across the throat. Meanwhile, Charlie Hardie tumbled forward awkwardly, snapping one of the arrows in half. He cried out. Hang on, buddy, she thought. Mann felt the girl's wrist. The pulses were faint and slow. She was on her way out. Mann did the same for Robin Hood, though that was easier. There was no pulse at all.

Satisfied that the two assassins weren't going to be pulling a last-minute resurrection (those were apparently all the rage), Mann walked over to Hardie's shaking, moaning body and used the tip of her boot to flip him over.

"Hello, Charlie."

Ooh, you passed out for a minute there. That was not good. You didn't even see the face of the person who had been attacking you, ripping your hair out by the fistful, gouging at your face with nails like fishhooks.

Your eyes pop open to see an old friend.

Your old boss, from your previous life.

"Such a waste," Mann says. "All of these years, all of this effort, to end here. How does that make you feel?"

She sits on your chest, legs squeezing your torso, which already feels like it's three times its normal size and on fire.

"I wish I could stop time. Or just slow it. Because I've been waiting seven long years to kill you, and I don't want it to be over."

She reaches down and for a moment you think she's going to pluck out one of your eyeballs just so she'll be able to drop it into a cocktail glass later that evening. Instead, she wipes the blood from your cheek. You didn't realize your face was bleeding so much.

"Fortunately, we do have one last piece of business to attend to."

She shows you the scalpel, taps the nonbusiness end against your forehead three times.

tap

tap

tap

You take stock of your situation. Your right arm: immobilized. There's the remnants of an arrow sticking out of it. Somehow, when you fell, you snapped the back end of it off. Lucky the damned thing didn't rip your entire arm open. Lucky. Heh. Yeah, that's you, Mr. Luck. In the process of becoming Charlie Hardie you've inherited his knack of being at the wrong place at the wrong time, as well as the general failure to see the big picture.

Your left arm: pinned down by Mann's right knee.

You can move your legs, but that's not going to do you much good, because Mann's full body weight is pressed against your aching torso, along with the length of arrow wedge through your side.

And now she's coming at your face with the scalpel.

"There's something in your head that I need to dig out. They sort of told me where it was, but I'll admit, in all of the confusion, I might have to do a little searching. You don't mind, do you?"

Fuck.

She knows, then. How does she know? You only figured it out back at that cheap motel when you were wrapping up the previous Charlie Hardie's head. You saw the scar and it answered the question of why you didn't find the maguffin inside the satellite. Despite the fact that you had a sensor specifically looking for it, and you searched every last corner of the craft.

They put the maguffin in his fucking head.

And while you were searching for it inside the craft, it was safely tucked away in Hardie's skull inside the gun-lined tube.

The only reason you didn't kill Hardie right then and rip it out of his head was because you didn't know if there was a kill switch or not. The host body dies, the information on that chip could be instantly erased.

Kind of brilliant, really. A double (triple axel) fake-out.

So then how did Mann know?

You need time. Keep her talking. Take advantage of the fact that this is personal for her. Just like it is for you.

"Where's my wife and son?" you ask.

The smile on her face is pure fucking evil. She's absolutely relishing this.

"Their bodies are in the basement. Had a nice chat with your boy. He's just like you, in a lot of ways. You should be proud."

You do the only thing you can do, the most Charlie Hardie thing you can do.

You start giggling. "I'm sorry."

Mann doesn't take the bait. "You wouldn't be giggling if you walked down into the basement and saw what I did to them. Maybe I should drag you down there and carve open your skull in front of them."

"Let's find out."

Which would give you a fighting chance as she dragged your pincushion body to the house and down the flight of basement stairs that only exist as images in your mind. At the very least, you'd like to see the interior of your family's house before you die.

Mann, to her credit, seems to think it over. "So tempting, but that wouldn't be professional of me. My orders are simple. Take the device out of your head and then finish all of you off. You. Your wife. And that darling boy of yours for last."

You start giggling again. "Really, I'm sorry."

No reply from Mann this time. Instead she grabs you by the hair and jerks your head to the left, which sends fresh new spasms of pain up and down your body.

"Right or left, right or left. You know, they told me there would be a scar, but I'm not seeing anything. Guess you heal fast, since you can't be killed and all."

Then she jerks your head to the right. Crazy intense explosions of agony all over, your body signaling all of its complaints in an urgent, frenzied, desperate way. To think that at one point, in your previous life, you fantasized a few times about sticking your penis into this woman. You have the desperate need to hurt her back, but you can't, because you're immobilized and in so much pain you can barely think. The tip of her blade presses into your scalp.

"Gotta start somewhere."

Then you realize something that would hurt her the most.

Two things, actually.

"Before you start digging around my skull," you tell her, "there's something important you should know."

"What's that, my dear?" she asks half-distractedly as she pulls the blade across your scalp.

"I'm not really Charlie Hardie."

29

SIEGE COULD MOVE his fingers. At first he thought it was an involuntary twitch, like your body jolting after a bad dream. But then he tried to repeat the jolt and he realized it was him consciously doing it, not some automatic part of his brain. The one-eyed bitch had said they'd be paralyzed for an hour! Well, she lied obviously. She lied about a lot of things. He focused on each finger individually. Pointer. Middle. Ring. Pinky. Back to the middle. If nothing else, Siege wanted to be able to shoot the bird to whoever came down here to kill them.

"Mmmmm," he said, trying out his mouth, trying to say "Mom," surprised to hear any sound at all.

"You're telling me you're not Charlie Hardie," Mann says, genuine amusement on her face.

"Nope," you say.

Mann pulls the blade from your scalp. There's already a lot of blood on it. Head wounds bleed a lot. She jabs the tip of the blade under your chin. You feel it cut into your flesh so deep you're worried she's made it all the way to the underside of your tongue.

"So," Mann says, "this is obviously a mask, and if I just cut here a little, I'll be able to rip it off and discover your true identity."

You need to be able to speak to convince her. So you start speaking:

"Moorpark, June, the school activist and his family, swimming pool electrocution. Barstow, July, the actor and the producer, car crash. Big Sur, also July, the money manager, car crash. Phoenix, again July, the writer, drug overdose."

As you blurt out the bullet points of your resume with Mann's team—starting from the very first assignment you worked together—you see it instantly sink in. There's no one who could know that information. Not unless you were Gedney, Doyle, or Abrams. Or you were a member of Mann's team.

Which you were. In a previous life.

"O'Neal!?"

"Yep."

"No. No fucking way," Mann murmurs, the fury burning in her eyes like jellied fire, and for a moment you think she's going to slit your throat out of sheer rage.

"Mom."

Siege's first word happened to be "Da," something that his mom liked to throw in his face now and again just to tease him. But now, seventeen years later, he was all about the word *mom*. Siege couldn't quite turn his head yet to see if she heard him, so he tried again.

"Mom."

There was a mumbling moan in reply.

She was still conscious. That was great. But only the first step. If his plan was going to work, he was going to need her talking...

HARDIE.

Once again, the name lit up in Mann's brain like pure neon.

HARDIE.

She knew they should have killed him in that hotel room, and then in the prison, and then in the secret hospital. You don't leave a man like that alive. Not after what he's seen. But her bosses wanted

HARDIE

kept alive, to be dealt with later, in a manner of their choosing. Well, now it was up to her to take down

HARDIE

no fucking around, no fancy shit, because a man who's too stubborn to die will be too stubborn to stay put, and god fucking damnit she should have listened to her gut on this one because now

HARDIE

was going to be the end of her.

She didn't understand it. The motherfucking motherfucker... oh, this motherfucker! Why was he cut to look like Charlie Fucking Hardie, of all people? Now that she knew his real identity, she could see the O'Neal beneath. Same eyes. You can't do much to change the eyes. How could she have been so stupid as to be fooled by this faux Hardie? She needed the real thing. If there was one last thing she would do on this earth, it would be proving that Charlie Hardie could be killed after all.

"So where is he, O'Neal?"

She rested the edge of the blade against his pulsing throat.

*   *   *

"Mom I just need to know one thing."

Siege could move his entire hand now. This was good. This was progress. But he was going to need more. He was going to need his entire right arm and, soon after that, his left. Fortunately, the more he struggled, the more his body opened up and let him back behind the controls.

"Mmmmrrrrmmrrr."

Siege had to admit, on any other day, his mother being unable to speak would be a fantastic thing. Not today. He needed her to be able to say four numbers.

"Mom, I need you to tell me the combination to the lock on Dad's steamer trunk."

"Tell me, O'Neal," Mann says. "Tell me or I'll slice your throat. You know me. I don't make idle threats."

She's speaking the truth. You do know her. She's going to cut your throat in about three seconds unless you tell her what she wants to know.

So...

You tell her what she wants to know.

"He's in the trunk of a black Lincoln Town Car parked up Fox Chase Road. He's badly injured but still alive. I have him on life support, to make sure nothing happens to the package inside his head."

"Thanks."

And then she goes to cut your head off.

"Wait."

She's not really listening; she's really going to cut your head off now.

"I have the trunk booby-trapped. You need me to open it."

Mann smiles this big warm smile, truly savoring your desperation. "You know, I can feel the bulge of your car keys against my thigh. Despite whatever you used to say about me, I'm not dead from the neck dow—"

As she's speaking she does two things: shift her body weight a little to emphasize the bulge of car keys between your bodies, and lean forward to give her a stronger position to chop your head off.

And the second after she's done those two things, you do three things:

Grab the back of her head.

Pull down.

And not-so-gently guide her good eye into the broken shaft of the arrow sticking out of your arm.

For Melissa McQueen, the mastermind assassin known to her peers only as Mann, a half-dim world went permanently black.

The second before her remaining eye was punctured by that sharp rod of wood and pushed back into her brainpan, she had an instantaneous revelation. And the revelation was this: Sometimes hard work and determination do *not* pay off. Just because you want something doesn't mean you'll get it. Just because you *think* you'll have the chance to destroy—down to the last atom—the person who ruined your life doesn't meant it'll happen.

Melissa McQueen died quickly, on a cold, browning lawn in Hollywood, Pennsylvania.

30

Them fellers up there are gonna wonder why you bailed out.
And I'm gonna tell 'em. You chose sides. Got yourself a little
nookie and chose sides.

—Bill McKinney, *The Gauntlet*

Up.

Get up and get inside the house. Just because you're shot full of
arrows (two, only two, you big pussy) doesn't mean this is over. Because big picture-wise, you're doing pretty fucking amazing. All of
your enemies—even ones you didn't know about—are dead. You've
got a long-sought-after prize on life support in the trunk of a big,
mean invisible gas-guzzling car. You're about a two-hour drive down
I-95 from the finish line.

But all of that means nothing if you won't have Kendra and CJ by
your side.

Part of you realizes how ridiculous this all is—a year ago, you
barely knew they existed. But funny how love works, isn't it. Love is
a matter of force of will. You've come to believe that.

As you limp across the lawn toward the back door of the house,
you think about what Mann said. *Their bodies are in the basement.* She
was trying to hurt you when she spoke those words. Was she imply-

ing that she'd killed them and put their corpses in the basement? You don't believe it. That's not how Mann works. She was sent here to arrange an accident, and, knowing her style, she'd arrange it to look like you—Charlie Hardie—had come home to murder them both. To do that, she needed you. Charlie Hardie.

So you prayed.

Through the back door, through the kitchen. There were drops of blood on the linoleum. Ignore that. Find the basement door. Of course, Mann could have been lying. She could have them bound upstairs, or she might not even have them here at all.

Come on, find the basement door.

You know the layout of this house from those countless hours of studying surveillance footage, but moving through the actual space has you temporarily confused.

Wait—there it is. The door.

For a moment you think the door might be rigged or trapped. Wouldn't take much for Mann to have installed a wasp's nest. You check the frame of the door for tell-tale signs. Scratches, but nothing obvious. A wasp's nest almost took out the previous Charlie Hardie all of those years ago. He managed to survive. You know you wouldn't.

Mann could have any number of surprises in this place—but you think about it. She wouldn't have time. No, the Kindreds attacked in the middle of Mann's preparations...

Stop overthinking this. Go down there and gather your family and bring them up to the car and drive to that complex in Virginia. You don't have much time. Shots were fired, screams *had* to have been heard, and you're better off doing this without the local police up your ass.

You put your hand on the doorknob, you twist...

There is no hiss, no wasp's nest. No death traps set by your former boss.

Just a set of carpeted steps, leading down to the darkness.

You're about to call out but change your mind. Never give away anything more than you need to. There could be something *else* down here, waiting for you.

So you take the first few steps down the road to your new life, hoping your new family will be there alive and waiting for you...

And that's when your chest explodes.

Siege lowered the .357 Magnum. He'd found only one slug— 158-grain, tip painted gold. Probably a show bullet, meant to impress friends or put on display. But it had worked just fine. Siege heard the sorry asshole tumble down the stairs and collapse on the concrete landing.

The basement was only half-finished. Carpeted staircase but bare floors. Drywall in places, foundation walls in others. Light fixtures half in, half out. The owner had been in the process of remodeling when his mortgage went underwater. Which was why he and his mom were able to afford the rent. This recent wave of mass killings wasn't going to do the owner any additional favors.

The bleeding person at the bottom of the staircase—who turned out to be a man—just groaned. Siege was almost disappointed. He was hoping to have nailed the one-eyed bitch. What's more:

"Seeeeeeeeej," the man said.

Something about the voice forced Siege to gasp suddenly, and his mother to start crying softly. A sudden realization smashed into his brain and all Siege could think was: no no no no *no*...

*   *   *

It had been easy to get caught up in the moment. Ten seconds ago Siege had heard the basement door open. Thirty seconds ago Siege had heard the back door open. Fifty seconds ago he had loaded the gun. A minute and a half ago he'd found the gold-tipped slug tucked in a corner of the steamer trunk. Four minutes ago he'd found the gun wedged under a deep pile of manila folders. Five minutes ago he'd squinted in the near-dark as he thumbed in the combination that his mother had managed to tap into his open palm, *Johnny Got His Gun*–style—

four seven three eight

—just five and a half minutes ago. Eight minutes ago he'd regained the use of both arms and his head and neck. Ten minutes ago he had been pleading with his mother to try, just try to speak...and somehow tell him the combination to the lock.

Ten minutes ago, it seemed like life couldn't get any worse for Siege Hardie.

Ten minutes later it had.

Ten minutes ago, he was a victim of circumstance, a kid at the receiving end of a long run of total and utterly bad luck.

Now he'd killed his own father.

Siege used his arms to crawl across the cold basement floor to the figure at the foot of the staircase and confirmed the worst. A narrow shaft of light from above lay over his father's face. Charlie Hardie Senior looked exactly how Siege remembered him—which was a complete shock. After years on the run, wanted for murder...the absentee father in Siege's imagination looked much, much worse for wear. And while his face was bruised and cut and bleeding from many places, it was an essentially young face.

All of those newspapers had called his father unkillable. It was the source of much teasing and much mental anguish over the years, but now Siege hoped—prayed—there was a glimmer of truth to that.

Across the room, Mom found her voice.

"Charlie."

And his father replied, with a slight gurgle in his voice:

"Hi, Kendra."

Siege laughed. He couldn't help it. A nervous twitch bubbling out of God knew where.

"You're going to be okay, Dad. You've been shot before and it turned out okay. You're going to be okay. Can you hear me? You're going to be okay."

You look up into the face of your son, your beautiful boy, and when you take a breath you realize...

You are not going to be okay.

31

How do I look? I mean, do I look Amish?
—Harrison Ford, *Witness*

THE SHOT WAS clean and good. Your son has skills, you have to admit that. Perfect center-of-gravity hit, just like they teach you at the police academy. And from the floor in a dark basement.

Probably not a good idea to tell CJ that now, though. Not with him looking at you with immeasurable grief and despair in his eyes.

You can hear your wife, Kendra, crying elsewhere in the basement. You can't see her; it's too dark. Which is kind of a cruel joke. Why hasn't she come over to you? Is she too grief-stricken to move? If you're going to die, the very least you can hope for is to look into the eyes of the woman you love as you slip away. Her real eyes. Not video images of eyes, eyes that can never look back at you. Her *real* eyes.

Then you understood what Mann meant when she said that Kendra and CJ's bodies were in the basement. She'd obviously given them some kind of paralyzing agent, keeping them alive but immobile, awaiting to be arranged in some sort of multiple-homicide-suicide narrative.

Which is all great, because they're alive, and the paralysis agent will likely wear off with no ill effects. But that does you no good, because you need an ambulance pretty much right now or it's all over.

Where did this all go so wrong? You've thought it before and can't help but think it again: Maybe you've inherited the previous Hardie's godawful luck along with his body and soul. Maybe that's just in the job description under the listing HARDIE, CHARLES D.

Still, part of you can't help but plot it out a little. If Siege can call an ambulance in time, there's a chance you can be saved. The bullet savaged your chest, but you've heard of people bouncing back from worse, right?

The narrative's easy: You came home to save your family from all of the creepy-crawlies who were trying to kill them. You took them out one by one. In the confusion you were shot. Simple, right?

You'll just have to pray that no one decided to look in the trunk of the black Lincoln Town Car parked up Fox Chase Road, near Roseland...

"Dad, I'm going to get you help. I promise. Just hang on, okay?

The phone was upstairs. No cell phone—the one-eyed bitch had taken it from him. Siege still couldn't move his legs. To get to the phone mounted on the kitchen wall, Siege would have to climb over his father. Which was something that could easily kill him. But without calling for help, he could die anyway...

No, that's just a fool's dream; you're going to die in this basement. The realization is settling in now. You can feel your damaged and rapidly failing internal organs all telling you the same thing: *Yer number's up, buddy.*

The look on your face must be obvious, because your boy is looking like he's starting to realize it, too. And, fuck, does that hurt worse than the slug that ripped you apart.

You look into your boy's eyes and for the first time you truly know what it is to be a parent. To suffer a parent's grief of watching your child fall apart. All of this time you've been play-acting. Assuming the role. Assuming the emotions. Now you feel it for real. It is unlike anything you've ever experienced. As if a surgeon had sawed into your skull and connected a few neurons and announced that you had an entire new set of senses to enjoy and experience. Now you get it. Goddamn it, *you get it.*

"There's . . . keys in my pocket," his father said.

"Don't talk, Dad," Siege said. "I'm going to figure this out." And he was. Siege saw that if he could pull himself up the banister, and if the banister would hold his body weight, he could somehow flip over the top and land in the middle of the staircase, then use his arms to crawl the rest of the way up to the kitchen. How would he reach the phone on the wall? Whatever, figure it out then. Go for the banister *now . . .*

"*Seeeeeeej,* please."

His father, pleading.

"Take the keys out of my pocket . . . trust me . . . just take the keys and go to a black Lincoln parked on Fox Chase Road . . . near Roseland, you know where that is?"

"Dad, no, I'm going to get you help."

"Looking in that trunk will help me. It'll fix everything, you've gotta trust me on this. What's in that trunk will save my life."

The boy—who you understand is not your own, though you wish it could be another way—finally agrees to your dying wish. There's a part of you that wants to explain more, but how can you? What would you say? You've said and done enough. For a while there, you were Charlie Hardie, and you came home to save your family.

Charlie Jr. reaches into your pocket, finds the keys, shoots you a quizzical look, as if he's waiting for you to reveal the punch line. When you don't, he gives you one last smile then tells his mother he'll be right back, he promises. You know why he says this. You would have said the same thing.

Then you watch with sorrow and pride as he struggles to crawl up the banister, up and over it, and lands hard on the staircase. You hear his mother gasp. But by the time he's crawled to the top of the staircase, he has his legs back under him. It's amazing. The paralysis has almost completely worn off. Then again, Charlie Jr. is his father's child, born after the Project Viking therapies. He most likely inherited the ability to bounce back from practically anything.

Unlike you.

The pain's gone now, which has you convinced that this is for real. Time seems to slow down and speed up at random. It's all happening so fast, yet you've been here a thousand years. You can hear something scuttling across the bare cement basement floor. Maybe it's creatures from hell come up to drag you down. You've lived a selfish, bad life. You've killed people. This is what happens to people like you. This is what you deserve.

Instead you feel warmth on your right hand. Something squeezing it . . .

Steady on.

Just steady on, man.

That was your mantra, wasn't it?

You're just a man who for a short while called himself Charlie Hardie. A man who used to call himself O'Neal, when you were a killer for hire. But you were actually born with the name Peter Jonathan Jordan in Muskego, Wisconsin. You die as your hopelessly damaged heart finally fails. You're not Unkillable Chuck, after all.

All of the hate, all of the rage, all of the questions, all of the lies, all of the distance, it all disappears. All is forgiven.

Kendra Hardie held her dying husband's hand because it was important for him to know this.

Life is cruel in that it underlines things for you this way, she thought. Kendra remembered visiting him in the hospital after the shooting ten years ago and holding his hand just like this, worried about their future, thinking things couldn't get any worse than that endless moment. Life showed her, didn't it?

Some part of her is relieved, though, because at least now she knew. She wouldn't go to her grave wondering why he'd disappeared, or if he thought about them at all. In the end, he'd come back home for them.

And that meant everything.

32

You pull a gun, you gotta be ready to kill somebody. And I'm telling you, it's better to run.

—Robert Culp, *Hickey & Boggs*

SIEGE HARDIE TOLD his mom he'd be right back. He saw the stark fear in her eyes—she couldn't move anything else—but reassured her. "I'll be right back. I promise. I have to check."

That was his dying father's last request, after all.

The rental home had turned into a house of horrors. Siege's limbs still ached and felt numb, which only made the short journey through his kitchen, out the backyard, around the side of the house, and down the front walk all the more surreal. As if he were a dead man, a ghost, doomed to haunt a crime scene forever. Maybe that was his fate. After all, he'd just blown away his father.

Anyway, there was his old friend One-Eye with a rod of wood sticking out of her eye. The other psycho chick with her throat slit. A guy with a bow and arrow (ah, which explained the wood sticking out of One-Eye's one eye). Around front, another guy stuck to their front door with a bunch of arrows. Then finally, a guy with his head almost cut off sitting in a van. Sure it was close to three in the morning, and this was a sleepy suburb, but Siege was half-surprised there weren't cops everywhere. I mean, shots had been fired. Guess everyone just assumed it was a car backfiring. Or they all really didn't give a shit.

As Siege trotted up Fox Chase Road he tried to imagine what would be in the trunk of that car. Would he slide the key in and open up the lid only to discover Laurence Fishburne sitting there, offering him the choice of the red or the blue pill? What else could possibly save his father's life?

Then he spotted the black Lincoln, right near Roseland, as promised.

Siege opened the trunk. After the shock at finding a body curled up inside subsided a little, he remembered his father had sent him here for a reason, so he'd better find out what. He pulled away the facial bandages.

Oh my God.

At first: relief.

Then confusion.

Then, as his trembling fingers reached for the man's still neck...

"MOM!"

UNDISCLOSED LOCATION—
11 MONTHS LATER

33

We all go back to where we belong.
—R.E.M.

THIS WAS IT, finally, at long last. Hardie thought he'd lost the taste for it, since it had been almost—what—seven years since he'd had one? The night before flying to Los Angeles. The night before Lane Madden. The night before everything. The doctors told him he'd never have one again. Too much damage to his system. He needed to eat right and focus on healing. They made him promise. Kendra made him promise. And for almost a year, he'd honored that promise.

But fuck it. Sometimes a guy just wants to crack a beer.

Hardie bribed the supply sarge, this brush-cut foul-mouthed guy named Phillips, to put aside a six of Yuengling Lager the next time a bunch of cases showed up at the base. Military bases, even super-secret ones like this, had a policy about rotating the beer selections so no regional brew was slighted. So every week a plane would bring in Shiners from Texas, or Buds from St. Louis, and so on. Hardie decided that if he was going to fall off the wagon, he'd do so clutching a can of his favorite beer, Yuengling, brewed in Pottsville, not too far from Philly. Oldest beer in America, they claimed, brewed continuously since 1829. Hardie had no idea what they did during Prohibition, but whatever. You've gotta love a survivor.

So now Hardie dug his secret six-pack out of the bottom of the fridge, hidden beneath a bunch of vegetables in plastic bags, plucked one can from the plastic holder, and carried it back to their modest living room.

It was close to 2:00 a.m., and all was quiet in this quiet, anonymous patch of the country. Where? Hardie couldn't tell you. No, literally. That was part of the deal.

Quite a bit had happened since he was gunned down on a dark highway in Nebraska. At the time, Hardie had been pretty sure he was done for, story over, check, please. Much to his surprise, he'd woken up a day later in the trunk of the fucking coma car with his boy looking down at him, utter shock on his face.

Hardie would learn the whole story—or as much as Kendra and Charlie could tell him—days later. In that moment though, once Seej started yammering about how he'd died, and how could he be here, and what the hell was going on . . . Hardie lifted up two fingers and told his kid to please shut the fuck up. He may have missed the main show, but he still had to save his family.

"Do you have a driver's license?" he asked, his voice cracked and weak.

"Permit," Seej replied.

"Go get your mother."

Seej made a motion to start untangling Hardie from the life support gear in the trunk, but stopped when Hardie waved those two fingers. No. Much as he hated this damned car—specifically, the

241

trunk of this car—he knew it was probably the only thing keeping him alive. If you could call this a life.

"No, please, don't. Just get your mother."

Even now, thinking back on it, the events of that night were disjointed in Hardie's head, like a hastily edited montage in a 1980s action movie. Some of it barely seemed real. Yet it had happened, otherwise he wouldn't be here, in this living room, with a beer in his hand, right?

Siege had indeed gotten his mother. Both were shaky, seemingly barely able to stand. Kendra was even more shocked when she saw him in the trunk. Shocked...then angry, for some strange reason. Whatever, Hardie thought. This wasn't the time for family therapy. This was the time for getting the hell out of town.

Apparently after much confused back-and-forth, with Kendra insisting that they needed to drive his shot-up ass to the closest hospital right this very second, Hardie somehow finally transmitted the message to his estranged wife:

Put the boy in the car and drive all of us down to NSA headquarters in suburban Virginia.

NOW.

No, I don't have an address. Look it up on the way. Figure it out on the road. The boy's smart. He probably has a magic phone that can help him out.

Once you arrive at NSA headquarters, ask for the most senior person you can find and open the trunk for him.

I'll live until then. Fuck, I've managed to survive this long.

The NSA is home base.

Getting us to the NSA as quick as humanly possible is our only chance.

(The Other Him kept talking about the NSA this, the NSA that . . . so they would know what to do, right?)

Kendra drove them south on I-95, leaving all of their possessions—and many, many dead bodies—behind.

Including a dead body that looked just like him.

Cut to:

The NSA, having no fucking idea what the hell he was talking about.

No, we did not carve one of our agents to look like you, Mr. Hardie. Nor did we shoot this fictitious agent, um, into space. Who are you again?

But once a junior-level agent began digging into the case, fireworks started to go off. Apparently someone had been investigating him all this time, thanks to some obscure document they kept calling the Arbona Memorandum, which Hardie didn't fully understand. Nor did he care to understand. Hardie had stumbled into this world by mistake and found himself caught up in it for seven years of pure misery. Now he had the chance to possibly stumble back out of it, and that would be just fine with him.

The important thing was, they knew about the Cabal, though nowhere near as much as they thought. They were looking for Doyle and Abrams, two lawyers who'd slipped off the grid some time ago. And once they recovered the crashed spacecraft from the Pacific Ocean floor, just off the coast of California, Hardie thought, they'd have evidence to destroy them all.

Hardie was content to let them. He was out of the destroying-the-evildoers game. All he wanted to do was heal his body to a reasonable degree. He didn't want to run marathons or stop bullets with his bare hands. He just wanted to live.

The NSA had access to an excellent private hospital; Kendra and Seej were put up in housing—under heavy protection—adjacent to the facility. They were as essential to saving Hardie's life as the surgeons who labored on his hopelessly wrecked body. But the real surprise came when they took a CAT scan of his head and found...

...a small computer chip welded to his skull.

They told a semi-conscious Hardie what they'd found. He asked what it looked like. Puzzled, the techs told him:

"A small black square of shiny plastic, mounted on four corners with some kind of gummy material."

Hardie started to laugh, which made the anesthesiologist worry, because he wasn't supposed to be having that kind of reaction to the gas while his head was cut open. Hardie, though, thought of the poor bastards doing a deep-sea dive to pull up a wrecked spacecraft...when all this time, he had the power to destroy the Cabal in his head.

Thank you, Glinda, Good Witch of the North.

See ya, Cabal. Your days are numbered.

However, when the NSA finally broke through the impossibly sophisticated encryption programs, they found that the chip welded to Hardie's skull had but one message:

FUCK YOU DOYLE

And nothing more.

The real bombshell dropped later.

NSA operatives found the pulpy, wood-chipped remains of a woman believed to be Abrams in the Pacific Northwest. A good old-fashioned forensic trail led them to her former partner, Doyle, who was holed up in an assisted-care facility in South Dakota. The man was clearly insane, babbling, "I wish I hadn't walked through her. I wish I hadn't walked through her." No one could figure out what that meant until they analyzed the footprints at the crime scene. All of Abrams's personal documents were in Doyle's possession, and they led to a safety deposit box in a small savings and loan in Santa Monica, California. Inside of which investigators discovered the complete operational secrets of the Cabal, and the Industry, and the Accident People...since the very beginning. Every last move, recorded on a series of forty-two flash drives. No password protection, no encryption, no nothing. They were even helpfully indexed.

Still, Hardie's testimony was invaluable. Especially after word of Hardie's cooperation reached Eve Bell and her secret army working all over the world to dismantle Cabal operations. In exchange for their cooperation, Hardie and Kendra and CJ were given new identities, a new life, on a secret base somewhere within the continental United States.

At least, that's what he'd been told. It was hard to make sense of anything these days.

Hardie's head still hurt, even after the operation. Time was kind of disjointed and fuzzy, and not entirely *real*-feeling. Sometimes he would blink and for a moment forget who he was, what he was doing here, what he wanted. This never lasted more than a moment or two, but it was nonetheless awful to experience. Imagine walking down the street and the sidewalk dropping away from your feet, giving you an instant and terrifying sensation of free fall...before the world righted itself again. Sometimes Hardie thought he was dead and his brain just hadn't processed the information yet.

The on-base doctor explained that this sensation was perfectly normal. After all, all three of them had been given memory shots after their transport. For a hellishly paranoid moment Hardie thought that this was it; that these NSA guys were just another front for the Accident People, the Industry, the Cabal, the Whatever...and that he'd just sentenced his family to death. But instead they'd woken up in this small but clean house. New construction. The usual appliances and furnishings. No phone, no open Internet, but still—better than death.

Meanwhile, the world thought Charlie Hardie was dead. After all, local police had found his body in the basement of his wife's rental home, fatal gunshot to the chest, with assorted assassins and psychopaths littered around the property. Pop culture changed its tune about Charlie Hardie. He was no longer the nutcase from Philly who'd snuffed an actress in a seedy Hollywood hotel. Instead Hardie was a hero, because Jonathan Hunter had been telling the truth about the Accident People and Hardie had sacrificed his own life to save his wife and boy. Whereabouts unknown, but the world assumed they'd gone into hiding. After all, wouldn't you? The body of Charlie Hardie was given a hero's funeral. There was even talk of a citywide Day of Remembrance, but then the Phillies start to pick up some heat and attention spans moved elsewhere.

Narrative over.

But the real Charlie Hardie, aboveground and recovering from six lifetimes' worth of physical abuse, was cooling his heels at a secret military base somewhere. Though it wasn't exactly a military base; it was a *suburb* next to a military base.

Yep, after all of his adventures, Charlie Hardie couldn't quite escape the burbs.

Hardie had been told that this place was housing for the employees of a government research facility, secret shit happening every-where. Everybody in town had the same deal: You just lived your life the best you could and didn't talk about what anyone did. Hardie asked for a job, to be able to do *something*, but his caseworker told him he'd done enough for his country. Hardie pressed the point, and the caseworker finally relented. "We'll call you if we need you."

That had been ten months ago. So far, no call.

So it was time, at long last, for a Yuengling.

Hardie's life was far from empty. He had physical therapy six days a week and was finally walking on his own again. He had occasional debriefings from anonymous men in suits who asked a few specific questions, then asked them another way and still another way, then departed without explanation.

But most of the time Hardie spent trying to reconnect with Kendra. They had parted under the lousiest of circumstances, and their reunion wasn't exactly roses and confetti, either. They had grown into different, older people. Still, somehow, their strange lit-tle shared spark was still there, beneath all of the years and hurt. Hardie felt it in her touch, in her kiss. If it had been extinguished completely, this new life would be unbearable.

Most importantly, the hate in her eyes was gone. Hardie took that as the best sign of all.

CJ was another matter. He was a young man, eighteen now, and full of rage and confusion. Hardie got it. You grow up thinking your old man snuffed some actress before disappearing for seven years...and then the next thing you know, you're living on some se-cret base somewhere...well, yeah, you're going to have some blame and rage issues.

Hardie twisted the top off the cold bottle of beer. He did the som-melier thing and even sniffed the top. There was no better smell than this. It only worked the first time. He put the top to his lips and tilted.

The on-base doctor had told Hardie confidentially that he probably didn't have all the time in the world. He'd burned too fast, too hot, too hard. No, he didn't know about any Project Viking. There was no trace of any kind of gene therapy or secret government projects. (*Then again,* Hardie thought, *this was a military doctor. Of course he'd cover it up!*) The doctor emphasized: You can't expect your body to absorb that kind of punishment without breaking down completely. You drink a beer, the doc said, and you're just giving yourself a good hard nudge toward the grave. The very idea gave him pause. Hardie didn't want to pull the grass and sod over himself until he had a chance to make things right with Kendra and CJ. As right as they could be. In this weird afterlife, every minute with his family was a bonus.

Hardie swallowed long. The beer was cold and fresh and felt like it had hit a part of his soul that hadn't been touched in ages.

Time fragmented again. Hardie blinked and found himself on the floor. His fingers closed around a bottle of Yuengling that wasn't there anymore. Did he finish it? Geez, did one sip knock him out? The ceiling looked strange, unfamiliar. So did the carpet under his arms. He was having a difficult time moving.

Which of course is when the alarms went off.

And somewhere, in the distance, in the direction of the base... gunfire.

At first Hardie thought he was having the mother of all death flashbacks, that eleven years hadn't gone by, and that he was lying in a pool of his own cooling blood in the middle of his Philadelphia living room, having just been gunned down by those crazy asshole Albanians. And everything that followed: exile, booze, Lane, Accident People, Alcatraz, Abrams, the double, the shootout in Hollywood, everything ... had just been a fever dream, experienced in a matter of seconds as the neurons in his brain misfired and gave him the pulp-action show of a lifetime ...

More gunfire. Rocket blasts ... were those rocket blasts? Hardie thought fast. Could it be some pissed-off remnant of the Cabal, coming after him finally to settle a score? No, he decided. If they were to come at him, they'd come at him directly. *And stop thinking everything's about you. Because it's not.*

Whatever it was probably had to do with the top-secret shit going on all around them, because wherever you had top-secret shit, you had people doing top-secret shit to steal the other top-secret shit because, Hardie supposed, nature abhorred a vacuum. This was the way the world worked. Hardie's world, anyway. He'd come to accept it. Bad shit went down, and for some reason fate kept nudging him into its path.

More gunfire, explosions, screams. This wasn't sounding good.

So go on, Hardie.

Get up.

Grab your gun.

Where is—

Oh God, where's your gun?

Hardie hadn't just bribed his way into a six-pack of beer. Six months ago he'd managed to get his hands on a Glock—again, from that foul-mouthed brush-cut supply sarge. This was a clear violation of the rules of this secret base. But Hardie had been through too much to be without a weapon ever again. He'd kept it a secret from

Kendra and CJ, naturally. Kept it in a locked table by his recliner, key on a chain around his neck, so heavy firepower would forever be within easy reach.

But now the table drawer was unlocked and open. No Glock. Damnit, did they do a security sweep of the house and confiscate it?

Not that a gun would matter if Hardie couldn't move. He grunted. His body responded with silence. His body had stopped talking to him. Why, after months of physical therapy, were his limbs failing to respond? So many agonizing steps, so many hours of sweat and pro- fanity and muscles worked to the point of absolute failure. Hardie slammed his eyes shut, trying to think back on those hours of ther- apy. Were they a dream, a ridiculously detailed and active dream? No. He did this shit. He knew he did. And his body should know better. Fuck you, body. We're getting up. Just like we always do.

When Hardie opened his eyes, he saw his boy, Seej, on the landing. He was holding the Glock. Pointed down, classic two-hand grip. Just like he learned from those video games he was always playing. But where's your sword, kid? Don't you need a sword, too?

For a horrible moment there Hardie thought his son had snapped. What a horrible thing to think about your own son, isn't it? Despite everything they'd talked about, the time they'd spent together, maybe Seej hadn't forgiven him after all. Maybe he'd stolen the gun hours earlier and had been sitting up in his room trying to work up the courage to finally do the Oedipus thing and take out the old man for good.

But the kid surprised him by saying, "It's okay, Dad. I've got this."

Part of Charlie Hardie could have died right then.

Thanks and Praise:

The Final Chapter

If life is a series of buddy films, then I'd want to co-star with these fine people: John Schoenfelder. David Hale Smith. And the man this book is dedicated to: David J. Schow. I couldn't have written this book without these tough guys.

Also, huge thanks to Richard Pine, Lauren Smythe, Danny and Heather Baror, Angela Cheng Caplan, Shauyi Tai, Jessica Tscha, and Kim Yau, as well as the whole gang at Inkwell Management.

It's not every day you encounter buddies like those at Mulholland Books. Huge thanks to Miriam Parker, Wes Miller, Michael Pietsch, Theresa Giacopasi, Betsy Uhrig, Barbara Clark, Christine Valentine, Janet Byrne, Peggy Freudenthal, and the rest of the stellar Little, Brown team. Ruth Tross and the amazing Mulholland UK team. Kristof Kurz, Frank Dabrock, and the rest of the team at Heyne in Germany.

My space doc, and the man who keeps me from making serious medical blunders in all of my books, is the legendary Lou Boxer. He's at once the most *noir* guy in all of Greater Philadelphia—yet, an absolute sweetheart. Explain *that* one...

Special Cabal Honor Roll:
Megan Abbott, Lexi Alexander, Scott Allie, Cameron Ashley,

THANKS AND PRAISE:

Janelle Asselin, Brian Azzarello, Jed Ayres, Josh Bazell, Eric Beetner, Stephen Blackmoore, Linda Brown, Ed Brubaker, Aldo Calcagno, Eric and Hannah Carlson, Jon Cavalier, Sarah Cavalier, Scott and Sandi Cupp, Bobby Curnow, Warren Ellis, Peter Farris, Erin Faye, Joshua Hale Fialkov, James Frey, Joe Gangemi, Jim Gibson, Rachel Gluckstern, Sara Gran, Allan "Sunshine" Guthrie, Charlaine Harris, Charlie Huston, Tania Hutchison, Jennifer Jordan, John Jordan, McKenna Jordan, Ruth Jordan, Vince Keenan, Anne Kimbol, Katie Kubert, Ellen Clair Lamb, Terrill Lankford, Joe Lansdale, Simon Le Bon, Paul Leyden, Laura Lippman, Elizabeth-Amber Love, Mike MacLean, Mike Marts, David Macho, Patrick Millikin, Scott Montgomery, Lauren O'Brien, Jon Page, Barbara Peters, Ed and Kate Pettit, Rickey Purdin, Keith Rawson, David Ready, Marc Resnick, Doug Robinson, Janet Rudolph, Chris Ryall, Adam Sandler, Jonathan Santlofer, Joe Schreiber, Brett Simon, Warren Simons, Evelyn Taylor, Mark Ward, Dave "Vigoda" White, Billy Wee, Elizabeth A. White.

Supreme thanks, as always, to my family: Meredith, Parker and Sarah. Without them, none of these books would have been written, and I'd be a wasted husk of a human being.

And I'm grateful to the following songs and bands, who provided the unofficial soundtrack for *Point and Shoot*. I always compile a playlist for my novels-in-progress; certain songs help me pinpoint a certain emotion (or batshit action idea).

"Zach's Fanfare #2" (MFSB)*
"Comeback Kid" (Sleigh Bells)
"Monkey Gone to Heaven" (The Pixies)

THANKS AND PRAISE:

"Spaceman" (Harry Nilsson)

"Going Down" (Freddie King)

"I'm Bad" (Rocket to Memphis)

"Pumped Up Kicks" (Foster the People)

"Nobody Does It Better" (Me First and the Gimme Gimmes)

"Skull & Crossbones" (Sparkle Moore & Dan Belloc and His Orchestra)

"Switchblade Smiles" (Kasabian)

"I Wanna Destroy You" (The Soft Boys)

"Drain You" (Foxy Shazam)

"T.O.R.N.A.D.O." (The Go! Team)

"Woman of Mass Destruction" (The Woolly Bandits)

"Tough Lover" (Nick Curran and the Lowlifes)

"(I'm Stuck in a Pagoda With) Tricia Toyota" (The Dickies)

"Apache" (The Sugarhill Gang)

"For Whom the Bell Tolls" (Metallica)

"We All Go Back to Where We Belong" (R.E.M.)

"Change Reaction" (David Uosikkinen)

"Satellite" (The Hooters)

"Fanfare for Rocky" (Bill Conti)*

Philadelphia, PA

---

* If you build this playlist, then have it loop, there's something awfully thrilling about the moment that "Fanfare for Rocky" gives way to "Zach's Fanfare #2." It doesn't get any more 1970s Philadelphia than this, motherfuckers.

Duane Swierczynski

Duane Swierczynski is the author of several crime thrillers, many of which have been optioned for film and television, including *The Blonde* and *Severance Package*. He's written for several DC Comics, Marvel Comics, IDW, Dark Horse and Valiant titles, including Birds of Prey, Bloodshot, Godzilla, Punisher MAX, Judge Dredd, X, Cable, Deadpool, Immortal Iron Fist and Black Widow, and has collaborated with *CSI* creator Anthony E. Zuiker on the bestselling *Level 26* series of 'digi-novels.' Duane lives in Philadelphia with his family. Say hello at secretdead.com or twitter.com/swierczy.

Want to find out how it all started for Charlie Hardie? Read on for an extract from the first book in the trilogy, *Fun & Games*.

Fun & Games

THE PIERCING screech of tires on asphalt.
   The screams—
   His.
   Your own.
   And then—

1

It's all fun and games until someone loses an eye.
—Popular saying

Los Angeles—Now

SHE DISCOVERED Decker Canyon Road by accident, not long after she moved to L.A. A random turn off the PCH near Malibu shot her up the side of the mountain, followed by twelve miles of stomach-flipping twists and hairpin turns all the way to Westlake Village. And she *loved* it, hands gripping the wheel of the sports car she'd bought with her first real movie check—because that's what you were supposed to do, right? Blow some of that money on an overpriced, overmuscled convertible coupe that popped a spoiler when you topped 75. She never cared she was going thirty miles faster than any sane driver would attempt on this road. She loved the ocean air smashing into her face, the feel of the tires beneath as they struggled to cling to the asphalt, the hum of the machine surrounding her body, the knowledge that one twitch to the left or right at the wrong moment meant her brand-new car, along with her brand-new life, would end up at the bottom of a ravine, and maybe years later people would ask: *Whatever happened to that cute actress who was in those funny romantic comedies a few years ago?* Back then, she loved to drive Decker Canyon Road because it blasted all of the clutter out of her mind. Life was reduced to a simple exhilarating yes or no, zero or one, live or die.

But now she was speeding up Decker Canyon Road because she didn't want to die.

And the headlights were gaining on her.

The prick had been toying with her ever since she made the turn onto Route 23 from the PCH.

He'd gun the engine and then flash his high beams and fly right up her ass. She'd be forced to take it above 60, praying to God she'd have enough room to spin through the next finger turn. Then without warning he'd back off, almost disappearing...but not quite.

The road had no shoulder.

No guardrails.

It was like he knew it and was trying to spook her into a bad turn.

Her cell was in the dash console, but it was all but useless. The few seconds it took to dial 911 could be a potentially fatal distraction. And what was she going to tell the operator? Send someone up to Route 23, seventeenth hairpin turn from the middle? Even the highway patrol didn't patrol up here, preferring to hand out speeding tickets on Kanan Road or Malibu Canyon Road.

No, better to keep her eyes on the road and her hands upon the wheel, just like Jim Morrison once advised.

Then again, Jim had ended up dead in a bathtub.

The headlights stayed with her. Every few seconds she thought she'd lost them, or they'd given up, or—God, please *please please*—driven over a bump of asphalt where a guardrail should be and tumbled down into the ravine. But the instant she thought they might be gone...they returned. Whoever was behind the wheel didn't seem to give a shit that they were on Decker Canyon Road, that one slip of the wheel was like asking God for the *check, please.*

She was almost two miles along the road now; ten to go.

Her Boxster was long gone; traded in after the accident in Studio City three years ago. Now she drove a car that suited her age—a leased Lexus. A car for grown-ups. And it was a fine machine. But now, as she took those insanely tight turns in the near dark, she wished she had the Boxster again.

Decker Canyon Road was notorious for two things: the rusted-out chassis of cars that dotted the hills, and its uncanny ability to induce car sickness, even with safe, slow drivers just trying to make their way up to Westlake Village in one piece.

She felt sick to her stomach now, but she didn't know if it was the road doing it to her, or the events of the past few days. The past few hours, especially. She hadn't eaten much, hadn't slept much. Her stomach felt like it had been scraped from the inside.

She'd been up for a job that seemed like a sure thing: producers, director, writer, star all in place, a guaranteed fast-track green light. It was a supporting role but in a higher-profile movie than she'd done in years. A role that would make people notice her again—*Wow, she's in that? I was wondering where she'd been.* And then it all had fallen apart in less than an hour.

She'd spent the majority of the past week in her Venice apartment, brooding, not able to bring herself to take much interest in feeding or watering herself or even turning on the satellite cable—God forbid one of her pieces of shit appear, or worse, a piece of shit she'd been passed over for.

So tonight she'd gone for a long late-night drive—the best kind in L.A. Enough wallowing. She wanted the ocean air to blast away the malaise. Blasting away the better part of the past three years would be nice, too...

And then the headlights were back. Rocketing toward her, practically up her ass.

Number of accidental vehicle crash deaths in the United States per year: 43,200.

She stomped on the accelerator and spun the wheel, tires screaming as she made—barely—the next finger turn.

The bastard stayed right behind her.

The worst part was not being able to see much beyond the span of her headlights and having to make lightning-fast decisions, one after the other. There was no room to pull over, to let him pass. If passing was even on his mind.

She wondered why she presumed it was a *him*.

And then she remembered why. Of course.

At some point she knew Decker Canyon Road crossed Mulholland, and there was even a stop sign. She'd happily pull over then and give him the double-barrel salute as he drove by.

How much farther was it? She couldn't remember. It had been years since she'd been on this road.

The road continued to snake and twist and turn and climb, the tires of her Lexus gripping asphalt as best they could, the headlights bobbing and weaving behind her, like she was being pursued by a forty-foot electric wasp.

Finally the road leveled out—a feature she remembered now. From here, the road would ease up for a quarter mile as it ran through a valley, followed by another series of insane uphill curves leading to the next valley. A few seconds after, everything seemed to level out—

—then she gunned it—

60, 70, 80

—the electric wasp eyes falling behind her—

90

Ha, ha, fuck you!

The Lexus made it to the next set of curves within seconds, it seemed, and all she had to do now was slide and skid her way along them and put even more distance behind her. She applied some brake, but not too much—she didn't want to lose momentum.

Halfway through the curves, though, the electric eyes returned.

Goddamnit!

Right on her, curve for curve, skid for skid. It was like the car behind her was mocking her. Anything you can do, I can do better.

When she finally saw the red glow of the Mulholland stop sign out in the distance, she decided to fuck it. Hit the turn signal. Slowed down. Used the bit of skirting that now appeared on the side of the road. Go ahead, pass me. I'm stopping. I'm stopping and probably screaming for a while, but I'm done with this. Maybe I'll take a look at your license plate. Maybe I'll call the highway patrol after all, you reckless asshole.

She pulled the Lexus to a skidding stop, her first since the PCH, which felt like years ago. Then she turned left and pulled off to the side.

The car followed her, pulled up next to her.

Oh, shit.

She reached for her cell and power-locked the doors at the same time. The other car appeared to be a goddamned Chevy Malibu, of all things. Some kind of bright color—it was hard to see in the dark. The driver popped out, looked over the roof, made a roll-your-window-down gesture.

Phone in her hand, she paused for a moment, then relented. Pressed the power window lock. The glass slid down two inches.

"Hey, are you okay?" the guy asked. She couldn't see his face, but his voice sounded young. "Something wrong with your car?"

"I'm fine," she said quietly.

Now he moved around the front of his car, inching his way toward her.

"Just seemed like you were having trouble there. Want me to call somebody?"

"On the phone with the cops right now," she lied. She had her finger on the 9 but had stopped. Go on, press it, she told herself. Followed by two ones. You can do it. That way, when this guy pulls out a shotgun and blasts you to death, your last moments will be digitally recorded.

"What the hell were you doing, racing up my ass that whole time?"

"Racing up what? What are you talking about? I didn't see anybody on the road until just now, when you slowed down. I almost slammed into you!"

The guy sounded sincere enough. Then again, L.A. was crawling with men who were paid to sound sincere.

"Well, we'll let the police sort it out."

"Oh, okay," the guy said, stopping in his tracks. "I'll wait in my car until they show up, if you don't mind. It's a little creepy, being out here in the middle of nowhere."

She couldn't help herself—she flashed him a withering *Duh, you think?* look.

But that was a mistake, because now he was looking at her—*really* looking at her. Recognition washed over his face. His eyes lit up, the corners of his mouth lifting into a knowing smile.

"You're *Lane Madden*. No way!"

Great. Now she couldn't be just an anonymous pissed-off woman on Decker Canyon Road. Now she had to be *on*.

"Look, I'm fine, really," she said. "Go on ahead. I guess I was imagining things."

"Uh, don't take this the wrong way, but should you even be driving?"

Lane's brain screamed: *asshole.*

"I'm fine."

"You know, I don't mind waiting, if you want to call this in, or check in, or whatever you have to do."

"Really, I'm okay."

The guy seemed to know he'd pushed the ribbing a little too far. He smiled shyly.

"You know, I promised myself when I moved here, I wouldn't be one of those assholes asking for autographs everywhere he goes. And I'm not. Just wanted to tell you how much I'm a fan of your movies."

"Thanks."

"And you're even prettier in person."

"I really appreciate that."

After a few awkward moments the guy got the hint, walked back to the driver's side of his Malibu, and gave her a sheepish wave before ducking back inside his own car and pulling away into the dark night.

Lane sped through Westlake Village, caught the 101. It was an hour or so before dawn. The freeway was as calm as it ever gets. She took a series of deep, mind-clearing breaths. Maybe when she had enough oxygen in her brain she'd be able to laugh about all of this. Because it was sort of funny, now that it was over.

Sort of.

The Malibu guy hadn't been riding her ass; he'd simply been

out cruising down Decker Canyon Road for the same reason Lane used to cruise it—the sheer thrill. It only seemed like he was trailing her. Hell, he was probably following her lead. Lane Madden had clearly seen too many action movies. God knows she'd been in too many of them.

They caught her in the Cahuenga Pass near Barham—a two-car team. Malibu had done this dozens of times before. His job title: professional victim. You find your target in the rearview, then start to make a series of subtle calculations that only truly exceptional wheel men can make. A small turn of the wheel, a tap on the brakes, then presto, Hollywood fender bender. Happens all the time.

That was the fun part. The boring part was the aftermath. Bleeding. Waiting in your own car for the highway patrol to arrive. Then more waiting for the EMTs to take you to the nearest hospital. Malibu was stone sober, of course, and his driving record was spotless, since it was erased every time he did one of these jobs. His volunteer work with kids with leukemia (fake) would pop up, as well as his Habitat for Humanity projects (also fake). No one would give him a second glance. Maybe they'd mention his name—an alias, and he had plenty of them—in a newspaper story or two. But mostly they would focus on the actress.

Malibu wanted to take her out on Decker Canyon Road, but it turned out she knew these roads just as well as he did. Sure, he could pull some fancy surefire moves that would nudge her sweet little ass off into the canyon. But that was beyond what had been discussed, so he'd called Mann on the hands-free. The word came back quick: *no.* This had to look as mundane as possible. Something that would make headlines briefly, but nothing that would be followed up.

No, better if she looked like another coked-up actress who was out too late and didn't know how to handle her Lexus.

So he trailed her to the 101. Now it was show time.

Malibu liked working with members of the acting community. They were fun. You knew exactly what they were going to do, exactly how they were going to react. Like they were following a script. They had the idea that they were above it all—

"I really appreciate that."

—that made it all the more gratifying.

Lane was approaching the exit to Highland Avenue—the Hollywood Bowl. It was still painfully early. The sky over L.A. was a pale gray lid. Maybe from here she'd go down to Hollywood Boulevard, then take Sunset all the way back down to the PCH, and then Venice. Make herself a big strong cup of coffee—one of those Cuban espressos she used to drink all the time. Put on some Neko Case, wait for her manager to wake up. Plan her next moves. When life finally stops kicking you in the teeth, you don't whine and count the gaps. You see the fucking dentist and move on.

She signaled to change lanes, and saw the Chevy Malibu in front of her again. Damnit, the same one from Decker Canyon Road. As the moment of realization hit her—*he's braking he's braking he's braking*—the vehicle came to a violent rubber-burning halt.

Lane's body was hurled forward just as the hood was ripped from its moorings and went flying up into the windshield. Glass sprayed. The air bag exploded.

Mann watched the accident from approximately fifty yards away. Now it was time to pull over to the shoulder and be one of those friendly citizens who offers to hold your hand until the police arrive. Only *this* friendly citizen would be uncapping a syringe containing a speedball and jamming the needle into the victim's arm. There would be no hello, no speech, no nothing. Just death.

The speedball contained enough heroin and coke to take down a Belushi-size human being; it would probably stop her heart in under a minute. And if it didn't, there was always something more exotic that could be quickly loaded into a syringe. But better if it looked like a pure speedball. That way, Lane Madden would die and go to Hell still wondering what had happened. The Devil could fill her in.

Lane was numb for a few moments. Her body was telling her she was hurt, hurt bad, but she couldn't find exactly where. The signals in her brain were crossed. She looked around, trying to solve it visually. If she could put together the details, she'd know what happened.

She had broken glass in her lap. The air bag had smashed her in the face. She half pushed it aside. Her right ankle was throbbing. Her foot had somehow wedged itself under the brake pedal.

A few feet ahead she could see the car she'd hit, or the car that had hit her—she wasn't sure what exactly had happened. The driver's head was slumped over his wheel. She prayed she hadn't killed him.

Then someone opened her driver's-side door, pushed the air bag out of the way.

She looked down and saw the needle in a gloved hand.

Even though she was still wrapped in a cocoon of shock, she knew that the needle was the one detail that didn't belong.

The stranger grabbed her left wrist, twisted it, jammed the needle into the crook of her arm, depressed the plunger. Lane's heart began to race. Oh God, what was in that fucking needle? Her vision went blurry. She clawed at the passenger seat, felt the smashed beads of glass.

Lane grabbed a fistful—

—and smashed it into her attacker's eyes.

There was a horrible scream of rage and suddenly the needle was wobbling loose, hanging off Lane's arm. She plucked it out it, threw it to the side, then tried to crawl out of the car. Meanwhile her attacker flailed around, blind, looking for her. Cursing, raging at her.

As Lane's palms dug into the asphalt of the 101, she realized that her right ankle wasn't working properly. The damned chunky metal weight strapped to it didn't make it any easier. Her heart was racing way too fast, her skin slick with sweat. The world looked like it had been wrapped in gauze. Lane crawled away on her hands and one good knee, all the way to the fence at the edge of the 101.

And then she hurled herself over it.

2

California is a beautiful fraud.
—Marc Reisner

WHEELS WERE supposed to be up at 5:30 a.m., but by 5:55 it became clear that wasn't gonna happen.

The captain told everyone it was just a little trouble with a valve. Once that was fixed and the paperwork was filed, they'd be taking off and headed to LAX. Fifteen minutes, tops. Half hour later, the captain more or less said he'd been full of shit, but really, honest, folks, *now* it was fixed, and they'd be taking off by 6:45. Thirty minutes later, the captain admitted he was pretty much yanking off / finger-fucking everyone in the airplane, and the likely departure time would be 8 a.m.—something about a sensor needing replacing. Nothing serious.

No, of course not.

So after two hours of being baked alive in a narrow tube, Charlie Hardie took the advice of the flight crew and stepped off to stretch his legs. After an eternity of standing around, his belly rumbling, he decided to make a run to a bakery over at the mall between Terminals B and C. Hardie had taken exactly one bite of his dry bagel when the announcement came over the loudspeakers: *Flight fourteen seventeen ready for takeoff. All passengers must report immediately to Terminal B, Gate . . .*

By the time Hardie returned to his seat, carry-on in hand, someone had already commandeered his space in the overhead bin. Hardie glanced forward and back to see if there were any gaps in the luggage where he could slide his bag. Nope. Everything was jammed in tight. Irritated passengers tried to squeeze by him in the aisle, but Hardie wasn't moving until he found a place for his carry-on. He refused to check it. He'd carefully planned his seat assignments so that he'd be one of the first on the plane, guaranteeing him overhead bin space. It didn't matter what happened to the rest of his stuff; Hardie just couldn't lose sight of this carry-on.

"Everything okay?" a gentle voice asked.

A flight attendant—young, smiling, wearing too much makeup, trying to ease the bottleneck in the middle of the plane. Trying to avoid some kind of incident.

Hardie lifted the duffel.

"Just trying to find a place for this."

"Well, I can check it for you."

"No, you can't."

The attendant stared back at him, catching the raw stubbornness in his eyes. She looked uneasy for a moment but quickly recovered:

"Why don't you slide it under the seat in front of you?"

Hardie had tried that once—during his first flight. Some snot-ass flight attendant had given him crap about height and width and keeping the aisle clear.

"You sure that's allowed?" he asked.

She touched his wrist and leaned in close. "I won't tell anyone if you won't."

The flight was quiet, monotonous, boring. Landing, too—a soft touchdown in the early-morning gloom. Hardie was thankful that the hard part was over. Within a few hours he would be back to work in a stranger's home, where he could sink down into a nice fuzzy alcoholic oblivion, just the way he liked it.

Hardie stumbled into his house-sitting career two years ago. He was between budget residence hotels and a friend of a friend had been called off to a job in Scotland, so he asked Hardie if he'd look after his place an hour north of San Diego. Four bedrooms, swimming pool, bunch of lemon trees outside. Hardie got $500 a week as well as a place to stay. He almost felt guilty taking the money, because it was a mindless job. The place didn't burn down; nobody tried to break in. Hardie watched old movies on DVD and TNT. Drank a lot of bourbon. Munched on crackers. Cleaned up after himself, didn't pee on the bathroom floor.

The friend of the friend was pleased, and recommended Hardie to other friends—about half of them on the West Coast, half on the East. Word traveled fast; reliable house sitters were hard to come by. What made Hardie appealing was his law enforcement background. Pretty soon Hardie had enough gigs that it made sense for him to stop living in residence hotels and start living out of one suitcase and a carry-on bag. Rendering him essentially homeless, but living in the fanciest abodes in the country. The kinds of places people worked all their lives to afford.

All Hardie had to do was make sure nobody broke in. He also was expected to make sure the houses didn't catch on fire.

The former was easy. Burglars tended to avoid occupied residences. Hardie knew the standard entry points, so he spent a few minutes upon arrival making sure they were fortified, and then... yeah. That was it. All of the "work" that was required. He made it clear to his booking agent, Virgil, that he didn't do plants, didn't do pets. He made sure people didn't steal shit.

Fires were another story. Especially in Southern California during the season. Hardie's most recent West Coast gig was in Calabasas, where he watched the home of a TV writer who was over in Germany doing a comedy series. Hardie followed the news reports between sips of Knob Creek, and then without much warning the winds shifted—meaning a wall of fire was racing in his direction.

There was nothing Hardie could do to save the house. So instead, he loaded up every possible thing that would be considered valuable to a writer—manuscripts, notes, hard drives—into his rental. He was still filling every available nook and cranny when the flames reached the backyard. Ash rained on his hood, the top of his head. Hardie made it down the hill and over to the highway, watching the fire begin devouring the house in his rearview mirror. Watching the smoke and choppers reminded Hardie of that old punk song "Stukas over Disneyland." The fact that Hardie was pretty deep into a bourbon drunk at the time made his great escape all the more amazing.

Because that's what Hardie did after the "work" was done and the house was fortified—drank, watched old movies. When Hardie stopped understanding the plot, he knew he'd reached his limit. He'd put down the bottle and close his eyes. He didn't worry about not being able to hear home invaders, or sirens, or any of that. The stubborn lizard cop part of his brain refused to shut off. Which, Hardie thought, was why he drank so much.

See, it was all one neat little circle.

After the Calabasas fire, and weeks of hawking black gunk out of his lungs, Hardie decided he'd had enough of SoCal for a while. He did some jobs in New York City, San Francisco, Santa Fe, Boston, even DC for one wretchedly humid week. The writer from

Calabasas was grateful Hardie had managed to save so much of his material, so it wasn't as if he suffered poor marks on his house-sitter report card. In fact, Hardie had more job offers than he could handle. His living expenses—booze, used DVDs, a little bit of food—were minimal. He sent the rest of his earnings to a PO Box in a suburb of Philadelphia.

When this new California offer came up, Hardie decided it was okay to go back. The house was nestled right on the Hollywood Hills, and the ground was just as dry, probably drier, than it had been the previous year. Which had been an especially bad year for wildfires.

But it was also coming up on the three-year anniversary of the day Hardie's life ended, and he wanted to be as far away from Philadelphia as possible. He didn't want to be anywhere near the Eastern seaboard, in fact.

Hardie made his way out of the cramped tube, trying to stretch his sore body while walking. Nobody would let him. Bodies rushed past him from behind, nearly collided into him from the front. He felt like a human pinball. Down a flight of stairs he came to the luggage carousel and waited for the bags to start being vomited up from below.

Nearby, a little boy, about eight years old, squeezed his mother's hand. He glanced over his shoulder at the automatic doors every time they *whooshed* open. Down the carousel was a girl—dark hair, pretty eyes, vintage purse tucked under her arm. She tapped her high-heeled shoe to a slow, slow song.

The carousel kept churning. Airport carousels always reminded Hardie of a suit of armor, dirty and scuffed, as if a knight had fallen into a trash compactor.

The bags were belched up one at a time. None of them looked like Hardie's. There was a loud cry to his left. The little boy was running toward the doors. A man in his late thirties stopped in his tracks, took a knee, then held his arms out as the boy tackled him. He lifted the boy up off the ground and spun him in a half circle. Hardie looked back at the carousel. The girl with the purse, the one who'd been tapping her shoe, was gone. He guessed her bag had come up.

Finally all of the bags were up and claimed, leaving Hardie to stare at the empty metal carousel, turning and turning and turning.

Figured.

The suitcase contained nothing of real value—a couple of gray T-shirts, jeans, socks, deodorant and toothpaste, some DVD standbys. And Hardie still had his carry-on bag, thank God.

But the loss was still annoying. He would have no change of clothes until the airline located his suitcase—*if* they located it, ha ha ha—and had it delivered. Hardie went to the airline desk near the carousel and filled out a form with boxes too small for even his small, tight printing. He wrote down the address of the house he'd agreed to watch, wondering how the promised courier service would ever find it.

The owner, a musician named Andrew Lowenbruck, had told Virgil that the place was notoriously well hidden, even to people familiar with the tangle of intestines that made up the roadways of the original Hollywood Hills. Some deliverymen insisted that Alta Brea Drive didn't even exist.

Hardie figured he might see his bag somewhere on old episodes of *The Twilight Zone.* Maybe tucked into the background behind Burgess Meredith, or in the overhead bin over William Shatner's head.

Still, Hardie dutifully filled out the missing-bag form, then hopped a dirty, off-white shuttle bus to the rental-car area. Hardie hated renting cars, because it was one more thing to look after. But you couldn't be in the Hollywood Hills without a car. What was he supposed to do? Take a bus to Franklin and Beachwood, then hike on up to the house?

Lowenbruck was supposed to have met him at the place this morning. But he'd sent an apologetic e-mail last night to the service explaining that he had to be in Moscow earlier than expected. Lowenbruck was working on the sound track for a movie by an eccentric Russian director who wouldn't let the unfinished reels leave his native country, so he had to fly out to watch an early cut to start gathering ideas. His original flight was canceled; the replacement left eight hours earlier. Virgil told him that Lowenbruck was known for his "pulse-pounding" action scores—the modern-day Bernard Herrmann, they called him. Hardie didn't know what was wrong with the original.

So...Hardie wouldn't be meeting him. But that wasn't unusual. He rarely met the owners of the houses he watched—it was mostly handled by Virgil at the service, who in turn handled things by e-mail and FedEx key exchange.

Which was probably for the better. If they had a look at Hardie, some owners might change their minds.

Instead, Hardie got to know his clients by the stuff they left behind. The photos on their walls, the DVDs on their shelves, the food in their fridges. Stuff doesn't lie.

As it turned out, Alta Brea Drive wasn't too hard to find. Just shoot up Beachwood, the main drag, until you hit a dead end at the fairy tale–looking houses. Hang a sharp left on Belden, which only looks like somebody's driveway—swear to God, it's a real road, don't worry, keep driving. Then, follow the intestinal tract straight up into the Hills until it looks like you are going to drive over the edge of a road and tumble down a ravine to your death. Then, at the last possible moment is another turn, and you find yourself in front of Andrew Lowenbruck's house.

Hardie was thankful it was daylight. How the hell did people do this in the dark?

These roads weren't meant for two-way traffic, let alone a row of parked cars along the sides. But that's what people did up here, apparently—good luck sorting it all out. Still, Hardie made it up the mountain without an accident, and that's all that mattered.

Hardie had been up in the Hollywood Hills before, watching other houses. But never in this specific area—the original Holly-woodland development known as Beachwood Canyon. The whole setup looked way too fragile to Hardie. Back in Philly, he'd had grown up in a $7,000 two-story row house, which was wedged in with hundreds of other row houses on flat tracts of land that stretched river to river.

Out here was the opposite—all hills and heights and precariously perched multimillion-dollar homes. Every time Hardie looked at the Hollywood Hills, he half-expected to hear a loud wooden snap and then *whooosh.* All of the houses would slide down from their mountain perches and end up in a giant pit of broken lumber and glass at the bottom of the canyon.

Which was just one of the many reasons Hardie drank a little bit more when he sat one of these houses.

Hardie pulled up in front and turned off his rental—a Honda Whatever that felt and drove like a plastic box. Forget Alta Brea Drive; Hardie wasn't entirely convinced this *car* was real. But it was part of the airline–rental-car package he'd found online. He didn't plan on driving it much, anyway. All he needed was a way to get to a grocery store to buy food and booze, and then eventually a way back to the airport.

There were two other homes on this twisting bit of road, one on either side of Lowenbruck's place, all three of them clinging to the side of the mountain. Across Alta Brea was a rocky cliff covered in foliage. A crew of two workmen in buff jumpsuits were busy hacking away at the brush with chain saws. On top of the cliff was another of what Californians called a "house." The only part you could see from street level was a turret, standing tall, looking like it was part of a full-fledged castle. That was the thing about these hills. No matter where you built your castle, there was always somebody with a bigger castle, higher up than yours.

From street level, Lowenbruck's place looked like nothing more than a wide, flat bungalow. Spanish-tile roof, freshly painted stucco exterior. On the left was a single-car garage. In the middle was a sturdy front door cut from solid oak, and on the right, windows that would offer you a wide-screen view if tall shrubs weren't in the way.

But Hardie knew this was just the top level. Virgil told him the place had three floors; the other two were built down along the side of the mountain. In his instructions, Lowenbruck called it his "upside-down house."

The house was famous in a minor way. In 1949 a film noir called *Surrounded* had been set here, as well as parts of a 1972 neo-noir called *The Glass Jungle*. This was no accident. The director of *Glass Jungle* was a big fan of *Surrounded* and had spent a lot of time on permissions for the location. Later still, in 2005, they re-made *Surrounded*—this time calling it *Dead by Dawn*—but left out the house altogether. Hardie hadn't seen any of the films, but Lowenbruck told Virgil there were copies at the house—the sitter should check them out, just for fun. Hardie would check out the first one, but not the others. He had a rule these days: he didn't watch any movies made after he was born.

Seems the movies were another reason Lowenbruck wanted a house-sitter. Every few days some noir geek would just show up and start snapping photos of the house. Some would even try to sweet-talk their way in, as if the place were just a vacant movie prop and not a real place where actual people lived.

FUN AND GAMES

Late last night, when he had to catch his sudden plane to Moscow, Lowenbruck e-mailed Virgil to say he'd leave keys in his mailbox.

Hardie looked.

Yep.

No keys in the mailbox.

3

Nobody came, nobody cares. It's still not about anything.
—Bill Cosby, *Hickey & Boggs*

LEAVING THE keys to your $3.7-million-dollar home in your mailbox is never a good idea. But Lowenbruck had in-sisted—there was no time to FedEx them to Hardie, and he didn't know any neighbors to leave them with. Couldn't Hardie just let himself in? They'd be in the mailbox, what, a matter of eight hours?

Or never.

Hardie pulled his cell phone out of his jeans pocket, pressed the auto-dial number of Virgil's office. He waited. Nothing happened. Upon closer examination, Hardie realized that there were no bars on the screen. Probably the damned hills, blocking everything.

Hardie decided he wanted a beer. Like, yeah, right now. It was super-early in the morning, but maybe that's what he should do. Get back in the Honda Whatever, drive back down to level ground, and buy some beer. Perhaps by the time he got back, the keys would have magically reappeared in the mailbox. If not, drink another beer. Repeat until reality conformed.

Yeah. Sure.

Hardie realized that unless he wanted to guard this damned place from outside, he'd have to figure out some way of breaking in.

He examined the front, looking for entry points, hoping for an obvious weakness. The oak door was solid, locked. The wide-screen windows were locked as well—and wired. Hardie spied the security transmitters mounted in the corners of the frames. Lowenbruck had given Virgil the keypad code, but that was useless with Hardie locked outside now, wasn't it?

Moving toward the right side of the property, past some eucalyptus bushes, Hardie craned his neck until he saw a wooden sundeck hanging off the back of the house. It was supported by narrow metal poles and fitted with a wrought-iron railing. If he could make it onto the deck, he could probably jimmy open the back doors. The only problem: there was no easy way up to the deck. From the edge, there was a fifty-foot drop to the ground. Not unless Hardie wanted to climb onto the roof, and then jump down onto the deck.

The latter, of course, seemed to be the only option.

Hardie sighed. Was he really going to do this? Who knows what kind of trouble he might get into up there. One slip and he could end up with a broken leg down in the ravine, bobcats circling him.

Hardie slid the phone into his pocket, climbed behind the wheel, pulled the Honda Whatever up closer to the garage door, then parked. He stepped onto the hood of the car and scrambled up the slanted tile roof. The tiles were warm from the sun. Hardie had a vision of the damned things breaking loose, sliding down the roof, and shattering on the pavement, one after the other after the other. Hardie was a large man; he didn't know if the makers of Spanish tile took his size and weight into consideration.

But he made it to the peak of the roof without incident. There he paused. The lush bowl of the hills was laid out beneath him, and off in the distance were the hazy glass-and-metal skyscrapers of downtown L.A. Hardie instantly understood the appeal of living here. Even though the sides of the mountain were littered with homes, there was the illusion that yours was the only one that mattered, that the rest of these properties had been assembled here for *your* benefit. No one else had a view like yours, not the homes above nor the ones below. You had a front-row seat to the big show. You could enjoy it anytime you liked... when you weren't slaving away on a sound track, that is. Hardie wondered how much Lowenbruck enjoyed his view. He doubted the man ever climbed up onto his own roof to catch this particular vista.

Okay, enough. Sooner or later somebody was going to look up and see Hardie standing here, looking like an idiot.

Hardie spied the deck and began to make his way over to it, arms out for balance. Still, he couldn't help but glance down at the houses below. The different-colored roofs, the pools, the terra-cotta patios.

And through a clearing in the trees, on the back deck of the house closest to Lowenbruck's, a nude woman sunbathing.

It almost looked like a mirage. The branches and trees made a perfect frame around her body, blocking out everything but her astounding and abundant nakedness. She was full-chested, with pink nipples that looked too delicate to be out in the bright California sun. Her body was muscled, perfectly shaved, and oiled—as far as Hardie could tell—from her nose down. Her skin practically glistened. Hardie wondered why Lowenbruck hadn't left the keys with *her*.

The woman's eyes were hidden behind sunglasses. She held a cell phone to her ear. And while her mouth moved, the words didn't travel the distance uphill.

Hardie froze in place, pitched precariously on the downward slope of the roof. He stared for a few moments before he realized that, fuck, she could probably see him, too.

Probably telling a friend on the phone: *You're never going to believe this, but some idiot is standing up on the roof of my neighbor's place, staring at my tits.*

Hardie continued his descent, placed a hand on the hot tile for balance, then jumped down onto the back deck. Something squished underfoot. Hardie was almost afraid to look...then did. Some kind of animal had been up here recently and had left a large deposit on Lowenbruck's sundeck. Not a bird; this beast appeared to enjoy a heartier diet than seeds and grass.

Shit.

Fortunately, Hardie had packed another pair of shoes.

Unfortunately, they were in his missing suitcase.

Hardie tiptoed over and tried the sliding glass doors. Miraculously, they were unlocked. Either Lowenbruck forgot or he wasn't in the habit of locking it.

The moment the contacts separated, however, the alarm was triggered—a shrill repeating *bee-BEEP bee-BEEP.* Thirty seconds and counting. Hardie knew there was a keypad by the front door. He needed to reach it fast or he'd have company soon, and that would no doubt push back his drinking by a few hours more.

bee-BEEP

bee-BEEP

bee-BEEP

Just as he was about to step inside he remembered the unidentified animal crap on his shoes. Hardie worked off one shoe hurriedly with the back of the other, reached down, yanked off its companion, then darted through the open doors looking for any-thing, anything at all, resembling a security keypad.

bee-BEEP

bee-BEEP

bee-BEEP

There were too many things hanging on the walls near the front door, too much clutter. Fuck. Fuck. *Fuck . . .*

Hardie found it and jabbed the code in with two seconds to spare.

The key situation would have to be figured out sooner rather than later—Hardie didn't want to leave the premises unlocked for any period of time, nor did he want to climb the tiled roof again to make a grocery run. Maybe he could have some booze delivered? No. Because that would require a working cell phone, and Virgil had told him that Lowenbruck didn't have a landline.

Anyway, first things first: house check.

The sliding doors from the back deck opened up into a media room—and immediately Hardie knew he'd lucked out. Wall-mounted plasma TV, stereo components whose brand name Hardie only recognized from other houses he'd watched. Over-stuffed black leather couch, which Hardie immediately decided would be his home base for most of the next month. The wall shelves contained row upon row of DVDs, many of them classics—which was fantastic. Old movies gave him something to fill the long days. He remembered the special Hell of a Myrtle Beach condo that lacked not just cable or satellite TV but a TV as well. Longest two weeks of his life.

The rest of the top floor seemed to be little more than a life-support system for the media room. The locked front door led to the vestibule and beyond that a winding staircase with wrought-iron rail, leading down to the lower floors.

The stairwell was lined with cardboard standees of 1980s white tough-guy actors, arranged *Sgt. Pepper*–style. Clint. McQueen. Bruce. Sly. Arnie. Van Damme. Segal. And, strangely, Gene Hackman. This was seventies Hackman. Crazy-man Hackman. *Night Moves* and *Conversation* and *French Connection* Hackman. The collage of 2-D tough guys looked like it had been stuck up there for a while. The edges of the cardboard were frayed, cracked, and torn in places, and the material itself was yellowing. The surfaces featured a film of dust, and various body parts—an elbow, a foot—had come unstuck from the wall. Either Lowenbruck really loved his action heroes, or some previous owner had, and Lowenbruck thought it easier to leave the whole thing up.

The next room was a smallish dining area, though clearly nobody ever ate in here. The table was covered in scripts, DVDs, CDs, old newspapers, staff paper, pencils. A peek inside a cupboard door revealed more battered scripts, yellowing newspapers, and about forty copies of a sound track called *Two-Way Split* on CD.

The galley kitchen was clean but spare. Seemed like not much cooking happened in here. No booze in the cabinets, no food in the fridge, except for a box of baking soda and a glass jar of martini olives shoved in the back.

Half bathroom off to one side. Handy. Probably thirty paces between the leather couches and the porcelain throne here. That would make life easy.

On the other side of the kitchen, a door led to a tiny two-person deck with a hard-plastic Adirondack chair and a Weber Baby grill, overlooking another part of the hills. Hardie looked through the window and thought he could make out part of the Griffith Observatory. No other nude sunbathers in sight, however. Which was a little disappointing. Would have been nice to have the ladies in stereo.

Okay.

So, three entrances so far:

Front door;

Back patio doors (if you felt like walking on the roof);

Side patio door (if you were to somehow climb up the side of the house and vault over the railing).

All locks in working order as far as Hardie could tell.

Hardie retraced his steps, passed the gang of action heroes, gave Hackman a respectful nod—

Gene

—then continued down the wide stairs as they spun him around to face…a closed set of double doors. Which seemed weird, until Hardie opened them up and walked into a large music studio, soundproofing everywhere.

Ah, so this was the padded treasure in the heart of the Lowenbruck castle: the recording studio. The space was tricked out with enough gear to make the upstairs media room look like a kids' Fisher-Price set. Huge, wide-screen plasma TV, a mixing console the size of a back porch, multiple keyboards, amplifiers, heaps of spaghetti cable.

Virgil had told him:

"Lowenbruck's insanely anal about his studio. Don't even go in there if you can avoid it. Just make sure nothing happens to it."

"I won't."

"I've got explicit instructions here. Like, don't even turn a knob."

"What am I, in high school?"

"Just telling you what's here on the form."

"Okay, Virge. It won't be easy, but somehow I'll resist the urge to record my *Pet Sounds* tribute."

Nothing else down here—was there room for anything else?—except two other padded doors. One was open a few inches, and obviously led to a bathroom. Hardie could see a white-tile floor and the edge of a silver mirror. He supposed that when Lowenbruck was in full-on work mode, this was all he needed. His keyboards and a place to take a leak or splash water on his face from time to time. The other door probably led downstairs to the third-floor bedroom.

Hardie was about to head down when the bathroom door flew open all the way and someone screamed and rushed at him and hit him on the head with something really, really hard.